The Househusband Contract

Agreement made the .... day of ....
It is hereby agreed that, in consideration of..........(partner's name here)
paying me the (weekly/monthly) sum of ...... , this being a sum
inclusive of housekeeping money and wages for work done, ...
(name of househusband) hereinafter known as 'the househusband' will
endeavour, strive, essay and resolve, to the best of my abilities,
knowledge and stamina to carry out the below mentioned tasks to a
reasonable standard, ... (partner's name here) being sole and final
adjudicator of the definition of 'reasonable standard' :

All household chores, including, but not limited to all:

— cooking.
— cleaning.
— laundry & ironing.
— shopping, this to include feminine hygiene products and other
    consumables peculiar to women.
— general appliance maintenance & repairs.
— waiting on tradespeople to call and supervising their activities
    in and around the house.
— diary maintenance including remembering all significant dates
    such as birthdays, anniversaries etc.
— providing on partner's demand, plentiful sex of the stress-
    relieving variety to partner.
— organising all festive occasions including Christmas, birthdays etc.
— establishing and maintaining good relations with neighbours
    howsoever obnoxious they may be.
— keeping an eye on personal horoscopes to forewarn of pending
    catastrophes.
— keeping up to date with television soap opera storylines as
    requested in order to be able to supply partner with casual
    conversation after her hard day's work.

This agreement shall be reviewable after a period of......(six/ twelve months.)
Signed..........................(the partner)
Signed..........................(the househusband)

Diary of a
Househusband

Carl Peters

The
X
Press

Published in United Kingdom by:
The X Press,
6 Hoxton Square, London N1 6NU
Tel: 0171 729 1199
Fax: 0171 729 1771

Printed by Caledonian International Book Manufacturing Ltd, Glasgow, UK.

Distributed in UK by Turnaround Distribution, Unit 3, Olympia Trading Estate,
Coburg Road, London N22 6TZ
Tel: 0181 829 3000
Fax: 0181 881 5088

ISBN 1-874509-60-3

To Mum

Wednesday December 31

Nikki's New Years Eve party instructions to me, exactly as typed:

    no politics.
    no religion.
    if sex comes up, try to keep it decent
    don't mention love scenes for actresses
    or casting couches or anything else that
    winds Malik up.
    don't point out the age difference
    between Antonia and her latest beau.
    no diet talk because that upsets
    Antonia.
    definitely no mention of rats or other
    members of the rodent family you are
    professionally acquainted with since
    that'll have everyone throwing up.

Apart from that I'm free to say what I like. I dust off my C&A suit. As always, Nikki looks drop dead gorgeous.

10 p.m. Dinner party gets going. Why Nikki has to invite her ex-boyfriends to a New Year's Eve party I don't know. Malik is so ugly, like a boxer after a thousand losing fights. Yet his girlfriend Debbie-Anne is a real babe, open and sweet and confessional. They make an odd couple.

1

New Year Resolutions flow free as the *Liebfraumilch*. I confide in Debbie-Anne my dream of giving up my day job at Environmental Health and becoming a full-time sculptor. "I've won a couple of awards." I state nonchalantly. Malik butts in "Where's the money in Art? It's for white people, not us." I surprise him by agreeing: "Yeah I should stick to killing rats!" Malik goes royal purple and his face blows up like a puffer fish. He throws up. *Splat, splat, splat* — a bellyful of jerk chicken shoots across the table into Ralph's lap. Ralph blithely continues feeding Antonia cheese nibbles. Debbie-Anne pours water down Malik's throat which just makes him splutter. Finally, Nikki revives him by mentioning her lucrative Latin American share investments. Instant recovery. Malik hangs on to her every word, not to mention her left bra strap.

Something soft and warm is crawling up my trouser leg. It's Debbie-Anne's foot. She's slipped off her slingbacks. We play footsie under the table. Malik's been neglecting her all evening, chatting up Nikki. I may know zilch about Latin American mining investments but I play good footsie. Debbie's legs are smooth and long. We get more and more risqué. Debbie whispers me a story about a woman who had an orgasm through her lover massaging her with a toe in some West End restaurant. She's wearing a pink 'A' — line silk dress, and a soft contour lilac bra that peeps out from it. Her pearl pendant ear-rings are an engagement present from Steve, she tells me when I finger them. She often calls Malik by his birth name, Steve. Debbie-Anne is great company. She's an actress with a full Equity card. Malik has promised to get her into films. You need a man who offers you more than just promises, I advise her, you can do better than him.

To my left Malik and Nikki are working their way through the crate of Australian plonk he brought. I tell Debbie-Anne more about my sculpting dreams. Malik leans over and says I haven't the bottle or brains to give up the day job. Nikki weighs in on my side, which is surprising seeing that she and Malik have been inside each others keks all evening. Everyone joins in a drunken chorus of support:

"Why don't you?"

"You've got the talent!"

"If any one can, you can, Harvey!"

A party game starts called planning Harvey's life for him. I leave them to it and finish off this playfully fruity bottle of Bulgarian Red while covertly admiring the luminosity of Debbie-Anne's cleavage.

12 a.m. New Year's Day strikes. Malik snogs Nikki under a sprig of mistletoe. Debbie-Anne twirls a sprig in her hand alluringly. Why not? I keep my eyes on the other two while I'm kissing Debbie. Nikki's lips are pressed full against Malik's, her eyes are closed tight. I've had enough. I pull Malik off Nikki. He swings a fist at me. I duck. He falls face down into the settee, where he lies groaning. I do my Ali shuffle, telling him to get up and try that again. Debbie-Anne giggles. So does Nikki. Ralph and Antonia are still spoon-feeding each other. Nikki helps Malik to the kitchen for a glass of water. There's a banging on the front door and I open up to a horde of people I don't recognise who hug me, charge in and head straight for the drinks. Someone puts a dance track on. The whole house starts to jump.

Thursday January 1

Last night's a blur. Did I get off with Debbie-Anne last night, or did I dream it? Descend stairs to find Nikki with a wet flannel on her forehead and a line of five Alka Seltzers by a glass of water. She frowns when I appear and asks can I not grind my teeth so loudly. I tiptoe to kitchen.

Nikki's party dress is on the kitchen floor. Flashback of Malik fiddling with her dress zip when I came in for more

Nachos. Can't remember any more. Dismiss it as hallucinations. The fridge is a huge American model I bought on a whim. Ten cans deep and twelve cans wide. Shelf after shelf of cold cuts, fruit, yoghurts, cheeses and snacks confront me. I find the raw eggs, my dad's sworn-by hang-over cure. He died face down in a Brummie brothel. What a way to go. Swallow five raw eggs, yokes and all, then wait to feel the improvement.

Throw up eggs. They join the other pools of sick on the Berber carpet. Luckily, my sense of smell has gone AWOL. House is a total mess. Upstairs there are two used condoms in the bathroom. So who was having sex up here last night? I ask myself pruriently. Malik wouldn't use one since he and Debbie-Ann are trying for a baby. So it was Antonia and her latest beau. Randy devils. Or maybe it was those gatecrashers.

12 p.m. My head still throbs like a Sunday bell.

1 p.m. My head groans like a loaded cement mixer. There's nothing for it but the hair-of-the-dog. Sidle off to fridge again and uncork that vicious Bulgarian Red. It produces a woozy contentment. Nikki serves lunch: beans on toast, two Alka seltzer and mineral water. I eat, then pick my way through the lounge to the large radiator by the bay window and curl up.

Woken by howling dog outside. It's 9 p.m. The lounge sparkles. Even the puddles of sick have vanished from the carpet. Tell Nikki she only needed to wake me and I would have helped out. She smiles, lovingly (I think).

Friday January 2
Wake up, do a press-up, collapse. Starting to recall more bits and pieces of the party. Some people were really depraved. I think.

Saturday January 3

Nikki asks whether I want to talk about her and Steve kissing? This is a confession. I vaguely remember them in the kitchen. Not sure what I got up to with Debbie-Anne, so I say it's OK. She says it was the mistletoe and the wine and she and Malik are just good friends now, and Malik's a very physical person. I shrug my acceptance. She smiles, relieved, and says she won't bring up my having my hand up Debbie-Anne's thigh all the evening. I don't know why but we burst out laughing. She kisses me hard. But then her autofax chunters: InterGlobe Sales Reports. She spends all day analysing them.

11 p.m. Nikki falls asleep over the fax machine. I carry her up to bed, kiss her full on mouth. She snores on. So much for sex. Watch Italian football highlights in bed. AC Milan 1 Roma I .

Sunday January 4

Manage 10 press-ups.

Malik rings and gushes that he's 100% behind my going for sculpting as a business, and he might even be able to broker a deal for me with one of his connections. This is not Malik. I thank him cautiously and say I'll chew it over. What connections? It all sounds very mysterious.

Look at myself in the mirror. I have a plump, dark walnut coloured face with a well maintained set of razor bumps. My hair is loose-curled enough to signal my Guyanese ancestry from my grandfather's side, and currently stands approximately four centimetres off my scalp. I am tall, broad shouldered enough to play centre forward for Willesden Borough Environmental Health Dept. football team, though in fact I am temporarily playing left back. Malik was right first time. The Western art world is not about to allow some black kid from Willesden to break in on their scene. Nikki says I'm a sculptor of talent, energy, ambition. Someone not afraid of rising to the challenge of the modern entrepreneurial art world. I nod agreement. Before I know it she's drawn up my very own Sculptor's Business Plan, Projected Cashflow and Income and Expenditure Chart. I only bail out when she begins an Equilibrium Price Product Proposal: Did Picasso ever ponder over an Equilibrium Price-Product Proposal? I ask haughtily. Nikki offers me an interest free loan for one year while I get on my feet. That's love for you. I accept fawningly. There are strings attached though. Since I will be staying at home, sculpting, I will also have to take over responsibility for all the household chores, meaning the cooking, cleaning, laundry, shopping, repairs, everything. I sigh OK. Before you can say 233MB MMX Hewlett Packard Laptop she's typed in and printed out a contract which she lays out for me to sign. I sign. She signs. She grins. Another day, another deal for her, I guess.

The Househusband Contract

Agreement made the .... day of ....
It is hereby agreed that, in consideration of..........(partner's name here) paying me the (weekly/monthly) sum of ...... , this being a sum inclusive of housekeeping money and wages for work done, ... (name of househusband) hereinafter known as 'the househusband' will endeavour, strive, essay and resolve, to the best of my abilities, knowledge and stamina to carry out the below mentioned tasks to a reasonable standard, ... (partner's name here) being sole and final adjudicator of the definition of 'reasonable standard' :

All household chores, including, but not limited to all:

— cooking.
— cleaning.
— laundry & ironing.
— shopping, this to include feminine hygiene products and other

> consumables peculiar to women.
> — general appliance maintenance & repairs.
> — waiting on tradespeople to call and supervising their
>   activities in and around the house.
> — diary maintenance including remembering all significant dates
>   such as birthdays, anniversaries etc.
> — providing on partner's demand, plentiful sex of the stress-
>   relieving variety to partner.
> — organising all festive occasions including Christmas, birthdays etc.
> — establishing and maintaining good relations with neighbours
>   howsoever obnoxious they may be.
> — keeping an eye on personal horoscopes to forewarn of pending
>   catastrophes.
> — keeping up to date with television soap opera storylines as
>   requested in order to be able to supply partner with casual
>   conversation after her hard day's work.

This agreement shall be reviewable after a period of......(six/ twelve months.)
Signed.........................(the partner)
Signed.........................(the househusband)

Monday January 5

Nikki back at work. I tell Shirl, I'm giving one month's notice of my resignation and what with my holiday entitlement and all that, I won't be coming in again. My boss comes on the line to say I'm to call back tomorrow when I'm sober, then hangs up. Shortly after, Debbie-Anne knocks on door! She and Malik are only two streets down and she remembered the address. We giggle over the New Years Eve party. She says something I don't catch about Steve and Nikki in the kitchen but won't repeat it so I don't press her. She's buzzing. Malik is lining up some promotional work for her. I tell her he's lining up something for me as well, and she titters.

7

Get on with this housekeeping lark. Debbie-Anne helps out. Upstairs, I make the bed while she opens up the windows. She has very long, lithe legs and a fantasy of a luridly sexual nature pops up into my mind. Debbie says she's often alone while Steve is out 'making another dollar'. She thinks he imports African textiles and sells them on, but she's not sure. He's away a lot. She gets lonely, especially now she's moved in with him because she's fifty miles from where she was brought up and she knows nobody around here. Except me, she adds. I tell her she's welcome to visit any time. As I'm dragging the vac up and down the landing carpet, the phone rings. It's work. My boss says he's changed his mind. They need some voluntary redundancies, so I'll do. Could I put my resignation in writing for him? There'll be a lump sum of redundancy money. Four thousand pounds.

Abandon vac and drive up to the depot with Debbie to hand in my resignation note. Boss asks for the keys to the Mondeo! I'd forgotten I was driving a company car. Go back to car and explain to Debbie. The cheque will wing its way to my house from Finance next payroll day, the boss promises me. He shakes me goodbye and does a jig back to his office. Was I that bad a worker?

Me and Debbie-Anne have £3.45 between us, which is not enough for a taxi, so we wait for a bus. It's raining. Two hours later we board the 234. The driver is smoking a small cigar and wants eight quid. I try haggling but he says he's not a charity. He'll take Switch and cheques backed by a valid bankers card. It's chucking it down. I fish my chequebook out of my black bin liner and write a cheque. Dick Turpin inspects my signature closely against my banker's card and is eventually satisfied. The bus belches on its way, with us inside.

Get home, boneshaken, fleeced, drenched and starving. All that's left in the freezer is frozen sprouts. Have eighteen sprouts for dinner, washed down with Lemsip. Cough, splutter and sneeze through the night. Nikki sleeps with mobile in charger under blankets.

Tuesday January 6

Do shopping. L-Mart is a revelation to me. Where has it been all my life? The banner across the entrance says, "Feel Groovy At L-Mart" A supermarket with retro chic! I pass through the automatic doors. It's a 15,000 square feet air hangar of consumer perishables heaven. The floor tiles are Mondrian. The piped music is Mantovani. The air is fresh bread and scented lemon. The shelf fillers smile and wink (yes wink!) as I trundle around with my trolley.

An hour and a half later I've found everything I want. Hand over my dosh over to the grinning cashier and head for the car park. A shiver of dread joins the shivers of flu along my spine. I Am A Pedestrian. I Don't Have A Car. I have no change and no cheque book this time. There's no way I can walk back with this load. I spy a Volvo-owning balding black man I've seen driving around our estate. Cadge lift. His name is Ivor. He speaks glumly of the riff-raff coming into the neighbourhood on dodgy mortgages. Just this week there was one helluva racket coming from that number 57. What a carry on. Loud, repetitive music, people fornicating on the lawn, peeing in the bushes, the women as well. The type of tenant this area can do without — they should be sent back to Brixton where they belong! Grateful for the lift, I agree wholeheartedly with everything Ivor says. Lie that I live at No 37. He drops me off there.

Stagger to 57, unbag everything and go to put it away. Fridge light blows on me. Where on earth do you get hold of replacement fridge bulbs? Dig out phone book. Megawatt want 33 quid (Two pounds for the bulb, ten pounds in handling fee, ten pounds in import line surcharge, plus the VAT) Rats to that! I delve in garage and find spare Mondeo headlight bulb. Fix this into fridge. It's a perfect fit. Fridge light works. Stuff microwave meals and rest of shopping into refrigerator.

Nikki back late. Declares her office is a war zone. They've just appointed a cost-cutter to oversee the London sales operation. He's a hatchet man with Corporate Slaughter previouses as long as his arm, the downsizing guru's guru, the forensic auditor's auditor. He spells efficiency with only one f. He's the one who cut Kentucky Fried Chicken down to KFC. It's dog eat dog now, she says. She opens her attache case and spreads InterGlobe plc sales reports out on the table. Microwave oven pings and I serve her chicken chasseur. Nikki gushes appreciation, then buries her head again in her papers. Her small talk consists of grunts and aahs. She is very fluent, able to converse on all subjects from Vampire Legends to Stock Exchange movements by subtle inflections of 'grunt-aah'. I mention I have to pop out and she grunt-aahs an OK and offers me the keys to her car. I grunt aah that I won't need them.

Brave the elements on foot to corner shop to buy Loot magazine. Back home I thumb through it, drooling and sighing over the big engine Probes and Mazdas, but know I won't be able to afford the petrol. My eye is caught by an advert for a Nissan Micra. Four hundred and fifty pounds o.n.o. Very Low Mileage. Owner Is Elderly Spinster Whose Arthritis In Hands Forces Sale. Phone up and frail spinster with very deep voice says yes, it's still on offer, due to time-wasters, and it's OK for me to come and inspect it.

Speed over to North London address by taxi and am greeted at kerbside by Norman. Norman is grandson to the old lady who owns the car, he explains — Rita's having her evening nap. Micra has only ten thousand miles on the clock. He lets me test drive it up and down street. Says he'd give me longer but he has to catch a train to Norwich for his church bell-ringing class. The car seems OK. I offer a cheque but he laughs and says Rita's still living in 1946 and only understands the folding stuff, nothing bigger than twenties. He drives me to a cashbank. I withdraw two hundred and say I'll have to write a cheque for the balance. Who should I write it to. He says to keep the payee space blank, and write four cheques for £50, each with my card number on the back. He takes the cheques and hands me the keys. I volunteer to drive him to the station for his train to Norwich but he merely chuckles, and disappears.

12 a.m. Nikki gasps sexily in her sleep. I listen in, hoping to hear my name. But she only whispers "Awesome price-performance ratios!" again and again and again.

Wednesday January 7
Nikki has left a Post-It note on breakfast table:
Harvey dearest,
Please sort out my laundry for me (as per our contract). I am going on a business trip to Rome shortly. The clothes I need are in the laundry basket.
Your ever loving concubine, Nikki.

Load ever loving concubine's clothes into the washing machine and . . . machine refuses to gurgle to life. Try twiddling machine dials again. Nothing doing. I need a drink. Open fridge door. Fridge light shines sweetly. Simultaneously, washing machine shudders to life. Feeling better already, I extract an L-Mart lager and close fridge door. Washing machine shudders to a halt. Deduce washing machine will only work while fridge door is open. Why this is, I cannot fathom, but fridge door is easily wedged open with beer can, so that's that sorted.

Am congratulating myself on my ingenuity when the doorbell chimes. It's Debbie-Anne. She declares her face is the wrong shape for an actress, and asks me to look at it, even takes off her earrings so I can have a proper look. I tell her that in my professional sculptor's opinion, her face is graceful, symmetrical, proportionate and complete. She is not interested in my professional opinion. She wants my personal opinion, she insists. My personal opinion doesn't differ. She has a beautiful face. She absorbs the compliment effortlessly, like a true thesp.

Get back to the laundry and Debbie points out that thousand pound suits are usually dry-cleaned not boil-washed. She's right. Disaster. But there's time to catch the High Street dry cleaners if we're fast. It's snowing. We reach Johnson's Dry Cleaners at one minute to five. I attempt to reverse between two cars, to find the Micra's reverse gear does not work. Traffic backs up for half a mile behind me. Abandon reverse gear and park a hundred metres further down the road, then dash through blizzard with full laundry basket in arms. Dry cleaners has just closed. I knock frantically on door. Pimply shop assistant opens up when I beg on hands and knees. Ask if they do a recovery service for thousand pound suits that have been accidently boil-washed. He says they'll do their best. I thank him profusely.

7 p.m. Nikki back. Says she hopes I don't expect her to leave her £16K Lexus out in the elements for all the Willesden joyriders and assorted east London villains to take a screwdriver to — while that tin-can I've acquired in a rush of blood is parked in the almighty garage. I tell her her skin glows beautifully when she shouts. She picks up a vase with her throwing hand. I go to move the Micra. I suspect this isn't the time to tell her about the little mishap with her suits. Nikki guesses dinner right: chicken chasseur. I try some small talk but she has her face in her laptop and keeps it there all night.

Thursday January 8

Another note from Nikki:

Partner dearest,

The shower-head bracket is loose, could you please fix it? Thanks. Also, windows need cleaning and furniture needs dusting; PS. re clothes: remember I will be leaving for Rome next Wednesday. You don't want me to go there naked, do you?

Your very loving partner, Nikki

I set about loving partner's list of fun things to do. Shower head is easily fixed by replacing 3 millimetre flathead with five millimetre posidrive screw. I run vac over the carpet, scrub inside surface of windows with clean cloth and chase dust off furniture with feather duster. Award myself one Holstein for effort.

Phone Johnson's, dry cleaners. Garments I handed in will be ready Friday. That's fine.

With what remains of the afternoon, I do some drawings of ideas I've had for sculptures. Not impressed with results. Maybe my sculpting phase is coming to an end? Drink two Holsteins to calm nerves.

8 p.m. Nikki back and tells me Hatchetman is extending her Division's inspection for a week. She's double worried. I broach subject of sex. Am told it is off menu. Nikki is 'directing all her energy into the cerebral'. I think this means Hatchetman has given her a headache.

Friday January 9

Collect garments from Johnson's. They look perfect. Tip youth £20. Drive back. Hang Nikki's clothes up. Sculpture ideas come to me — thousands of them, like rats to a skip! I get through five sticks of charcoal.

9 p.m. Nikki and I watch an old movie together snuggled up on the sofa. James Stewart is about to confront the killers and berate them for the iniquity of their deeds when Nikki starts snoring. Sex is off, then. But my libido is definitely returning. Maybe because I've not inhaled rat fungicide for a whole week now. Spank the monkey imagining I'm the only guy at a Hollywood chorus line backstage party.

PS. I have perfected the art of crossing Willesden without ever having to use reverse gear.

Saturday January 10

The basketball fan in Nikki is revived. We take the Lexus to the Arena to watch London Towers whup the ass off Manchester Giants. Nikki's screaming and cheerleading herself hoarse for the Towers. Wonder how much of her zeal is due to the sight of tall, hunky, black males in shorts and singlets? We lick our Haagen Dazses on the drive home. KISS FM is playing. Why is licking an ice cream so damn lewd and suggestive?

Get back and sex occurs. The real, physical thing. It was the ice cream that did it. Must Remember This. After, Nikki says she enjoyed it (sex) and would like to do it more but she's usually too exhausted from work, weekdays. My suggestion: Work late next Thursday, then come home early on Friday, and we can do it then? She says she'll see what she can arrange. I am to ring her at work on Friday morning. All calls to her Division are being recorded by Hatchetman so we will have to use a secret code for talking about 'it'. The code is 'Will We Be Having Digestive Biscuits?' If she answers 'yes' it means afternoon sex is on.

Sunday January 11

Antonia visits. She's having problems with 'the phallocentric academic mafia'. She's the only woman psychology lecturer in her Department. She drinks off a bottle without any help, then she and Debbie go for a stroll together. They'll freeze to death. It's minus 3 centigrade. I put on two coats then drag my ancient oxy-acetylene and welding kits out of the garage and begin welding strips of steel according to those sculpture doodles I did. The torch flame sings, sparks shower into the frosted snow. I'm in the groove and have half completed the first sculpture when the oxy kit packs up. My hands are totally numb with cold by now anyway, so I quit. Nikki and Antonia return from their stroll. They compliment my work. I tell them it ain't finished yet.

Lazio 4 AC Milan 2

Monday January 12

Debbie phones, excited. She's won a theatre part for a theatre-in-education company. The director is very influential in Children's TV. It could be her big break. I promise to come and watch her first performance. Set fire to my Van Heusen white shirt trying to light gas hob on cooker. Thought: I Need An Apron.

Late evening, Debbie phones again. Malik's gone missing again. I tell her it's probably nothing and he'll be all right He was always late to class at school. She cheers up at this. She hadn't known we went to school together — so I was at Westminster Choristers too? Tell her neither of us was. We both went to Willesden Community Comprehensive.

Tuesday January 13

Get call from Colonial Direct Insurance Company: Do I want to buy life insurance? Ask them why — is there a contract out on me? Am cut off. I'm sufficiently amused by my repartee to be still smiling half an hour later. On a whim, I drive to Kitchen Rejects and pick up some kitchen shelving. I also grab a melon ball maker, a runner bean slicer, a kitchen cabinet deodorising cube and a Frenchy, blue and white striped apron. On way back, Micra breaks down, right outside municipal pool, radiator hissing. It is raining heavily down, still, unlikely to collect enough water in bare hands. Approach Willesden Municipal Pool & Fitness Centre in search of water. Bright spark behind the grille says "You've come to the right place then, mate!" He eventually points me to a vending machine. Pool noticeboard advertises beginner's swimming class, every Wednesday afternoon. Vending machine wants two pounds for tiny blue bottle of mineral water. Load machine with coins. It spits out a baby bottle of Evian. Dash into rain, fill Micra radiator. Radiator gurgles with pleasure.

8.30 p.m. Nikki back late. She was caught speeding by a police patrol. . She clocked fifty on their radar, which can't be right. she wails, she never does less than sixty-five on that stretch. Her Rome trip is off: she needs to be around the office while Hatchetman is there. I mention I might take a swimming lesson tomorrow. I've always wanted to be able to swim. She disappears into her laptop with a grunt.

Wednesday January 14

A sixty-strong double column of Venezuelan ants marches its way across the kitchen worktop as I'm washing up. I stop and marvel. Have seen their brothers and sisters in restaurants the lengths and depths of Willesden. They're no great health hazard, but they do compete ruthlessly for food. Tell myself I will dig out some powder and kill 'em off later.

Malik calls when I'm in the middle of dusting. He laughs at my new apron. I look ridiculous, he says. Nikki has me under too heavy manners. Anyone would think . . . well . . . I'm supposed to be a man, aren't I? I tell him I flattened him on New Year's Eve and I'll flatten him again if he gives me any more lip. Still, I get self-conscious and take the apron off.

Malik's full of his latest deal. If I understand it right, an Eastern European copyright-free (i.e. bootleg) recording factory is offering to barter CDs for a stock of, priced-to-sell (read factory reject) fluffy toys that Malik's obtained from God knows where. He stands to make a quarter million if it comes off, which it will, he boasts: " I'm Aries, you see. My element is air. I'm a natural high flyer. " I am about to explain Aries has nothing to do with air when his mobile warbles and he vanishes in a roar of over-sized engine. It's now too late for that swimming lesson. I finish off the dusting and run the iron over a few things.

Thursday January 15
Nikki home late and collapses on sofa. I ease off her shoes, throw blanket over her, and plug her mobile into its recharger.

Friday January 16
Catch Nikki at her 6am breakfast. Ask her if she'll be home early this afternoon. Her eyes twinkle with promise. I am to ring her midday. Midday arrives. Will She Be Having Digestive Biscuits This Afternoon? She whispers, yes, then hangs up. I scrub, bathe and pomade myself, pull on Jockey Sports underwear (she likes them), a Polo T shirt (easily ripped off) and moleskin trousers. I don't know why moleskins turn her on, but they do. Then wait. Doorbell chimes. Answer it. Window cleaner at door says I smell nice. I tell him to push off. Phone rings. Debbie-Anne. Problems with Malik. I say I'd love to listen to her but I'm waiting on Nikki and when she arrives we are going to get it together and, since we haven't done it since Cable TV was invented, I'm sure she'll understand. Debbie-Anne giggles and wishes me luck. At 4 p.m. there's still no Nikki. I'm starving. I penetrate the microwave with a hard chicken chasseur. The microwave holds it in there till it's all hot and bubbling, then I take it out. It satisfies me.

10 p.m. Nikki back with apologies. Hatchetman detained her over her turnover to margins ratios. Nikki in tears. This is what the pressure's doing to her, she says, but she won't buckle. She'll smash the glass ceiling before she buckles, she sobs. I warn her that modern office glass is usually bombproof and doesn't shatter. She rails at me: "I'm not talking materials science, Harvey, I'm talking equal opportunities! And what's more if I lose my job I don't think one of your pathetic sculpture things will pay the mortgage for even one week! And don't you dare ever, ever ask me to make you a cup of tea!" She then phones Antonia. I retire, dazed and confused. What's making tea got to do with it?

Sex: half metre chastity chasm separates our bodies.

Saturday January 17

Get a call from Ira. Bazza has sprained his ankle and Jaycey has defected to another team. Can I turn out for Ajax-Willesden in half an hour? Turn out? I reply, I'll be their midfield dynamo! I unearth my football boots, and gulp down two tins of strawberry Nutrament. Malik rings. He's heard a rumour Ajax Willesden haven't got enough players and he's thinking of phoning Ira. I tell him he's heard wrong.

We play at Fog Park, a place aptly named. We lose seven nil. Though the result was bad from the point of view of the team, my own individual contribution was impressive. I introduced them to Dutch distribution skills, Brazilian ball control, and German movement off the ball. I'm sure to be picked next week. Can tell from the way Ira slapped me on the back after the game saying, "Amazing Harvey, amazing!"Ira does not lavish praise like this on every one. After, me and Nikki go see the London Monarchs hockey team. Nikki roars herself hoarse as they tcream Newcastle Cobras, and clambers over the perspex trying to join in one of the players' brawls. Go, Nikki, Go!

Sunday January 18

Nikki and Antonia go off plotting Hatchetman's downfall. I waste four hours trying to fix my oxy equipment. Then do some figuring. I have four finished metalwork pieces in the garage, and some breeze block carvings. If I sold these I might have enough for a new oxy-acetylene lance. I need new stuff. The old oxy lance is all corroded. My goggles are scratched from spitting metal. And the asbestos gloves are wearing away. At the moment all I can afford to do is sketch.

AC Milan 3 Roma 1

Monday January 19

Get card from the Willesden rat pack: "Please come back Harvey, all is forgiven!" Signed Babs, Kate, Kwame, Fat Paul and Robbo, of the South Willesden Area Environmental Health team. I almost shed a tear. I feel more and more lonely holed up in this big house on my own all the time. We had some good times, in between kebab house inspections and run-ins with psychotic absentee landlords. Feeling all nostalgic, I decide to phone them in the afternoon when they'll all be writing up their reports.

Get drill out for new kitchen shelf. Debbie-Anne rings in tears, Malik is missing again and she can sense something's wrong. I suggest to her she treats his absence as the norm and only phones me when an unusual situation arises like when he's not missing, but she's too upset for sarcasm. She thinks Malik's seeing someone else. I reassure her Steve's vice is money not women. She brightens up at this and says she might pop round.

Debbie-Anne doesn't show. But the Venezuelan ants do. Watching the ants reminds me to phone the rat pack, but when I do I get the answering machine and I hang up without saying anything.

Tuesday January 20

Note from Nikki:

Dear Harvey,

I'll be at my company's annual sales conference in Birmingham, tomorrow-and will be hotelling overnight today and Wednesday. Here's a number in case you need to dialogue with me.

Your most ever loving partner, Nikki.

Late in afternoon, Malik shows at the door, eyes heavy with emotion. I sit him down. He tells me they are no longer together. She meant everything to him. He used to wash her down, polish her, sponge and wax her. I tell him I don't want to know about his perverted sexual practices, I have my own to be getting on with and he is pathetic and it is no use sitting there crying and the way he's been treating Debbie-Anne it's no surprise she's walked out on him. Malik mutters he's talking about his BMW not Debbie-Anne. Someone pulled out right in front of him, the front end is all mashed up and he's had to garage it. Insurance have provided him with a courtesy car. A Vauxhall Corsa. He'll die of shame . . . Pathetic. I kick him out. Spend the evening working on sketches.

Wednesday January 21

Get up early. Aware must do shopping and get Micra to a garage. Also aware am spending more time farting around than sculpting. Head for L-Mart thinking will buy in bulk to save time. Take two trolleys and load up with a Weight Watcher Escapees' party's worth of food. Notice the shelf fillers don't nod and wink at me today. They must have picked up that don't-mess-with look in my eye. At till, cashier says I shall have to replace the goods. They don't accept credit cards. Smile my 'absolutely livid' smile and ask to see the manager. Manager breezes over and says he'll personally guard my trolleys for half an hour while I dash back and get my chequebook and cashcard. I hear him whispering to the cashier "Single, lonely people are often grumpy, Gayle. Humour them." Weird.

Half an hour, twenty seven pounds cash and two cheques for fifty pounds later, I steer my SuperLoad trolley out of L-Mart and load up the Micra. I have to drive with six three-kilo bags of patna rice in my lap.

Sculpt or swim? I choose swim, guiltily. There are eight of us in the beginners' class. Our teacher is called Teresa. Teresa is very impressed with my ability to get into the water and says she can tell I'm going to be a fast learner. I get an inexplicable hard-on and have to splash about in the pool after lesson ends until it goes. We non-floaters have a little get-together in the café afterwards and discuss matters of swimming technique (the men) and sex lives (the women).

6 p.m. Malik calls round again looking glum. I give him a lager to cheer him up. He asks if it's really lager. I say yes, they brew it smooth at L-Mart. Two per cent alcohol smooth, he retorts, squinting at the small print on the base of the can. I say hey, it's wet, right and how's the Corsa? This really cheers him up.

Thursday January 22

Sketch all day. Early evening, Nikki gets back from Brum and flings her arms around me. She is InterGlobe's Best International Sales Team Leader! It was declared at the conference by Hatchetman himself! But wasn't he the one who insulted your marginal turnover ratios? I quiz. He was, but she outwitted him, she boasts. Hatchetman was getting confused as to whose reports were filed as Nic.date.doc. He thought they were from some Nicholas of Northern region. None of the admin staff wised him up. So, at conference, InterGlobe MD reads out Hatchetman's findings and declares Best

International Sales Team Leader to be Nicholas Jamieson and would he step forward? Well, she did! She won a £3,000 deferred bonus and has been promoted into the International Taskforce. I tell her I'm astounded — intelligence she's always had, but guile is something new. We get drunk and chase each other round the house naked. Then Antonia comes round and the two of them go off in a taxi to celebrate. Taxi delivers a roaring Nikki home around 3 a.m.

Friday January 23

Nikki comes back mid afternoon, has a quickie (she on top) then zooms away again. Where she gets the energy I don't know. I'm too lethargic from yesterday's bonking and drinking even to pick up a charcoal stick. Try Nazar's beef lasagne, thick, treacly minced beef in sauce, and robust, chewy pasta. Wash it down with an L-Mart lager . Then drag out the old oxy-acetylene equipment and melt metal in the last hours of daylight.

Saturday January 24

Nikki lends Steve-Malik her Lexus 'just for the weekend'. She has never lent it me! Ira rings. He asks if Malik's around or do I know anyone who can play a bit, they're a man short again. Such a joker, is Ira. I tell him not to be coy, he's rung the right guy, but I can't keep bailing them out like this and a few other teams have approached me with offers. Ira sighs over the phone. He's so relieved I've volunteered to play I guess.

We lose twelve nil to AC Brixton, though I personally play a blinder. Take Ira to one side after the match and tell him he needs to go out and sign a few quality finishers to get the balance on the side right, I'm in a different class from the rest of them at the moment. Ira says, "Fe true, you're different class, Harvey!" Straight after match, I whizz Nikki in the Micra to watch London Towers outjump Leicester Riders 98-64. Nikki still doesn't explain why she lets Malik drive the Lexus but not me. Nazar's Beef Lasagne definitely tastes good.

Sunday January 25

Early afternoon catch Nikki and Malik in an embrace by the garage. Nikki explains Malik's just returning the car. "How about simply handing over the keys? That's how it's done normally." I riposte. Malik sniggers, Nikki says "Don't be so possessive". Maybe I am possessive. Don't trust Malik though. Beef lasagne is excellent.

Fiorentino 1 AC Milan 1

Monday January 26

Phone Willesden EHO. Babs answers the phone. They're arranging my leaving do. I say I didn't know I was having one. Babs says I have to. It's bad for morale if I just leave and it's this Thursday, an Italian meal out and maybe dancing later. I say fine, so long as it's not Italian. I've had my fill of beef lasagne. Babs says she'll ring me back with details. Debbie-Anne comes round. I speed-sketch her face and she asks to keep the sketch . Even asks me to sign it.

Tuesday January 27

Malik round, miserable. His Eastern European deal has collapsed due to lack of finance. He drove there and back last weekend in Nikki's Lexus to set it up. The banks wouldn't give him a bridging loan. Do I know how it is for black businessmen out there? he sighs. This is how Malik cues himself into his 'hassled black businessman' aria. I know it word for word:

Malik's Hassled Black Businessman's Aria

Bank managers won't lend you shit. They're mostly surprised you can even add up. Nobody trusts you. Your credit's always checked out. You can cut a deal just fine on the phone. All you do is you put on the white voice. But when they meet you — wham-wham-wham! Tills close all around. They're just not expecting a black man. Asian is fine, no problem. But black? No, thank you. They think we can't add up despite us inventing arithmetic, right brother? We built the pyramids while they were still running around playing Flintstones and nobody even today can figure out how we built them, we were so smart. But do they acknowledge that? Do they s***. Maybe I should just settle for driving a bus. But no, Malik fights on. Bloodied but unbeaten. I believe in myself and one day the world will wake up to my mighty talents!

Malik tells me he knows this Rastaman who runs a garden store. The Rasta thinks Rasta gnomes will sell well nationally, even internationally, but he can't get a supply and have I considered making gnomes? I tell Malik I'm not sure and I'll sleep it. Malik explodes. It's a sure thing! He drives off in his Corsa cursing the entire British nation of petty racist shopkeepers including the black bourgeois artists who'd rather paint gift horses than sell them!

Wednesday January 28

Cannot get iron round shirt sleeves. Resolve to wear ponchos from now on. The Mexicans have it figured. Debbie-Anne rings. Malik's talking about remortgaging his house on this stupid Chechnyan tanks deal and would I talk him out of it? I'm his best friend and she's sure he'll listen to me. Wonder how bootleg records deal became Chechnyan tanks deal but don't bother to mention this. Tell her I'll try. Ring but his mobile is switched off.

Sketch Debbie. She's a good sitter. She tells me she was

adopted twice and fostered three times and she met Malik at the National Exhibition Centre last July when she was demonstrating WigWam Personal Organisers. He bought two. So how come he's so unorganised then? I quip.

Wild-haired, urchin sandwich seller calls at door with wicker basket of pathetically thin, overpriced sandwiches. Suspect she's a scout for a burgling team. Urchin sees the sketch I'm carrying and comments, that's not bad, Mister — are you an artist? I puff my chest out and buy two ham, two egg mayonnaise, and a bag of pork scratchings from her for a fiver. Well, you've got to support youth enterprise.

Thursday January 29

Tap water turns tangerine. Soon after there's a knock on the door. Man in an expensive suit, holding clipboard. They are laying cable right past my house and the benefits of cable are threefold etc. etc. I tell him I don't watch TV and by the way is their gang the one that's turned my tap water tangerine? He says I shouldn't turn my back on the technology of the new millennium. I'll be left behind, besides phone calls are cheaper with cable etc. Declare myself perfectly happy to be left behind but can I have my water back to its usual chemically foul, clear colour? Clipboard man leaves, snorting. Soon after, all lights go out. The cable diggers have accidentally sliced through my power supply. They'll get someone out to repair it, they say and by the way, have I changed my mind about cable yet? Mutter obscenity and close door.

6 p.m. Throw some smart casuals on for my works leaving party. It's at The Andalucia, the place I condemned two years ago. They thought I'd like that. Luckily, the proprietor, Senor Ramsbottom doesn't recognise me. Team has endless argument about opportunities for debauchery at different Spanish holiday destinations. Five tequilas each later we stagger into Heaven & Hell. Babs tries to kop off with Robbo, Fat Paul dances lecherously with Kate, and Kwame saves his strength for later. Suddenly miss them all like hell. Chase ice cubes at the bottom of my glass. Ice cubes remind me I forgot my swimming lesson yesterday. Mention this to Kwame. Me and Kwame take to the dance floor and practice front crawl upper body technique. Everyone joins in. Think we've started a whole new dance craze.

Friday January 30

House still utterly dark. Only power is on phone line. Utility company, MegaWatt says it's the cable company's responsibility. Cable company blame the Council for laying the electricity line where they did. Meanwhile, freezer contents are slowly melting.

12.30 p.m. Phone Malik. He's not going to remortgage his house to finance the East European deal any more because sterling is riding too low against the kopeck. In fact, he's abandoning the deal. He sounds upbeat about this and asks if I've thought any more about the gnomes project. I tell him I'm still thinking. He tells me not too think too hard because my brain's not used to it and can I get off the line now please because he's expecting someone important to call.

3 p.m. Lug entire freezer contents in Micra to Nikki's mother, Ruby. She thinks it's a gift from me and says I'm a good son-in-law and she's going to cancel Meals on Wheels because they charge too much and they don't cook anything but slop and the youth at the West Indian Centre are eating the old people's meals which isn't right and even a man on a galloping horse could see that, and she's going to make an official complaint. I settle further down in the armchair as Ruby flows on. She's having problems with the NHS prescription forms for free dentures and the chemist shop staff were rude to her and the wig shop plucked the wig right off her head when she said she could not afford the NHS top-up charge and she has a little money in a building society but it might run out any time, and cat thieves have stolen her cat, it's been gone a week. Apart from that she feels good and thanks me for visiting and here's some Jamaican bread and to make sure Nikki gets some. I feel all of seven years old again scoffing the bread on the drive back to Cherryville. Get back by 8 p.m. Lexus is on drive, but no lights on in house. Guess power supply still cut off.

No electricity means Nikki has had to give up her machines to conserve batteries. Laptop, mobile fax etc. all ghostly quiet and unbacklit. We make do with candles. which produce an unexpected intimacy about the house. We cuddle up among the red glow, shadows and wax. Nikki drops Barry White on the hi-fi . . .

Saturday January 31

Mention to Nikki that I visited her mother to drop off the frozen food and that her mother seemed a bit down. Nikki accuses me of trying to poison her mother: those frozen meals are hardly edible, she exclaims. This is news to me since she has been eating them apparently happily for weeks. Nikki phones her mother in a panic. I eavesdrop on upstairs extension. Ruby says not to worry, she threw my meals in bin. She hadn't wanted to upset me by refusing a gift and at least her prospective son-in-law comes and visits her, unlike her daughter. Ruby lets out a little sob at this point. Nikki promises to visit her tomorrow and Ruby perks up. She says I'm a very attractive man and should produce good, healthy grandchildren and when are we two getting married?

Sunday February 1

Oxy equipment packs up completely. I fling lance into brambles in despair. Later sheepishly go and search for it again. Need to finish the metal series before I can hawk them round the galleries. Nikki comes back from her mother's subdued. Goes off into bedroom. Miracle occurs: MegaWatt sends a gang out on a Sunday and they not only dig a hole, they actually fix the electricity supply and refill the hole. Nikki asks me just to hold her and not to say anything. I know it's about her mother, but that's all.

Monday February 2

At breakfast, Nikki seems more her old self again. Explain my redundancy money will be coming through any day now but until then all the freezer food needs replacing and I'm a bit short. She writes me a cheque for a couple of hundred and asks how sculpting's going. I say I've got a few ideas. I phone some galleries to brownnose the owners. None of them can see me till next week.

12 p.m. Take my shopping list to Aftab's Delicatessen. Aftab bought the Deli from the Poles when they retired. Drool at plantain, aubergines, ginger, garlic, cauliflower, watermelon, cow peas, gungo beans, lentils, corn meal, chapatti flour, tins of 'reines noires' black olives, bean sprouts in water, Jamaican Callaloo in brine, cooked fave beans, real German frankfurters, 'labhina dahl', black eye beans medium spiced, 'moong dahl', mild spiced mung beans, jerk seasoning, beef seasoning, beef and steak seasoning. There's a butcher's at the back and a sign in Urdu and English sign says:
"Fresh halal meat, mutton, lamb, chicken, available daily 2 p.m. to 7 p.m."

On a wave of hunger-inspired enthusiasm I buy everything in sight. Aftab watches puzzled as I sit in loaded Micra for ages, waiting until I can pull out without using my non-existent reverse gear. Too tired to cook. We have peanut butter and jam sandwiches, which Nikki says reminds her of her student days.

Tuesday February 3

Bored. Why are DayTime TV presenters so relentlessly cheerful? Zap box off. Load washing machine and open fridge door to get it going. Notice spores floating in fridge air. They're from an old pepper core that's gone mouldy. The spore shapes are amazing. I get oxy equipment out and begin cutting and welding. I finish last two pieces of series in the style of the fridge spores and they are the best thing I've ever done.

Delivered to my door today: one block of clay, and one bag of plaster of Paris. PS. Never understood this. why plaster of Paris? why not Rome? Or Birmingham? Store it all in garage. Remember I'm supposed to be cooking the big meal for Nikki. Put gungo beans on to boil. Nikki finds my gungo bean soup 'unusual'.

Wednesday February 4

Debbie-Anne calls round. I show her the spore metalwork pieces. She loves them. I tell her I'll be going round to the galleries next week and I might take the sketches I did of her. One or two of the galleries may be interested. I want to do some full figure studies to complement the face drawings. She asks if this involves taking all her clothes off. I nod and plead it's for art's sake and if it makes her feel any more comfortable, I'll strip off as well. I shouldn't have said this. She takes me up on it! She demands the keks off as well. Says I've got a fit bod. Awkward moment then and I think of rats' intestines (an old trick) and my member goes flaccid again. There's a knock at the door. I pull on my dressing gown and answer. A window cleaner: can I fill up a bucket of water for him? Upstairs again, and Debbie tells me Malik's latest wheeze is precast driveways Then she giggles. Follow her pointing finger and discover window cleaner poised on ladder. He is goggle-eyed. Apparently I assented to him cleaning my windows by filling up his bucket. I tell him to sling his ladder elsewhere. He says he won't be lectured to by the likes of me, and what kind of lark am I up to up there with nude girls and all? When I get back upstairs Debbie-Anne is fully dressed. I apologise about the window cleaner. She tells me to get net curtains or I've lost a model.

I'm late for my swimming class. Class all cheer when I step into the water. They thought I'd given up. Manage to swim one breadth. After the lesson, I play ping pong with Siobhan. She's an au pair from Germany and was getting changed in the cubicle next to mine (the changing rooms are unisex). Over the game she tells me they've nicknamed me 'Splash' because of my swimming style.

Back home, Nikki eats only a mouthful of my fried aubergine and cauliflower paella. Says she's dieting. All that swimming has given me an appetite and I wolf it down. I make overtures under the blanket, but Nikki rolls over and whispers, "Not tonight, Napoleon". This strikes me as quite a sexy way of saying you have a headache.

Thursday February 5

This evening, Nikki eats token amount of my lamb fettuccine. I ask her what's wrong? Debbie-Anne liked it, Debbie-Anne had two plates full. An argument ensues along the lines of why's Debbie-Anne coming round here anyway? I say I'm sketching her. Nikki asks to see the sketches. I say that's my professional work, I don't ask to see her sales projections. She says I can see her sales projections any time I want and where are the sketches? I show her the face sketches and harmony is restored. I go to bed early to surprise her with something. She comes up and finds me in bed wearing an old Carnival pirate hat that I've converted into something Napoleonic with curtain fringes. "Ah, Josephine!" I whisper in my best French accent. That night Josephine and I ride on a sea of ecstasy and all my love cannons are fired.

Friday February 6

Nikki has left note:

Dear Napoleon,

I will be home late due to a Company campaign meeting.

Our big continental battle is approaching and we have to work out our troop positions and check that our spies are giving us correct information. For this reason, and this reason only, I will not be able to present myself at your tent until very late tonight, though my heart is with you always.

Yours most passionately, Josephine.

For lunch, I deep fry some chicken and smother it with beef seasoning. It looks almost KFC. Debbie-Anne isn't hungry, though she has some rice. I eat two chicken legs washed down with L-Mart lager. A gallery rings to say they have to postpone my visit. They are receiving Damien Hirst that day. I'm mad enough to saw a sheep in half myself, but accept their offer of a short audience next week

Nikki returns at eight and is too tired to eat. She hints that the chicken smells off. Off? That's the beef seasoning! I explode and junk the remains of the chicken and rice. My culinary masterpieces are as a flower in the desert, unappreciated. Nikki says don't be so petulant.

Saturday February 7

Spend first two hours of the morning throwing up last night's chicken. My temperature stabilises in the low hundreds. Ira rings and is sorry I'm ill. I tell him not to panic. There's nothing wrong with me that a couple of Diacalm tablets can't put right. Unfortunately, the Diacalm tablets are not full-strength and am forced to spend most of the ninety minutes cross-legged on the left wing. Nevertheless, my mere presence steadies the lads and we beat The White Horse Winkers 4-3! Two Diacalm, one glass of Lucozade and a paracetamol and I'm fit to go with Nikki to see the London Towers. They thrash Derby Storm 88-36. Nikki is quiet during the game, and even quieter in the car home. She talks French philosophy in a flat voice: "We are born, we live, we die." I ask is it that bad at her workplace? If it is she should chuck the job, we'll get by, we always have. She says no, work's fine. We stay in and watch Bette Davis in 'Whatever Happened To Baby Jane'. Nikki gets through a box of Kleenex. It's a safe guess something's troubling her.

Sunday February 8

This morning, Nikki gets half way to to her mother's then turns back. She can't face her, she says. Ruby's lonely. She'll cling. She'll say she wants grandchildren when we've both agreed now isn't the right time, especially with Nikki's career just taking off. I say I'll go with her if she wants, despite her mother having thrown away all my Nazar's frozen meals. I'm not one to bear a grudge.

Get to her mother's to find there's a party going on. Full of oldies. Her Axminstered floor's jammed with creaking bodies. A Lord Kitchener calypso is playing on a bumpy 78rpm. Everyone looks sloshed, there's even a whiff of ganja in the air (old time ganja no doubt). Ruby catches Nikki looking on aghast and turns us out: we young people are too much party poopers, she says.

Nikki laughs with disbelief all the way home — and she was worrying about her lonely old mum! She cooks lamb provençal to show me it is possible, and tells me to find a cook book and follow the instructions if I want to cook it.

Monday February 9

The morning rhythm at No. 57 is established as follows: Nikki gets up at 6 a.m. and leaves at 6 30 a.m. I laze under the covers until the dawn chorus of wheezing car starter motors ends. Then I get up.

Today I decide to make a real go of vacuuming. Sprinkle Shake N Vac all over the house and switch on vac. Middle section of vac inflates hugely, then there's a bang and a pall of dust. Vac motor whines frantically then goes phut! Walk away from scene. Stuff washer with clothes, hit the buttons and wedge open fridge door. Washing machine shudders to life. Check fridge. Notice there are more, bigger spores floating around in the fridge, and they are a different shape from the last ones I sculpted. Maybe spores are like snowflakes, no two are ever the same.

Load vacuum cleaner and oxy equipment into Micra and trundle all down to Rufus's Garage and tell Rufus — the man himself — I've got three jobs for him: fix the *rahtid* reverse gear on this Micra, sort the vacuum cleaner motor, and see what he can do about the lance on the oxy equipment. Plus a fourth job. I want him to present me a bill for this that doesn't make it into three figures. Rufus tells me to take a stroll, cos I'm stressed out, and he has it all under control.

Stroll down the High Street as far as The Record Shack. *Second Hand & Collector's Records* proclaims the hand painted shop sign in Rasta colours. It looks like a record shack should look, before Virgin-HMV created music supermarkets. I peer through the rusted wire-mesh fronted window glass at the record sleeves. Millie Jackson, Ann Peebles, Bob Marley, Elvis — Hits of the 70's. Time stopped in the mid-Seventies for this window display. There are some great Afros on the sleeves and Bob Marley's knitted, stripey waistcoat looks natty. But who in hell was Ann Peebles? There's a base pumping inside. A little black butterfly bell at the heart of several hand painted orange, yellow, black and chrome circles on the door behind the padlocked gate says *Ring Me*. I ring. The bell goes, "tinkle tinkle." Hardly surprisingly, given the pumping bass, no one answers. Back at Rufus's, the reverse gear on the Micra is smooth, the vac motor hums perfect, but he couldn't do anything with the oxy kit. The bill is seventy pounds cash. I pay up grudgingly and he hands me back the Micra keys. Back home I dash some moong dahl into a saucepan and boil up some rice. Nikki chews in silence. I guess she doesn't like it. Her palate has been dandified by the cordon bleu in InterGlobe's Executives' Canteen.

Tuesday February 10

I pass through L-Mart's automatic doors. Johnny Mathis is playing. A huge sign by the entrance announces *Try Home Body Massage! Discount Vibrators : Only 5.99 !* What kind of a supermarket is this? Things become more bizarre when I'm handed a single red rose by a winking, adolescent shelf-filler of uncertain gender. I accept cautiously. Reach the second aisle and a strange middle-aged man wearing a huge badge introduces himself to me as the Manager and asks if I've met Susan. She's over by the yoghurts and likes country dancing and quiet nights in, has high personal hygiene standards and expects the same of her man. Grinning, he points to his badge. It reads: *Tuesdays are Singles Days at L Mart, Where Lovers Meet and Staff are Discreet*. He looks like he's about to call Susan over and introduce us. Hurriedly, I explain there's been some mistake.

Leave L-Mart with a variety of frozen wonders, plus the rose. Later, Debbie-Anne calls and I get sketching. She's quit the T.I.E. dolphin role, she tells me, the piece was too shallow for someone of her talent. Her agent has lined up some proper theatre auditions.

Late evening, Nikki storms in. She says she's been shafted

by The Four Bastards. She fulminates for a good hour then asks how my day was. I say actually a very interesting thing happened to me at the supermarket. She stops me with such a look of pity for my empty life that I dry up. Serve microwave fish and chips supper. Nikki won't eat it because of the calories. She kisses me for the rose which she finds in the fridge. Then launches into a long and complicated explanation of what the Four Bastards are up to. I accidentally yawn in the middle of this, which upsets her. We then argue over which TV channel to watch, and are currently not on speaking terms.

Wednesday February 11
Vacuum landing. In afternoon, I try to swim half a length with only one armband. I'm drowning when Teresa cleaves through the water and rescues me. I cling to her neck as she tows me to the side.

Thursday February 12
The receptionist at Gallery Electra is a camp delight. We gossip over cups of Darjeeling about the art market: how cruel it is! — how arbitrary! — how capitalist! — how tame! until the proprietor finally deigns to see me. I arrange my sculptures on his floorspace. He tugs his goatee and dismisses them as derivative, substandard Giacomecci, art school efforts, and do I have anything else? I feel like blowtorching his backside, but instead pull out my folder of sketches. He likes the sketches. He has discovered a rare, new talent, he declares. Can he show them to a colleague and get back to me tomorrow? I nod mutely, stunned, and he disappears with my folder. The receptionist helps me load my sculptures back into the van, commiserating. I tell him the proprietor liked my sketches. The receptionist says, "Yes darling, his way of softening the blow. Don't raise your hopes too high." I return home under a grey cloud of rejection.

Friday February 13

Gallery phones. They're buying four of my sketches for £300, and want me to follow them up with fully fledged paintings! Nikki comes home mid-afternoon to find me air-guitaring to Jimi Hendrix. She asks what's the news. We make ecstatic love on the sofa to Jimi Hendrix's *All Around The Watchtower*.

Saturday February 14

I score a superb diving header, mesmerise the opposition midfield with lightning diagonal runs creating huge gaps that Ira and the lads pour through to score four more. The final score is a puzzling 4-1. Ira explains that since we'd changed ends my superb diving header was an own goal. We all get pissed at Mullarky's and stagger home at midnight, singing, There's only one Ajax-Willesden!

Sunday February 15

Nikki evicts Mushy, Dumpling and Silk from our sofa. Ajax's midfield must have come home with me last night. Nikki's mother rings. Nikki refuses to visit. After that sob story her mother gave her last week she just will not go. She will not be emotionally manipulated. I go on my own. Ruby entertains me with some old time, back-a-yard stories while I tuck into ackee, stuffed breadfruit and sweet potato pone. Ruby admires my appetite. I admire her cooking. I wobble back to the Micra, ease the seatbelt round me carefully and drive home smacking my lips. I Must Visit Ruby Again.

Monday February 16

Washing machine fails to work even with fridge door wedged fully open. *Appliance Repairs R Us* wants a Princess's divorce settlement just to come and take a look. *Discount Washer Repairs* have never heard of my model and ask am I sure it's not a dishwasher, chuck? *Willesden Mobile Appliance Servicing* have no call-out charge and can come straight away. Edward of *Willesden Mobile Appliance Servicing* could give any funeral director a run for his money with his mournfulness. He nods sorrowfully at my machine: "It's a very unreliable make, most Washer-Dryers are. Washer. Dryer. Two as near as incompatible technologies as you can get." He closes machine door. Do I want him to take the back off and look inside? If I do, he has to charge a £20 inspection fee. Grudgingly, I agree to his inspection charge. After shining at torch at the wiring, he pulls plug from wall, coils flex ceremoniously round the appliance. He declares solemnly that it is not the wiring, rather, the engine has passed over to the other world. He will replace it for seventy five pounds plus VAT. I tell him I'd rather visit the other world and get it back than pay him his lousy seventy five plus VAT. He presses his card into my hand and says I'm to think about it and if I change my mind, don't hesitate, just call. No apology necessary, he'll understand. He sees himself out.

Start washing clothes by hand then realise we don't have a line to dry them on, so abandon them in the sink. Phone Willesden Council finance department to find out about my redundancy money. They say they are still sorting it out. That gallery cheque hasn't cleared yet either. Eat beans on toast for lunch.

Tuesday February 17

Am greeted at *Willesden Bubbles Launderette* by none other than Edward, the washing machine bandit. He owns the launderette as well. I concede defeat. Look around. An assortment of students, poets, grannies and other natural born suckers is on the plastic benches. Nobody talks. Half the machines have Out of Order signs on them. The false ceiling has multiple tide marks and bulges from flooding. Drop a pound coin into one of the dryers. It whirs for about twelve turns then stops. Call Edward over. He says I'm just to feed it another coin and it'll start again. He recommends I feed it at least a couple of quid at a time.

I contemplate the unbearable sadness of launderettes. Way back in the old tradition of African washing we'd be down by the river, engaged in a communal act of renewal, sharing and intimacy. We'd be scrubbing clothes on the banks of the Nile, healing each other with our laughter and swapping village stories. We'd have a quick swim in the river before wringing out the clothes,and spreading them out on the rocks to dry. Now we sit here mute on plastic chairs as the machines click, spin and thunder. The machines have dried our tongues, stolen our powers of conversation. And Edward the washing machine bandit owns the river . . . I wake up from this soppy nostalgia to find my dryer stopped again and the clothes still damp.

Wednesday February 18

Debbie-Anne gives me the inside dope on this TV show she's been working on, The Dancing Detectives. It isn't a speaking part she's got, though at one point she does sigh very loudly. The hunky one in the star role is gay. the Director thinks she's Spielberg's sister and goes around with a fish eye lens in her eye all the time. One of the extras used to be a big name star and lets everyone know. The show will be on Carlton TV next Autumn.

Teresa removes both my armbands. I cling to the rail in panic. I'm a Scorpio, I lie — I am not a water sign. Teresa's voice drips reassurance. The class is lined up across the pool, waiting. I take a deep breath, and flail in an all or nothing frenzy and surprise myself by reaching the other side. Teresa says well done and anyone would have thought there was a shark chasing after me. I get a certificate to say I have swum one full breadth of the pool unaided. I blue-tac it to my kitchen wall.

Thursday February 19

Dear Harvey,

So glad to learn of your swimming success. Please apply your remarkable talents now to the cleaning of the house!

Your buoyant partner, Nikki

Vacuum cleaner packs up. The world is a conspiracy of repairers. No wonder Rufus drives a neat little silver soft-top Audi. Decide I'll Do It Myself. Take the Vac apart, lay bits on floor and examine them. Blow dust clear of wiring and circuitry, flick the On switch and stand back. The motor whirs a dream. Begin to put vac parts back inside casing. Three hours later I have most of the parts more or less inside the casing. Make a mental note to write to the company telling them it is the most poorly designed appliance I have ever taken apart. Switch on vac. It sucks carpet up so fiercely I can't move it unless I switch vac off again.

Nikki comes home stressed. The lavatory fails her inspection visit. Ditto my bathroom. Ditto landing and lounge carpets. She digs out the bristle broom and sweeps the carpets herself in a sulk until I offer to take her clubbing. We go to a little club on the other side of town, with one tiny dance floor, and a reputation for the latest import music and easy vibes. There are only five people there, but it's no problem. We dance slow and close. At midnight people flood in. At 1 a.m., just when the Mad Professor has got the crowd jumping, Nikki's bleeper reminds her she has to leave. We push our way out, pretending we're on our way to another, better club. Nikki's mother's right — we are party poopers.

Friday February 20

Mop kitchen floor, do dishes and run a cloth around the bathroom, all before breakfast. Smell pile of dirty clothes festering in corner. I have a brainwave. Nikki's friend Antonia's latest boyfriend is an electrician. Maybe he can fix my machine.

Late night, there's a 'Little Green Men sited in Willesden' story on the TV news. Nikki says aliens are always little because that's cute, and green because we human beings are many colours but never green, and men because it's inconceivable to the powers-that-be that women could be running some planet out there, isn't it?

Saturday February 21

Ira rings to say I am not in today's team. He explains players need resting from time to time, especially the best players, and also, it's raining buckets and my delicate ball control skills are unsuited to today's mudbath conditions It's a day for the donkeys. I wish the donkeys luck. Malik rings. There's a black art shop in Islington with a small exhibition space. He's got the owner with him right now. Can I get down there Thursday? I say I'm jetting off to Brussels Friday, but yes, I can squeeze it in. Later, Malik calls round in person. He says he loved my hype.

Ajax-Willesden lost 14-3. That will teach Ira to drop me.

Sunday February 22

Carve three breeze block sculptures of Willesden rats in poses: the Rat Rampant, the Rat Dormant and the Rat Contemplative. Am I getting nostalgic for my old job? Nikki retrieves Ralph's phone number from her Psion Organiser and suggests I ring him to get the washing machine sorted out. What is Ralph's phone number doing in her electronic memory banks, I wonder.

Monday February 23

Poison myself trying to clean oven with chemical cleaner. It takes two cans of Hofmeister to resuscitate me. Discover a wallpaper scraper cuts through the burnt gunge faster than any chemicals, and doesn't give off noxious fumes. Open up the New World Cookery cookery book Nikki has left on kitchen table. Unfortunately it is written in some kind of code. For instance: *Sift 6oz (1 cup) icing (confectioners') . Drizzle on stiff dough.* I am attempting to decipher this when Debbie calls round. She hasn't a clue about cooking either. Why do people do it, she asks, when they can just get a take-away? Debbie talks sense. Lunch is a doner kebab each from The Casbah. Find invitation card on doormat. *Anne at 65 Cherryville Estate is holding a morning party. and cordially invites the residents of 57.* Decide to go. We've only lived here nine months and know nobody.

Tuesday February 24

Morning TV puts me off my breakfast. A grinning black man in lurid pink and purple lycra cavorts under the guise of teaching aerobics. This is not what the nation's househusbands want to tune into while eating their Coco Pops.

Ralph sorts out the washing machine by the bizarre if simple expedient of removing the light bulb I'd fitted into the fridge. I must obtain a bulb of 15 watts or below for the fridge if I want the washing machine to work, he chides. He goes on to condemn the wiring in the kitchen as an obviously amateur job, like that shelf — whoever put that up wants shooting, it is so unlevel the pans are practically sliding off, he makes half his money putting right bodged DIY jobs, he sighs. I ask how's it going with Antonia? Are the two of them getting on as well as they did here on New Year's Eve, in the kitchen, on the lawn, in the bathroom? He gets out of my kitchen.

The washing machine works a dream. Respect due to

Ralph. I load it, get it running, then whizz round in the Micra and pick up a 15 watt fridge bulb, oil paints, canvas, brushes and solvent. Tomorrow, I paint! Go, Picasso!

Wednesday February 25

Speed through ironing backlog. Then change toilet light bulb. First one I fit is a 100 watter and shows up every tiny dirt mark, so I find a 40 watter instead. Debbie arrives. She's feeling lonely and neglected. I paint her. Her skin has this marvellous luminosity. She's a real pleasure to paint. All is not well between her and Malik in the sex department, she tells me. Malik has no drive. I snigger behind my paints.

Thursday February 26

Lunchtime is graced with a visit from Nikki's mother, Ruby. She's brought lunch for me. Pumpkin soup, then banana bread. I tell her it's amazingly good and she confesses she lied to me about Meals On Wheels. She's never used them. I can tell why. Chatting away I realise I'm due at that art shop Malik rang me about. Explain I've got to dash. Ruby invites herself along.

The shop owner, Wilbert, seems OK. He takes one of my Love In Chaos metalwork pieces and a couple of rats on a sale or return basis, and says he'll take the standard fifty percent, is that OK? I turn to Ruby. She nods. Later Ruby tells me you can always trust a man who wears brogues. I Must Remember This.

Friday February 27

That window cleaner knocks again. He says he'll clean them for nothing. He shins up on his ladder to the studio window first. His look of disappointment when he sees there's no orgy going on today is actually worth paying for.

Tired of ironing. Make a mental note to shop only for nocrease clothes. Ironing is a primitive custom probably invented by the Ancient Egyptians. Have you ever noticed how flat everything is in ancient Egyptian paintings? Turn on the radio and find a pirate station. From the crackle and fade, sounds like it's one guy and a shoebox transmitter in some pokey high rise flat. The single DJ reads all the commercials in different voices, which is as funny as it's cheap. He does Oliver Samuels for a nightclub plug, Sergeant Bilko for a comedy venue, and Frank Bruno for a herbal tonic, one after the other. The guy's a star.

7 p.m. Nikki rings, says she's ball-and-chained to her desk putting the finishing touches to a three year European Region-By-Region Corporate Sales Roll-Out Strategy Document. I tell her if the document is anything like the title, its sheer weight will crush all opposition. Get out some breeze blocks, but I have no inspiration, not even for rats, and end up merely sitting on them.

Saturday February 28

I'm back in the team, Ira declares. We play away at The Moon. Goggle at pitch. It's ninety minutes of churning through craters but the other team is strangely chicken of getting dirty and we win two nil. Home team captain then informs us the showers are not working. Mud begins to cake on my skin. Traipse home to find Nikki's been cleaning. Toilet smells like a Bavarian pine forest, bathroom tiles gleam like mirrors and there's a new vase on the window ledge. Take a bath. Later, Nikki disappears with Antonia. I think they went to the pictures because when she comes back she smells of popcorn.

Sunday February 29

Loll around all day.

Monday March 1

Daytime TV Channel 1: Three women Sharing One Man — Is It Possible? Channel 2: Can Men Give Birth? Channel 3: Household Objects As Erotic Devices. This last show intrigues and I do some experimenting around the house. Washing machine does nothing for me despite sitting on top of it, legs crossed. I also fail to be moved by straddling the vac, though I forgot whether it is supposed to be turned on at the time. Ruby delivers lunch and stays for a beer. No sculpting done.

Tuesday March 2

Knock on Anne's door, ready for her morning party. Four female faces appear around door. Gales of laughter when I say why I've come . Charming hostess in a scanty French Mistress costume says there appears to have been a misunderstanding. Her name is not Anne — it's Gillian, and this is an Anne Summers brand, erotic lingerie party. Retreat home feeling foolish. Then fantasise about the party for at least half an hour. Debbie phones, emotional. She thinks Steve has gone off her. "He's so cold, he won't come near me," she says. It's probably nothing, I reassure her, he'll have business things on his mind. Privately, I tire of making excuses for him.

Recognise I am not a brilliant cook. The fancy food I bought yonks ago is slowly decomposing in the fridge because I don't know what to do with it. Go down to the newsagent and ask for a Cordon Bleu video. Newsagent says to come back in a week and he'll have me sorted. Notice newsagent has a strange tic to his face.

Whizz the Micra up to L-Mart. Shop to the dulcet tones of George Michael's Greatest Hits. There's a special offer on Lovers' Feast Food. Manage to emerge from L-Mart unpropositioned. L-Mart oyster dips in seafood sauce and hot garlic bread fail to do the trick with Nikki. She has eyes only for her laptop screen.

Wednesday March 3

I vac everything and wipe down the kitchen surfaces. Then it's painting with Debbie. Debbie thinks Steve doesn't love her and is tired of her. I tell her she's a very interesting, lovable person. She cries. Over lemon tea I ask her about her acting. She's going to some TV auditions. Her agent feels she comes across better in close-ups than in theatre because she has expressive eyebrows. She's not having much luck in theatre to date. One director told her, "You can't cut the ketchup, Deborah — you just can't cut the ketchup!" I say I thought the expression was 'mustard' and she says that's what she told Mr Sweaty Arse Director too. We have a laugh and drink to her TV success. She's doing in-store demonstrations at Debenhams tomorrow. She's learnt the sales jingle already. She sings it me:

> *Rap T'ou Multiblender*
> *The latest thing in kitchen splendour*
> *Great to mix with, great to beat with*
> *It's the only Multiblender you wanna be seen with!*

I say I'll come and see her and she tells me to stop kidding. Venue: Debenhams first floor 2 p.m.

Go to my swimming lessons feeling nervous. No polystyrene floats and no armbands now. This is the big league. Lesson goes well. Get back to my cubicle and realise I've forgotten my towel, knock on the next door cubicle, and get the all-clear to enter from Siobhan. I enter. She's starkers. She doesn't miss a beat. She apologises for inviting me in. She thought it was Lola. Lola arrives just then and giggles at us both. I try to explain I came for a towel. Eventually Lola lends me one. All three of us play table tennis afterwards.

Thursday March 4

Turn up to Debbie-Anne's in-store demo. She dies of embarrassment so I say I was just passing. She looks great in the Rap T'ou uniform. We give each other a parting hug. She asks if I've been sculpting; she can feel a chisel in my pocket. Her little joke. I hide around the corner to watch her routine. She's very accomplished. She makes five sales at the end of demonstration. She comes across as honest and fun. The jingle is catchy and I hum it all the way back in the Micra: "Rap T'ou Multiblender, finest thing in . . ." Nikki says the house is a mess, what have I been doing all day and our arrangement isn't working. I promise to try harder.

Friday March 5

Listen to Ruby's back-a-yard stories while tucking into her cooking. She shows me how to do rice and peas. Realise Ruby has become my lunchtime meals-on-wheels service. Early evening, Ira and the entire football team rendezvous at my place to plan tactics for tomorrow. Ira appreciates my tactical brain so much he wants me by his side on the touchline, so I agree to be substitute. Then Crazy Phil finds my lager stocks and they all get stuck in. Half an hour later, they are carousing on my freshly vacuumed Berber carpet and some lager gets spilled. I get the vac out quickly. They find this amusing and all start ribbing me about aprons, dusters, milkmen and bored housewives until Ira calls them off. Ira punches me on the shoulder and says there's no shame in being tidy, and it's only right that we men should help out around the house. Afterwards, I thank Ira privately. I manage to clean everything up and air the house before Nikki gets back.

Saturday March 6

Nikki sits me down in the morning, holds my hand and asks me is there anything I want to tell her? I know the correct answer to this one and say yes, that I love her. This is a good answer, but she is not satisfied. She asks me if I have a drink problem. I say not that I know of. She sighs and says I'm in denial, but when I feel like talking she will always be there for me, so long as it's not office hours. What' she on about?

Ajax-Willesden lose 12-0. The team's tactical naivety astonishes me. Kick and rush went out with kipper ties. Besides, the opposition are all about ten centimetres taller than us so what was the point? Ira looks like he's about to cry when I ask if he's going to send me on to sort things out. He tells me to save my strength because this match is lost already. In the dressing room he says I was Man Of The Match and I didn't even play.

Nikki takes me to a minimalist Asian restaurant doing halal food. I call for the wine list. Nikki tells me it's a non-alcoholic place and am I comfortable with that? I say I'll bear up, so long as she'll allow me an extra glass of lassi.

Sunday March 7

Malik calls round 'for business advice' from Nikki. He spots my Modern German Football Tactics Manual and asks if Ira felt sorry enough for me to give me a game yesterday. I let slip that Ira said I was Man Of The Match. His jaw drops. Malik has Debbie-Anne 'on tow' (his words) and asks if he can leave her with me while he confers with Nikki. I tell him to confer away. Debbie-Anne waits till Malik has gone off with Nikki in the Lexus then shows me something: a MultiBlender. It's her demonstration model, the deluxe version, complete with all attachments. The promotion is over and they gave it to her for free and she wants me to have it. I say I can't possibly, but she insists. I kiss her all over. She laughs and says she didn't know a blender could mean so much to someone. It doesn't. But she does. Debbie watches me do some welding in the garden. I wear the full protective kit. I'm all hammer and tongs and flame-thrower and cursing — like the devil incarnate, she says, and the sculpture reminds her of that Picasso guy's stuff. I don't think she realises just how much what she said means to me. I tell her I'll give her one when I'm done. She laughs. She has a filthy mind. She leaves late afternoon to rehearse for another TV audition, a barmaid "in a tits-out TV thriller." I read this book I picked up from the library: *Daily Meditations For Tired Out Londoners*. Nikki returns late in the evening, minus Malik.

Monday March 8

Debbie rings and says Steve had lipstick all over his shirt collar when he came home yesterday and it was the shade Nikki wears. I say I don't think it's Nikki and anyway people kiss, even business people, in fact it's all the rage in business circles now, they've all gone kissy-kissy like the Continentals. She asks me do I think she, Debbie, is attractive? I tell her she is a very smart, intelligent woman, and yes, sexually attractive, Steve is a very lucky guy. She blows me a kiss over the phone, says she's off to audition for that barmaid part and hangs up.

I put phone down and catch myself daydreaming mildly erotic thoughts about Debbie for a good five minutes while washing plates. My mind drifts unexplicably from erotica to ephemera. Like: why is an occasional table called an occasional table? Is an occasional table also, occasionally, a chair? Or a cupboard? Or a hat rack? Or a jumping frog?

Remembering Ruby's tips from last week for lunch, I cook red kidney bean paste and fully boiled long grain patna rice. It tastes delectable. Finally I can cook perfect rice! I chomp through three bowls-full for lunch. Reach into the fridge and realise I'm all out of lager, thanks to the football crowd.

Someone calls at the door. I open to a tall, white, sixtyish man, wearing high green Wellingtons. He lives in the semi that adjoins ours, he declares. Swarms of midges are descending from that jungle that is my excuse of a rear garden, onto his rare Himalayan petunias. He has come to exterminate them. He looks emotional about this. I invite him in.

Tuesday March 9

Dear Harvey,

There is mud all over the carpets. An infestation of ants in the kitchen. The vacuum cleaner needs attention (it has too much suck). Generally the whole house is a mess. I expect to see a significant improvement upon my return. (please refer to contract if you need to refresh your memory that the above is all your responsibility). PS. There are some mysterious earth mounds in the back garden. Is a giant mole loose there? Yours, Nikki.

Edward is a retired tax inspector. He's going to lime and drain the land, and rebuild the garden. I pay only for the plants, though I have to lay on an endless supply of luke warm, unsweetened tea for him. While Edward's digging, I bring my favourite 'Love In Chaos' sculpture out of the garage and gaze at it. Then blaze away for an hour. Edward asks what the devil am I doing? He likes the sculpture. He thinks it looks like a three dimensional Kandinsky. An art-loving ex-tax inspector! His wife appears half an hour later with a deck chair. She's wiry, cardiganed, Polish and very knowledgeable about many things including gardening, Catholic theology and lager strengths. She directs Edward's digging from her deck chair.

Ruby calls close to lunchtime. She hasn't brought any cooked food. Instead, I am to cook under her directions, she declares. So that's where Nikki gets her Voice of Authority. An hour later, we're all tucking into Sweet Potato and Saltfish

Balls, and Barbados Snapper, washed down with Pils lager which Edward brings over.

Nikki returns. I didn't get much housework done because her Mum came round, I explain. My saltfish balls pacify her. She falls asleep with half a saltfish ball in her mouth, muttering "He's weighing my out-trays." I lift her chin off her keyboard and carry her to bed. Dream I'm sculpting. I finish the 'Love In Chaos' sculpture brilliantly in my dreams. Wake in the middle of the night to sketch it, but by the time I've found a piece of charcoal and paper from the studio I've forgotten the entire vision. Groan back to sleep.

Wednesday March 10

Debbie-Anne tells me all about her TV audition. She gushes about the script, the cast, the crew and the outside catering. She's so alive, I tell her. She says I'm the first man she feels she can really talk to, I have manners, droolsome eyes, and a large vocabulary. All this flattery makes my pecker rise and, since we're both starkers as usual, she notices. This time she doesn't laugh. She gets up and comes over to me. One thing leads to another . . . I feel like a rat, a complete rat. How could I have sex with my best friend's woman? How could I be unfaithful to Nikki? Debbie is untroubled. It happened, she says. She calls it our little secret.

Swimming lesson goes well. I am buoyant without floats or armbands. In the pool café afterwards I learn Lola is a post grad theoretical mathematics student, working on number theory, and Siobhan is learning English. I tell them I'm a sculptor. I'm not sure if Siobhan understands. Her English is a bit ropey. Lola is worried about her PhD. Will she be able successfully to defend her thesis when the Professors start taking it to pieces? If not, it will be 3 years wasted. Lola says she comes swimming to clear her mind. I say I do too, and somehow the water inspires my sculptures. Siobhan says,

"I would very much like to see your erections." Lola doesn't bat an eyelid. I stutter maybe sometime when it's convenient.

Nikki arrives home late. I say there's some Nazar's microwave chicken chasseur in the freezer. She microwaves the chicken chasseur huffily. She doesn't put one in for me. How petty!

Thursday March 11

Go to L-Mart with Debbie. The manager greets me, smile on full beam. "So, you've got lucky," he whispers. I ignore him, restock on lager and cereals, then we take to the High Street for some real food. Afterwards, Debbie and I decide to go play squash. I fling myself all round the court while she hardly breaks sweat. It's all in the wrist, she says. We're in the foyer about to leave when who do we see there but Malik, restocking the vending machines! We hide in the High Aerobics class till he's gone. I'm all shagged out from doing Steps by the time the coast is clear. PS. learn Malik has promised to get Debbie into the movies.

Nikki swallows my mange tout & black bean stir fry valiantly, I tell her her skin looks great in the candlelight. We make love, the lion and the cheesegrater.

Friday March 12

Spend morning browsing Bertrand Russell's *In Praise Of Idleness*, then laze in a patio chair. I fall asleep imagining shapes, dream erotic dreams, and wake up with that sculpture again, almost fully formed in my mind. This time I get it down on paper. I blaze away with the oxy equipment like a madman on LSD to get the sketch into three dimensions. All this effort. Mr Russell wouldn't have approved.

Later a BMW pulls into my drive. Malik and two others emerge. I imagine Debbie's blabbed our secret and he's come to break my legs. But Malik is all warmth and supplication. He and his friends can't make it to the mosque. Can they do their prayers here? I say go ahead and feel even worse about my coupling with Debbie-Anne. I am an abject sinner. But discretion is the better part of survival, so I resist the temptation to confess all. Leave Malik in charge of the house while I shop for vac. Late p.m. Nikki returns. I find myself going through tomorrow's shopping list instead of listening to her long tale about her work troubles. Maybe she sensed this and that's what caused the argument.

Saturday March 13

We are losing two nil and hanging on by the skin of our teeth when Ira sends me onto the pitch. I reorganise the midfield, switch Dobbo to sweeper and tell Mohammad and Leroy to spray it about a bit. We win the tactical battle, though four more fluke goals go past our feckless goalie. I whisper in Ira's ear that Scooby might not be up to it. Ira nods sagely. Scooby gets his nickname from the cartoon tune: "Scooby, Scooby Doo, where are you?" since he's never in the right place when the opposition shoots.

Me, Nikki, Antonia and Ralph head for the Moviedrome. Nikki roots for Murderous Transaction, a corporate thriller in which Demi Moore loses her clothes and saves the Company. Ralph wants to watch it too, though I don't think for the same reasons as Nikki. Antonia votes for Clarissa's Castle, a high gloss, Gothic lesbian weepie. I want to watch The .45 from Mantegna but I say I want to watch The Garden of Meaning — the latest French offering, because I want to impress Antonia. We all watch Murderous Transaction. In the interval I buy the popcorn and ice cream, and guess who's the aisle-girl — Debbie! This is what Malik meant when he said he'd get her into the movies, she giggles, and I'm not to tell the others. She slips her shades back over her eyes.

Sunday March 14

Late morning, Nikki and Malik drive off in power suits. Nikki's Armani suit smells of Malik's insecticide-strength eau de cologne when she returns. Maybe they swapped jackets. She flees upstairs and changes. I hope Malik is not tempting Nikki to risk our house on some jam-tomorrow investment scheme he's dreamed up. I saw them drooling over some Financial Times stock exchange indexes before they left. I ask Nikki what they're scheming, but it's all hush hush. I vac aggressively around her.

Monday March 15

The guy at the art shop Malik introduced me to begs me for more stuff. He's sold one k.s worth so far, he says, the steel sculpture and two rats. I do a fast calculation. After the shop's cut that leaves me with £500. I instantly plan a party to celebrate. The first barbecue of the year, provided it doesn't rain. I get busy on the phone with invites.

Nikki gets back late, flops on the couch and goes straight into REM dreaming. She lies there twitching and grasping.

Tuesday March 16

Get Party Invitations printed by the AutoCard Machine at L-Mart, then distribute them around to the neighbours. Ruby gives me another cooking lesson. We all four devour it, together with some Polish beer Roxanna fetches round. The Polish beer kicks like a Wimbledon centre forward. We are still all agreeably half-comatose when Nikki arrives back. She censures me for getting her mother and the whole neighbourhood drunk, and for having an easy ride while she's having her back flayed at InterGlobe plc. I tell her yesterday's news about my stuff selling but she merely says she has a report to write, can I clear up? I dutifully chairlift her mother into a taxi, then shake 'n' vac.

Wednesday March 17

This day is pure Ealing farce: Debbie and I are kekless as usual in the studio when the doorbell chimes. I pull on some underwear, chinos, a smock and go down. It's Nikki. Her eyes are dancing. She's just brokered a megadeal. "Success makes me so horny. Take me now! In the hallway!" She has my chinos down and is soon pulling off my smock. Then she stops and titters. I look down. I'm wearing Debbie-Anne's Tangas. No wonder I thought they were tight. When Nikki has finished tittering she looks at me with her kind psychiatrist's look and asks if there is any particular reason, though she isn't distressed by it, whatever turns me on, as long as I continue to buy my own and not wear hers. Bluffing like mad, I say I like the feel of silk, which is true. She says if she'd known I'd felt that strongly about it she'd have bought me the silk shirts I've been asking for. She offers me a deal. She'll buy me silk shirts if I take a rain check on women's undies. Her passion gone, and still tittering, Nikki staggers back to her Lexus, saying my secret is safe with her. I wave her a 'see ya!' from the hallway. Step into the studio to find Debbie rolling on the floor in silent hysterics, using a pillow as a gag. I don't know how long I want to continue risking these nude sessions.

Siobhan mentions to Lola they have a Turkish sauna at the baths and we should try it out. *Turkish sauna*. The name conjures up a huge bubbling hookah, steam, hypnotic Eastern music. I daydream: Swedish sauna: naked, sober, taut Aryan bodies, on hard pine slat benches, withstanding rigorous, mutual beatings with birch twigs to improve circulation. English sauna: everyone keeps their clothes on and the steam is somehow very cold. Italian sauna: three swaddled godfathers sweating, a huge bowl of spaghetti in the middle, in the background Gina Ferrari holding a strategically placed towel. Jamaican sauna: a beach, three bouncing . . . I come out of my daydream to hear Siobhan and Lola talking in English.

They're discussing the rise of neo-Fascism in Germany. Siobhan is speaking fluently. I invite them both to my celebration party, but they have dates with their boyfriends.

Thursday March 18

Putting finishing touches to latest sketch of Debbie for the day, when my (new!) mobile phone rings. It's Nikki, checking on how I am. I tell her I'm fine, just as Debbie-Anne says, "Here's your underwear," Nikki asks who was that? I tell her I'm in a shop, buying some underwear, but not to worry it's not silk, or women's. This satisfies her until Debbie-Anne bellows: "Have you seen my bra?" Nikki insists I put her onto the shopkeeper. I whisper staccato that the batteries are going, before cutting her off.

Even now I can hear the purr of Nikki's Lexus heading this way home. I drive Debbie-Anne into town. While there, I buy some underwear. Later that evening Nikki asks to inspect it. I explain away the bra reference by saying it was one of those unisex outfitters and someone was in the cubicle next door. Nikki is only half convinced, but she approves of my underwear (burgundy and white jockeys — Debbie-Anne chose them). She makes her ritual grumbles about the state of the house and I remind her about the barbecue party I'm throwing tomorrow.

Friday March 19

Ruby used to wring the chickens' necks herself when she was a girl, and she got the knack of big scale cooking from preparing wedding receptions. It's party time. Malik arrives in jeans for once. He mutters he doesn't want to smoke out any of his two thousand dollar suits. Debbie-Anne looks exquisitely happy on his arm. I recognise some of the Anne Summers party people even with their clothes on, and smile broadly to them. Nikki arrives late. She wears a black and white, flowerprint sarong and her natural face instead of the office make-up. She looks sublime. She gives me a quick peck which I convert into a long hug, then drifts around the guests.

I'm the barbecue chef and serve marinated chicken, corn cob, veggie and lamb burgers. Debbie eats a sausage before me very sexily then dashes back to Malik. I overhear a delicious exchange between Malik and one of my artist friends, Max:

Malik: So, Max, what's your biggest success this year?"

Max: I don't understand the question.

Malik: I made twenty k. clear profit on one deal last month.

Max: I feel I've come to a greater understanding of myself, of how materialist values have been eroding my spiritual well-being.

Malik: Huh?

Later on, when too much Polish beer has been drunk, things get disorderly. Antonia falls into one of Edward's earthwork ditches. Ralph is the hero of the evening for pulling her out single-handedly. Party ends abruptly with monsoon rain.

Saturday March 20

Nikki is up early in the morning filling in Edward's excavations. She's in tears and bans him from the house. I ask how Antonia is. Nikki says under the circumstances she was remarkably forgiving, and can I just see all the mess everywhere? I borrow Edward's shampoo vac and shampoo the carpet. But Nikki trudges in all muddy and I have to do it again. Phone Ira and explain that I can't make the team this week. He tries to mask his disappointment. "We'll cope, somehow, Harvey, we'll cope."

Nikki and I watch Sheffield Sharks destroy the London Towers. The behaviour of the referee was abominable, the Towers players played patheticically and the whole Towers Board of Directors should go, Nikki rails, as she scythes through traffic in her Lexus. I've never seen her happier. Malik comes round. Ajax-Willesden won 5-0. Malik played central midfield. I should have poisoned one of his halal lamb burgers last night. He drives off with Nikki for another of their business meetings. How come all his business gets done on a Saturday? I ask myself. And why does he always need Nikki?

Sunday March 21

'Anne Summers' Gillian drops by. She says she's moved into Betterware, it's like Tupperware, but cheaper and the same quality. She leaves me a catalogue and says she'll call round for my order and to give the date for her first demonstration party next week. There are a lot of things in the catalogue which I never knew existed, like lemon zesters, and plastic bag holders. Wonder why someone living in a 100K plus house has to be selling Betterware. I guess the mortgages on these Cherryville Estate mansions are enough to make anyone desperate. Nikki and me share a bath. I tell her my latest thoughts on saunas and she offers me a Hawaiian massage. We are soon both covered in coconut oil. I collapse exhausted and satiated and fall asleep to the sound of Nikki talking about restructuring stress. I dream of sculptures.

Monday March 22

Resolve to improve my cooking skills. The trick is to get the right cookery guide. The daytime TV cooking gurus are all bores with puffed-up hats, hammy spiel, souffléd egos and preposterous recipes. I want good-tasting, low cal, nutritious meals for two that are easy to make, startlingly good to eat and have ingredients I don't have to shop in Harrods for. Lunch is beans on toast. I find Ceefax's recipe page, blend a couple of these with the New World Cookery instructions, fold in my tapes of Ruby and after an entire day's culinary experimenting I come up with:

HARVEY'S DEJEUNER FOR TWO
flamed pork chops
cheese banana with Wan Ton noodles.

Practice a couple of times before I get it perfect. Nikki absolutely loves it. Consider applying to the producers to become a TV chef.

Tuesday March 23

Washer blows again. I trundle down to the launderette and scrutinise the settings on the LoadStar II like a safebreaker inspecting a combination lock:

1 hot wash
2 warm wash (with pre-wash)
3 synthetics (with pre-wash)
4 wash 'n' wear
5 cold wash

Everyone has theirs on 2 *warm wash* but I like the sound of wash 'n' wear (sounds like no ironing). I load up, feed the machine with coins and go for wash 'n' wear. The machine roars to life. I turn away satisfied. I was fortunate to have turned. Seconds later hot steam jets out from all sides of the Loadstar. The machine stops. Then every other machine stops. Faces turn towards me, and they are not smiling. I do not want to be stuffed into the spin extractor. I am saved by a rumble above. Everyone looks up. Water avalanches through the false ceiling tiles. As I leave, I glimpse a sign on the door:

"End your washday drudgery — service washes
with pleasure — see attendant.
While you do other things."

I make a mental note to next time see the attendant.

Cook chicken korma. Nikki nods yes, she can taste the

natural yogurt base. This wins her a peach melba dessert. She makes noises later about where her laundry might be. I say it'll be all dry cleaned and hung up for her tomorrow. She nods approval. She spills some peach melba on the new tablecloth, but I don't mind.

Wednesday March 24

Debbie-Anne comes round beaming like she's discovered a rich aunt. She says she's pregnant. I'm pleased for her but suggest perhaps it's a bit early for celebrations when she's missed just one day of her period, but she says she knows her own body and can feel something's changed. She fidgets with happiness throughout the sketch session, then lunches out of my fridge on two boiled eggs with curry powder, two slices of dry toast and a bowl of cold custard. If this is a phantom pregnancy the phantom is soon going to be obese. I drop Debbie-Anne off on the High Street where she's going window shopping for baby clothes.

Today's swim class is basic lifesaving technique. I nearly get to snog Siobhan but spoilsport Teresa finds the lifesaving dummy. It's Teresa's birthday. We've bought her a furry otter toy and she blushes and says we needn't have. Then we sing Happy Birthday. This has her hiding under the table with embarrassment. She stands up eventually and says we've all come on lengths and breadths since we started and that obviously none of us is attending singing class but that she's very proud of our swimming achievements and that she doesn't feel anywhere near forty years old. Then she has a little cry and is lost in hugs.

Thursday March 25

What happened to the 'Friday Is afternoon Sex Day' idea? I ring Nikki and ask her about today. She whispers she can't get away. I hear some bullfrog in the background croaking about

Target Slippage. Nikki hangs up. Ring the Council finance people. They promise my redundancy cheque is in the post. I ask how much the cheque is for. The size of the cheque is confidential, I'm told.

Nikki returns, jumps into the shower then an evening gown and her best Hollywood Premiere shoes. Where are we going? I ask. She intends to get well and truly drunk tonight and it's all going on her Gold Card so I'm not to take her to any place cheap.

We start out at the Lido and end up at a Mayfair jazz club where African millionaires' wanton daughters rub flesh with the sons of plastic surgeons. Nikki exudes class. She has the jazz band play all her favourites, and at fifty quid a request they are an expensive juke box. Her Gold Card ends the night two millimetres flatter than it started. The jazz band leader whispers to me they're available for private bookings.

Friday March 26

Nikki wakes with a hangover. I drive her to work in the Lexus, then catch a tube and taxi back to Willesden. She dents garage door with her front bumper on returning. Her head's sore as a squashed hedgehog's and no, she doesn't want to look at my sculptures. She chooses two cans of rice pudding over my cooking, then collapses in bed.

Saturday March 27

Malik calls round early morning with Debbie-Anne. He's full of himself as usual. He's the smartest black entrepreneur in London. He's Samuel L Jackson out of Berry Gordy of Motown Records Inc. (Sample speech: "It's a tough business, not a pretty one. You have to know how to hold your own. Face down the challengers on your territory, 'knowhaddamean?'") I tell him he sounds like a 50's B-movie gangster. He says he feels like one sometimes. I ask him innocently if many shoot outs occur in Sports Centres since that's where I saw him last, emptying the vending machines at Willesden Pool. He doesn't miss a beat, boasts it's a very lucrative sideline, and he has winner written right through him. He, Malik, is not one of life's Substitutes, he finishes. He stands there grinning broadly. Something comes over me and I give him a friendly headbutt. He ducks and we fall to the floor, wrestling. I soon have a half Nelson on him. Somehow, he rolls me and is about to plug my mouth with his gold braceleted, left fist when Debbie-Anne screams

"Stop it! I'm pregnant!" Malik freezes mid-punch.

Ira rings. Can I help? Malik has pulled out. He wants to go to Mothercare. I do my duty for Ajax-Willesden. I marshal our defence and we scrape home 2:1 against The Harlesden Bucanneers.

Sunday March 28

Fact 1: I like sex best in the mornings. Fact 2: Nikki prefers evenings, outdoors. Nikki says she's happy for Debbie-Anne that she's pregnant but she herself is having too much fun to stop and change nappies for a decade. She promises me a dishwasher when she gets her next rise.

Monday March 29

Not sure I have the right temperament to be an artist. It's a lonesome vocation. I need a studio somewhere in one of the artists' warehouse places that are springing up. But I don't have any rent money. I don't have any money. I haven't sold sculpture in at least a month. Neither has the redundancy money arrived. I am living off the house-keeping Nikki gives me. Why am I not an international sculpting star yet? I am deeply depressed. I go shopping.

Harvey's Beginners' Guide To The Shopping Trolley

Trolley Selection:
Do you have the correct coin? Many trolleys cannot be accessed except by the insertion of a one pound coin. This is not a mean way of getting you to pay for the pleasure of shopping, but an anti-trolley theft device. You can get the coin back when you return the trolley. Just jam the projection from an unused trolley into the neck of the locking device of your own and your pound coin pops out. Usually.

Trolley Size:
Size matters. Choose you trolley size carefully. If you choose a large trolley and fill it do not queue at the checkout behind someone with a small trolley. This is because most supermarkets use a trolley rotation system which is too complicated to explain, so just don't do it.

Trolley Manoeuvring
Test your trolley for manoeuvrability. Trolley wheels are as unreliable as jazz musicians. No four trolley wheels ever want to move in the same direction at the same time. But some are better behaved than others. If you see people battling at a stack of trolleys while there is a good-looking one nearby that no-one's going near, do not touch it. It is certain to be a rogue wheeled trolley.

Trolley Media
If your trolley has an advertising plaque on the front, do read it. Whether you like it or not, you are now in the walking billboard business. Do you want to be advertising an alcoholics drop-in centre? Or the next visit of Torville & Dean to your local theatre? Choose your advert as you would choose your wardrobe.

Trolley Inspection
Look inside the trolley. Clear out all the junk that's been left behind by other people. However, keep any very long shopping receipt you

find, and swap it with your own to impress your partner with how much you are spending on the weekly shop.

Aisle Navigation
Junk food is always in the first aisles so the slobs don't have to look far but beer is always furthest away next to the dog food tins so you will have to go all round the supermarket. Try to memorise where things are. If you really can't find anything then, as a last resort, look at the signs hung over the aisles.

Washing Powders
Don't let the experts fool you. All washing powders are the same. They all wash clothes. Buy the most brightly packaged ones and you won't go wrong.

Trolley Loading
Load heavy, uncrushable goods first. However, when you get to the check-out, load these onto the conveyor belt first since things go off the conveyor belt and into the new shopping trolley on a first on first off basis. If this sounds complicated, that's because it is complicated.

Tuesday March 30

I pass Ruby's rice-cooking test with flying colours. She also trusts me to chop up a chicken and prepare the orange sauce. I eat my laurels. Debbie-Anne rings. She is definitely pregnant. I offer her congratulations and she says the congratulations may be mutual. I ask, but what does she mean? She says Malik fires blanks and I'm the only other person possible. But we only did it once . . . Debbie gets weepily happy. Meanwhile I can see Ruby eavesdropping so I have to put the phone down but I promise we can talk tomorrow. Ninety nine percent of me would consider it a mind-boggling disaster if Debbie really was pregnant by me. But there's this tiny other part that's thrilled. I'd be a Daddy.

Wednesday March 31

Debbie-Anne calls round and says merrily she was only joking and of course the baby's Malik's. She's been to the doctor and she got the date of conception wrong. It was six weeks ago, not two. I go along with the story and this visibly calms her. She poses well. She glows with health as only a pregnant woman can. Can I see a slight bulge at her abdomen, or am I imagining it? I tell her she's more beautiful than ever and she likes that. She raids my fridge again and eats all yesterday's lunch leftovers: Chicken à L'Orange, rice and peas, peach slices. She says I cook like a TV chef.

Thursday April 1

I ruin a sculpture and can't patch it. I have to start over. Three weeks' work wasted. Edward and Roxanna ring the doorbell. I don't let them in. Just carry on getting the metal together for the sculpture, version two.

Friday April 2

Malik shows, settles himself on my sofa and does a rambling half-apology. I shouldn't be messing about being an artist, he advises. We men are muscle, strength, hunters, big car drivers, impregnators. He says that last bit with deep satisfaction. He has a new deal lined up for me but he needs me to change my image. He's already booked me a seat at his barber's, and he'll fix me some decent threads. It sounds like he wants to turn me into Malik Mark II but today I have low resistance to anything whatever involves getting some money so I capitulate.

7 p.m. Nikki comes home talking numbers and marketing. Her drift is she's got important work to plough through tonight. I tell her I don't mind. I sit in the lounger in the back garden all evening, watching the clouds scud by. Inside, Nikki's laptop screen bathes her in a lurid, neon-blue light.

Saturday April 3

Nikki goes away for a conference. Ira rings — Malik has taken my place on the team again.

Sunday April 4

Go Bergmann's. Bergmann's is an oasis of African artists. Besides Claudine there's James ('Not Jim, not Jimmy. James.') the tall, check-shirted choreographer, Arnulfo the beefy, yellow-looned, crazed lead guitarist, Samia the bandanna-ed short and scatty, demo-tapes singer, Filo the stick-like, bewigged, Bermuda-shirted acid cartoonist, and Sappho the

African-robed lesbian poet. Is insanity a prerequisite of being an artist? Seems so. We spend the evening dissing (1) the art establishment, (2) the insolence of promoters, (3) the perfidy of gallery owners, (4) the racism of hot dog sellers, (5) the ignorance of academics, (6) the myopia of the beancounters, (7) the crassness of Bergmann's menu and (8) the inevitability of the bill. In the end Sappho paid by plastic. It was an entirely refreshing moan session.

Nikki returns but has to drive all the way to some emergency computer recovery centre because her hard disk has crashed and she's lost everything. She looks close to tears. I say I'll drive her but she declines the offer. She's going to sue the ass off the manufacturers, she says, as soon as she's got time. They can stand down their lawyers for a couple of years then, I conclude privately. I wave her off, then vac and tidy a bit. She returns late, relieved. The whizzkids at Recovery managed to get back everything except her last two days' work. She spends the rest of the evening in the neon blue.

Monday April 5

Volvo Eric pulls up across my drive. Through the studio net curtains, I watch him stride up the driveway. He raps sternly on the door. Curiosity beats my better judgment and I go down and open. Eric says he knew all along I was the occupant, and he is willing to overlook past transgressions. I thank him profusely. He has a pair of binoculars around his neck. There have been a few burglaries, he explains. These are interesting times. Even the lower middle classes have a role to play. The Cherryville Active Citizens Watch, of which he is most senior member, is on a recruitment drive. Can I swim ten lengths of a pool, do fifty sit-ups, twenty press-ups, read a map upside down in a gale in the dark and live off wild plants for a week? If so, I can join the Watch immediately. I can do one pool length I tell him proudly, so I don't qualify. Though if he says the word I'll have a runner fetch some top class ganja for the Watch's exclusive use, free of charge, to show my moral support. He stamps off muttering about black riffraff and and nancy boys swamping the estate.

Try to entertain Nikki with story of Volvo Eric but she grumbles about not being able to find a clean glass, then starts mopping the kitchen floor. What has a clean glass got to do with mopping the floor? I ask her. A chilli-hot argument ensues which ends in Nikki calling me an artistic nonentity and a slob and me slamming the kitchen door, pulling on my coat and driving aimlessly round in the Micra listening to the car radio. When I get back she has turned out all the lights and gone to bed.

Tuesday April 6

Robbo from Environmental Health rings, officially pleading with me to return. The boss is offering me a salary increment, my choice of shift hours, a bigger desk and three trainee rat catchers to do all the crawling behind fridges etc. Things are that bad? I ask. Robbo answers, yup. They've been set targets and the manager's job is on the line. Maybe all their jobs. This is their hour of need. It's time to come back. I wish them luck. Low as I'm feeling, I will not go back to rodent extermination. As I put the phone down I imagine rats dancing on the streets of Willesden.

Spend the rest of the morning on the sofa musing on the sculpture I botched last week. And about the rickety kit I can't afford to replace. And Nikki's insults. And the still awaited redundancy cheque. Ruby wakes me out of my slumber. She's brought round lunch. Sea breeze salad. She asks how her daughter is. She's worried Nikki's overworking. I can find no good words to say about her daughter so I say nothing. Ruby doesn't push.

Wednesday April 7

Debbie-Anne doesn't show. I ring her and she says she'll start coming round again as soon as she stops throwing up.

I do three full lengths at the pool, dive and tread water. We are rewarded with a game of sharrrrk! I even get to be the shark. This is hard work what with the the flippers and the snorkel and holding on to the shark fin, but I really get into it. Their screams are delicious, Siobhan shrieks with a fantastic mixture of fear and delight whenever I go near her. Just when I'm getting into it, Teresa gives someone else a turn. I almost sulk. In the café afterwards everything is mellow until I have to leave. Then Siobhan smirks, why — do I have to go home to wifey? I say, actually I'm not married. Lola says
"There!" to Siobhan. Lola takes me to one side and apologises on Siobhan's behalf. Siobhan has a crush on me, she explains.

Thursday April 8

Go with Malik to Mohammad's Barber Shop on High Street. There are three barbers on duty and still there's a queue. I take a rickety, black vinyl seat. Malik stands. He calls the older man Duggie and nods in my direction. Duggie nods, but he's busy. His deft fingers whirr, his scissors flash, hover and swoop around a black and very bald, glistening pate. Duggie spends ten minutes clipping air as the old-timer goes over his 'I was a pilot in the RAF during WW2' stories. This is not the white people's three straight white strands of long hair being trimmed and pampered situation. It is not the very short patch of fuzzy grey and black situation. This is a completely bald head situation. "It still growing?" the old-timer asks.
"Growing fine" Duggie replies. He snaps off the Wahl electric clipper, whips off the cover sheet. The old timer smooths his bald sides in the mirror, dusts imaginary coils of hair off his shoulders, then gets off the chair. With a satisfied grin he parts

with three pounds to Duggie who trousers it without blinking. I consider setting up a barber shop next to an old folk's home.

Malik pushes me into the chair vacated by the old-timer and shouts to some youth in the back to get some scissors in hand and take six inches off this sad man's Afro and give him a more down-with-it style. My head is pushed this way and that by the youth as his scissors fly. Malik placates the queue-jumped customers by handing out complimentary tickets to a Tina Turner concert (I'll bet 20 to 1 they're forgeries). I ask my barber what's fashion now with the youth, the zig or the zag? Geometrical stripes? Bald heads? Wigs?

"Afros are back," he replies, "we just bought in a big stock of Afro combs. Whassamatter? You got one yourself." I explain my Afro is the result of neglect, not fashion and am subdued at the thought that afros may be making a come back. What next, I call out to Malik, flare pants? Kipper ties? Black power salutes? This sets the whole shop off on a dizzying retro trip. The banter works through mohair suits, velvet suits, fat lapels, ties, platforms, James Brown, Sly Stone, Funkadelic, Bob Marley, kaftans, Pharaoh beards, hot combs, Hope & Justice, strikes, protest marches, fat sideburns, chicks in minis, drummers, cymbals, crystal balls, tinsel suits, wigs, big tam hats, berets, and Marvin Gaye. It's a scream. And so is my new haircut. I have a dome as shiny as the old man before me. I could kill Malik but he beams with satisfaction. Anyway, what is this deal he's dressing me up for? He says he'll explain tomorrow. Then nudges me forward. We have to leave the scene fast before anybody realises the Tina Turner tickets are fakes, he tells me. I wear a hat all evening and Nikki either doesn't notice or else thinks I'm trying to attract her attention so studiously ignores it. I sleep in hat.

Friday April 9

Malik arrives late morning with a suit for me that's sharp as a skinning knife. He says all I have to do is sit in the car and not show my teeth. He drives to a nondescript location somewhere near fields. On the way, he leans back, pulls away a blanket and hands me a shoulder holster. There is a gun inside it. A real one, I think. I panic. Suddenly I'm in the middle of a Victor Headley novel. Malik says to calm down, the gun's loaded but mostly with blanks. All I have to do is lean on the car with the holster showing and not show my teeth. The suit and haircut will do the rest. Mostly. What does he mean by mostly?

Several sweat-drenched minutes later, a big aquamarine Mercedes arrives. Two men get out. One is a short, wiry, white military looking guy. The other is black and seems to have gone to the same barber and tailor as me. The wiry one walks over with a suitcase. Malik meets him midway, signals for the wiry one to open the suitcase. I check that I'm showing no teeth. The suitcase is opened. Malik inspects it. The case is closed again. The wiry one hands it to Malik. Malik walks backwards towards me. He opens his driver's side door. He calls me to get in. I jump in. He reverses fast and swings the BMW away. I watch the rearview mirror to see we're not being tailed. I've read enough pulp fiction to know to do this. We are not. Malik refuses to explain other than to say it was a little debt collection service he was doing for a friend. He drops me off at my place. I can keep the suit, he says generously. He hands me a bundle of notes too. He's off to the mosque. I count the notes when he's gone. Five hundred. Not a bad deal for an afternoon's work. But I'm buying a wig and a false moustache.

Nikki returns, laughs at my haircut, it's the only laugh she's had all week she says, and Malik must have done it for revenge because I look like a hitman. I say nothing. Malik, I'm sure, would not want her to know about this afternoon's escapade. On the plus side, as Nikki would put it, at least we are talking again.

Saturday April 10

I buzz over in the Micra to Bergmann's. Filo is planning a huge mid-summer African artists' exhibition. The world and their chequebooks are to be invited. Only the top black artistic talent will be showcased. We quickly agree that this means all of us here at Bergmann's, plus a few friends. James is not convinced that the idea is viable, and talks about the impossibility of getting a park licence, the inevitability of bad weather, the inability of black people to get their act together generally, the unavoidable need for expensive insurance, the critical absence of an advertising budget etc. etc. etc. He almost kills off the idea with his own pure and no doubt copyrighted pessimism but Sappho agrees to bankroll it "if that's what it takes." We all get drunk at that. Even James gets tight. A jam session breaks out and draws a sizable crowd. Sören the owner, a huge barrel of a man with a shock of red hair and Scandinavian vowels who claims he used to roadie for Abba, gets all excited at this and starts glad handing us. It's the first time he's acknowledged our existence.

Get back. Nikki's on the phone to Malik. I can tell because she always goes all hushy-hushy when I come in and Malik's on the line. I'm right. She calls me two minutes later and says Malik wants a word. But all he does is boast about scoring two goals yesterday and making the third. I yawn to him and pass him back to Nikki. I distinctly hear her call him Stevie-babes.

Sunday April 11

Nikki refuses to increase my household money. She says one hundred pounds a week is more than enough, especially since she pays all the other bills. I sulk off, thinking I'll simply stop buying food — starve her into seeing reason! Late in the evening, I press Last Redial and Malik's number comes up, so Nikki has phoned Malik some time this evening. (I phoned the speaking clock about 9 p.m.)

Monday April 12

Nikki is annoyed that the washing up isn't done. She delivers her "I'm out there working my butt off while you loaf around all day" speech. I've spent all day trying to rebuild that sculpture but she doesn't want to know. I tell her what she needs is an au pair, not a partner and I'm going on strike.

Later, she says the new project she's heading up is driving her loopy, having to sumo wrestle lower management every time she wants to get anything done. Is wrestling them the best way? I ask her. Wouldn't gentle persuasion work better? She snorts. I don't get any sculpting done today. I think I'm stressed out from hitmanning, last Friday.

Tuesday April 13

Debbie-Anne rings. She's coming round tomorrow. We chat on the phone. Malik is really tender, fussing over her since she got preggers. He hasn't let her go out all this week "in case she miscarries", but she's had enough, says she's bored as a eunuch at a wife swapping convention, and she misses my cooking!

6 p.m. Nikki comes back and says the phone bill is ridiculous and she'll have to call-bar it so nobody can can ring out. Nobody means me. She says Dickhead at EuroMarketing is stressing her with his stupid costings, and her nerves are splitting like bamboo. I say something innocuous, I can't remember what, and she lowers her head like a rhino about to charge. I retreat to my studio. When I see her next, she's on the sofa eating trifle while cradling the phone, talking to Antonia. She must have bought the trifle on her way back. You can get anything from a takeaway nowadays. Fried buffalo? No problem. Boiled antelope's brains? You got it.

Wednesday April 14

Debbie-Anne lets me feel her stomach. It's soft and hot. She says she can feel the baby kicking already. She doesn't say anything more about whether its Malik's or mine. I guess in her mind she's decided it's Malik's. She's keeps spitting due to the baby's hormones or something. She models for me with a bowl by her side into which she spits regularly.

I skip the swimming lesson and drive over to Bergmann's. Sören says either someone starts singing or we're out since collectively we don't buy more than one drink an hour. No one's in the mood for performing so I invite them all back to my place to look at my sculptures and paintings. We get five in the Micra and six in Sappho's Astra. At my place everyone spends two minutes wandering around admiring my art work and the rest of the time emptying my fridge of lager. They all end up drunk, stoned, sick and attempting to fornicate. Except Filo, who is standing alone, gazing at my sofa. I ask why. "Turquoise is very sad, you know, Harvey? Very sad," he says.

Nikki returns, thoughtful about the underwear incident. Why now, after all this time's passed, I don't know. Some of her friends said it would happen, I'd start wearing women's underwear. Men who do housework do these things, she's been told. But why? Seizing the opportunity, I repeat earnestly it's not that it's underwear, it's that it's silk. She agrees to buy me some silk shirts from her own funds if I stop wearing women's underwear.

Thursday April 15

The phone's on fire. First caller is James — can I find his necklace anywhere? It may be down the back of the sofa, or else on the landing or else on top of the washing machine. I take a look and don't find anything. Hang up phone. It rings again instantly. I pick it up, say, hello. Silence. Maybe its a bad connection. I try 1471 to trace the call but the caller has withheld the number. Probably double-glazing salesmen. Next ring comes after two minutes and this time it's silence with a slight sigh, then nothing. Is it a heavy breather hoping a woman will answer? This happens three more times after which I don't bother answering phone for a while.

Friday April 16

Newsagent says he's got hold of a cordon bleu video for me: The Food Of Paradise. I'm too cowardly to say I don't want it any more. He puts it in my bag with the tins and things I've bought.

Get back and slot it into the VCR. Screen fills with fuzzed and snowing porn. Watch it anyway. The video stars are very agile. I sit on the sofa, slurping wan ton noodle soup, watching. It's forty minutes long. I never knew so many sex positions existed, and I would definitely pass my biology exam now, if I sat it again.

Nikki comes home, sees the video on the coffee table, smiles her encouraging smile and before I can stop her she's slotted it in. I shrug. We watch it together. She checks if I'm wearing knickers. I'm not. She clambers over me. We end in a position we call the Gymnasts, copied from the video, until she gets cramp in her thigh. We untangle. I find James' necklace embedded in my elbow. The sex leaves me feeling numb. We argue about something immediately it's over.

Saturday April 17

Ira says I'm playing in place of Malik. Malik is as unreliable as Scoobie, Ira says. I agree totally and grab my boots. We're at a place known as the Ski-Slope. We lose nine nil, six nil the first half (uphill), and another three the second (down). This is Malik's legacy to the midfield, I tell Ira. It will be a couple of matches before I've repaired the damage.

Antonia sees the London Towers with us. Nikki screams

herself hoarse. Antonia never gets into the swing of it like Nikki and me. She's got too much reserve. On the way back Antonia congratulates Nikki on the way she "projects all her professional anxieties onto the team." They have a few drinks back at our place while I'm out in the garden. When Antonia is ready to leave, I say goodbye and she smiles disapprovingly at me. Nikki avoids me for the rest of the evening. I know the vibe. I'm in Nikki's bad books for something and she's told Antonia.

Sunday April 18

Malik calls round and goes off with Nikki. They are both dressed casually even though they claim it's business. I do some sketches for another series of sculptures.

Monday April 19

Nikki leaves one of her little notes telling me the cushions should be plumped up each and every day, the windows opened at least 10.5 centimetres so the house is properly aired, the setting on the vacuum cleaner should be adjusted so that when I vac, the dirt is actually sucked up and the nap raised. I am tempted to write a little note back saying I am not a housework zombie and go to hell, but I content myself with washing the plates as badly as I can and putting the creases in her clothes slightly out.

Nikki stomps in. Another bad day at the office. She quickly gets into her routine of criticising my lack of effort on the housework front. I am pissed off at her carping and I chew off half my lower lip keeping myself from saying anything when she (1) drips juice across the kitchen floor (2) messes up the freshly plumped cushion arrangement on the sofa (3) leaves her shoes scattered about (4) spreads her work papers all over the house. This house is too small for both of us.

Tuesday April 20

Debbie-Anne calls round. She's fresh, lively, spirited. I complete the portrait I've been working on. She loves it. Even I have to admit it looks good. It's not just a likeness. It captures her pagan, spunky spirit. We're downstairs and she's amusing me with Malik's latest ventures when Ruby knocks on the door. She says she can come back later if I'm busy. I say come in, come in, and introduce her to Debbie-Anne. Debbie-Anne says hello, then dashes to retrieve her knickers from upstairs. Ruby gives me a glance. She's pregnant I say I'm looking after her. This doesn't explain why she's left her knickers upstairs but I don't try. When Debbie-Anne has left, Ruby comments on the mess the house is in. She doesn't stay long, and leaves without cooking anything. I think Nikki sent her to spy.

Wednesday April 21

Nikki catches me and Debbie in the studio, starkers. We had Gabrielle pumped up loud and didn't hear her car pull up. Debbie-Anne makes a dignified exit, then there's a big row. I tell her Debbie-Anne has been nude modelling for me for the last three months, actually. So! It's been going on for months, Nikki wails, behind my back! She starts throwing paints at me. I counter attack by saying I hope she doesn't think I haven't noticed what's been happening between her and Malik; all those clandestine business meetings. Well, this is my business. I'm an artist, remember? She says her business with Malik does not involve taking her clothes off for him. I say people take their clothes off for me in the ordinary course of my business, just like for a doctor. She throws the painting I made of Debbie against the wall, then storms off, saying she is not going to speak to me, ever. I shout after her that that's going to be reaaally tough for me. I'll miss all her juvenile tantrums and petty complaints. She gives me the silent treatment for the rest of the evening. I sleep on the turquoise sofa.

Thursday April 22

Didn't get much sleep yesterday. Still, I crank up the old (very old!) oxy-acetylene equipment and start metal bending. I can't face going into the studio and seeing the painting Nikki ruined. Debbie-Anne rings. I tell her she's not to blame, I should have squared it with Nikki first, and say I'll let her know when things have calmed down.

Nikki comes back late and works through the evening still not talking. I try to be civil. She goes to bed early. When I get under the covers she is turned away from me. I feel something cold and hard in the middle of the bed. It's the screwed off, plastic pole of the kitchen brush running down the middle of the bed. A demarcation zone. I guess I am not to cross it. I consider maybe peeping a toe over and seeing how she reacts. But don't bother.

Friday April 23

Slept OK last night, though I had some strange dreams on account of that pole in the bed. The oxy fires first time and I have an inspired hour. I make my best sculpture ever. I must have some more sleepless nights with poles pressing into the small of my back.

Get a strange call in the afternoon. An early twenties female voice, fast, confident, London, almost Willesden: "Hello, is that Harvey? I'm Susie of Susie's Mobile Massage Parlour. I'm new to the area and I have some special introductory offers. I can do you an intimate massage for next to nothing. Are you interested?"
After checking I'm sober and in the right house I laugh louchely and say I'm tempted but what exactly is an intimate massage? She laughs knowingly and says she's not allowed to say over the phone but she's not talking about a simple hand job. I laugh connivingly and ask is she allowed to say how she got my first name then? She laughs coyly, and says I'm in the

phone book. I laugh affectionately and tell her I admire her enterprise, and, thinking strictly of some friends, I'll take her number but that's all. She laughs smartly and says she can't give me her number: this is a take it or leave it, once-in-a-lifetime offer. Tell her, sorry, maybe some other time and hang up the phone. Strange this as I'm not listed in the phone book. The phone's in Nikki's name.

Nikki still giving me the silent treatment, though she has removed the pole from the bed. She's wearing a new, baggy nightie with a double drawstring drawn tight to the neck. She must have got it from a Mormon friend. She is all elbows and knees when I try to get close to her. I fall asleep guarding my side of the bed.

Saturday April 24

Nikki leaves at the crack of dawn. probably to Antonia's. Ira rings to say I'm not wanted today. Thanks, Ira. I wander around the house nostalgically. All the happy times Nikki and I had together here. Peckish, I notice there is a mango in the fruit bowl. It wasn't there last night. Has Nikki left it for me as a peace offering? I wonder. She knows I love mangoes. Or is it there to tease me, to make me obliged to thank her for it? There is no way I am going to do that. I'd rather eat the carpet than thank her for anything. I eat L-Mart cornflakes instead. They taste so stale they might as well be the carpet.

Hop around the commercial radio channels. A jingle catches my ear. A hypnotically peaceful Devon male voice intoning in a Gregorian chant:

"PeaceGlade Cloistered Monastery. Novices from all walks of life now being accepted. Tranquillity, chastity, solitude, and two hundred acres of rolling hills to contemplate."

I call the number. An answering service asks me to leave my number and address, a time when I can be visited and, briefly, my reason for wanting to join. I say I'm sold on the package and think it will do me good. They can visit anytime.

Five cans of L-Mart Pils lager later, I get a call back. It's the head monk.

We need a breadhead, he says, and from my answering machine message, I sound like one. He tells me the commune was originally a group of "poll-tax monks", hippies who got religion a decade ago to avoid paying the notorious poll tax, but who stayed on because, without being corny, they found God and enjoyed the monastic life. Chastity is enforced (how? I wonder), but they have a vineyard. They need a few more people to help run it, hence the little jingle. Can I send a cv, also any evidence of horticultural or business management skills? I have no problems with any of that, I lie. One of the brothers will call round in early June to interview me, he says. I thank him and he blesses me, then hangs up. June!! I suppose that's fast for them. I envisage myself as manager of a hippy monastery vineyard. It sounds a dream come true.

Nikki returns late when I'm still dreaming on the sofa. She cuts me dead, plucks the mango out of the bowl and bites into it, then heads upstairs. The monastery idea seems better and better. In truth, I've forgotten what me and Nikki are supposed to be arguing about. I watch a late night TV comedy alone. There is nothing unfunnier than watching a TV comedy alone. I dream I sculpted a thousand mangoes and Nikki ate every one of them.

Sunday April 25

Get up and am surprised to see Nikki at the breakfast table eating bite-size Shreddies. I didn't buy any so she must have got them herself. I ask if it is OK for me to take some. There's no reply so I reply for her, "Go ahead, help yourself". Then I reply to my reply. "Thank you, don't mind if I do". I see the glimmer of a smile flicker across her face, then her inscrutable mask is back.

Phone rings while we're munching silently. I answer it. It's for Nikki. I call out to her. Without a word, she takes the phone from me. Then she starts gushing to Antonia. She's still on the phone when I say, *Bye, I'm going for a drive. She ignores me like I'm invisible.* This is becoming boring.

Drive to Bergmann's. James is there and I give him his necklace. He kisses me. Filo is morose as usual. Claudine, witty. Samia is on some heavy narcotic and asleep, Sappho and Arnulfo are trying to drink each other under the table. Sappho's winning as usual. I'm not really in the mood for them and I leave and drive up and down High Street for a bit, stopping off to watch the grass grow in the park.

Nikki's not in when I get back at 8 p.m. At 11 p.m her mum, Ruby, rings to say Nikki's at her place and is on her way back now, then rings off. Ruby sounded distressed. I open a tin of chicken curry. The front door slams and Nikki comes in. Her eyes are red-rimmed but she isn't giving me any eye contact. Or talking. She dumps some vegetables on the kitchen table. As she turns on her way out her eyes catch mine just an instant. There's pain, fury and fatigue in them. "You OK? How did your day go?" I ask her cheerily, but she storms off upstairs. Ruby rings to check Nikki reached home. I say she has and there's a pause, then Ruby sighs goodnight. Bedtime is the usual cold shouldering. Wake in the middle of the night to find her cuddled up in my arms. Wake again and she is far away on her side of the bed once more. Did I just dream the cuddle?

Monday April 26

Ruby calls round in the morning. A clipping from a magazine happens to spill out of her bag. She shows it me.

Top Ten reasons Why Couples Split :

1 Falling out of love
2 Perceived lack of money
3 Jealousy over arrival of first child
4 Adultery
5 Mid-life crisis
6 Unequal burden of household chores
7 Obesity of partner
8 Male competitiveness
9 Boredom
10 Personal hygiene
(Marital & Couples Therapy Centre, London)

Ruby asks which one are we? I tell her every one of them except number three. Ruby says do I know her daughter is prone to depression and I should not carry an argument on too long whoever's fault it is. I should apologise and make up with her. I want to say, it's her daughter who ought to be apologising, not me. But keep shtum and knead my dumpling mix as she instructs, like a dutiful sous-chef. She tells me how her husband would never have hung around a kitchen cooking, and Nikki is very lucky to have me, and Nikki says I might have a drink problem but I'm in denial and is it true? If I bite my tongue any more I'm going to bite right through it.

Ruby leaves as fast as I can get her to, which is still slow, when Nikki's mum wants she can go slow as a Monday morning Post Office queue. Then I ring Debbie-Anne. She is heaving up all over the place at the moment on account of the baby. In between pukes she suggests getting down on my hands and knees and begging Nikki, failing that, writing her a note since Nikki likes notes.

Nikki returns. I speak to her in the third person. "How is Nikki feeling today? Would she like me to cook a microwave meal for her?" Nothing doing. I try thinking aloud. "I so much appreciate quiet. I've contacted a monastery recently." "Does she have any preference in cheese when I visit L-Mart tomorrow? a rise of the left eyebrow is sufficient to indicate "yes" and the right can indicate "no"." The eyebrows stay level. "I presume then you have no preference," etc.

I imagine little green aliens watching us from some other planet. Would they know what was going on? I don't any more. I watch the sun go down in the back garden.

Come back in with frostbite. Nikki has left the oven light on but there's nothing in the oven. Cruel trick. The opposite of love is not hate but indifference. I go up to our nocturnal jousting field (i.e bed). She is wearing twenty layers of clothing and is far away on her side of the bed. I lie awake for a while, listening to her breathing. Then I get up, go downstairs, watch black and white films with the sound turned down. Finally go back to bed. The whole situation is daft. It's hurting me and I know it's hurting her. There must be a way to get her talking again. Name one then, I challenge myself. Flowers would be too traditional. A note would be too heavy, too permanent. Talking hasn't worked. An apology is impossible from her, and I've done nothing wrong so why should I be apologising?

Tuesday April 27

Paint furiously. Then do a lot of telephoning.

When Nikki comes back there's an oil painting standing on an easel in the middle of the hallway. It's a head and shoulders of her. I did it from a photo. "That's wonderful, Harvey, so . . . wonderful!" She's spoken! I take a bow and with a flourish introduce Surprise Number 2. — we have guests. Malik and Debbie-Anne step forward from behind the kitchen door, dressed to the nines. Dinner for four's already made and the settings are in place. Malik uncorks some wine he's brought over. "Let's eat, drink, and talk!" he says. Just for a moment I actually like Malik.

Malik says it's OK by him if Debbie-Anne models for me. Debbie-Anne says of course it's OK with her, and there's absolutely nothing going on between me and her, but if Nikki doesn't think it right then ... Nikki mutters that she damn well doesn't think it right. She talks to me directly and with some vehemence. "Since when have you started drawing nudes? You were into abstracts before." I am about to riposte when Malik weighs in again, all smiles, saying I paint good nudes. "He's in demand, our Harvey," he beams, "he's a highly rated nudist!" I think it's Malik's faith in me that wins Nikki over. He trusts me with Debbie. Also, it's good company for Debbie, he says. If there are any problems with the pregnancy he'd rather she were here with me, than on her own. Nikki slowly allows herself to be talked round to the idea.

Malik then explains to me his frequent business meetings with Nikki. Nikki needs to close a Saudi distribution deal but the Saudis don't want to deal with a woman. Malik is going to pretend to be her boss, while she goes as his secretary. Their meetings have been to brief him on how the deal is developing and to rehearse and get to know the details of the business so he doesn't get caught out. In return for Malik doing this, Nikki is going to help him shift some Five Vibes pop group merchandise to Israel, now that they've peaked and fizzled in Europe. Nikki confirms this story. It sounds far-fetched, but that's why I believe it. Everything in Malik's life is far-fetched. There's a toast to their success. To my success. To Debbie-Anne's success. Then we just drink for drinking's sake. By the end of the evening it's almost as if the last few days between me and Nikki have never happened. Malik and Debbie-Anne slip away as we begin feeding each other segments of orange.

Wednesday April 28

I get up late with a steel orchestra in my head. Find letter on doormat. It's my redundancy cheque! I do a jig, then collapse on the sofa. Head feels like a foodmixer on Full. Debbie-Anne rings to say she's feeling seasick and can't make it. Which reminds me of my swimming lessons. Can't miss two weeks. I make it to the Pool OK, but the chlorine smell turns my stomach. Teresa gets me into the water anyway. It's not so bad. I swim six lengths before throwing up in the showers. In the canteen Siobhan's hand lands in my lap a couple of times. I explain to her I'm in a long term relationship, almost married, so there's nothing doing between her and me. She says she understands but we can be good friends, can't we? I say yes, so long as we understand our boundaries we'll be OK. Lola sighs laconically at all this. Siobhan tries to kiss me on the mouth when I leave.

£2,465 is not to be sneered at. After some vaccing and wiping surfaces, I sit with a glass of beer and dream of spending that redundancy cheque . . . my own studio space . . . a holiday. I deserve a holiday. Nikki comes back and unburdens. Rumour is, her new boss doesn't think she's up to the job. She's going to have to work harder to get on. She doesn't have the lunchtime football option like her male colleagues for getting inside information. She will just have to impress with her brilliance — be twice as good as the rest of them. Which means putting in all hours she can find. I say I'll support her any way I can. Later I tell her about the redundancy cheque. She agrees I deserve a holiday. In fact, my going away might even help her by giving her more space, she says, to put in some overtime at home. So it's settled. I am to book a holiday for myself. We make love for the first time in at least a month. At least we try. I think Nikki falls asleep half way through and I don't actually remember getting as far as having an orgasm.

Thursday April 29

Go to travel agents. Leave unmoved by package holidays to Torremolinos, Kos and Barbados. At Bergmann's spot a flyer advertising 'Iron John' experience holidays. Phone them on the spur of the moment. I'm lucky, there is one place left on the May Camp holiday and at only two hundred pounds for a week, accommodation included, it's a steal, they say.

Tell Nikki I've booked Iron John holiday. She says she understands cleaning the house has bruised my male ego. If an Iron John camp is what it takes, she says . . . her voice trails off. I tell her it's not that I've got a problem with my role, it's that everyone else seems to have, like Malik, all the artists, the neighbours, even her mother! Whatever, if it's going to make me happy, she says. We watch an old vampire thriller together over pizza. Nikki keeps hugging me, even when there are no scary bits happening.

Friday April 30

I am a sculptor, sculptors sculpt. Chanting this mantra, I set to work. Edward puts his head round the fence. He's bought a plant for us to put in place of the brambles he ripped out. It's a tree, actually — very rare. I can see he's just itching to come round and dig it in, so I let him. Two hours later No 57 Cherryville has a bona fide Japanese fuchsia tree. It blossoms only once every decade, Edward tells me, but it looks interestingly tropical even without the flowers. Shortly after Roxanna appears, then Ruby. It's just like old times. Nikki comes home and joins everyone on the patio. She even has a lager. I stop burning and welding as the light deteriorates. The sunset is a spectacular lemon-orange blaze.

Saturday May 1

Early am, Ira rings. He has Type A flu and is off to see his solicitor to prepare a will in case he dies of it. Can I be Manager for the day? I insist I must be free to employ my own tactics. Ira groans whatever. So is all progress greeted. Eleven turn up at the Mudflats, plus me, which makes twelve. Surprise, surprise, Malik is one of the eleven. Does he not like the fact I am manager today! Purely to get the balance of the side right, I make Malik substitute while I play in central midfield. We play with passion and intelligence and lose 9 — 1 (I scored from the penalty spot — a delightful chip into the top right hand corner of the goal). I tell the lads not to hang their heads. Once they understand the new system I've introduced we'll be unbeatable.

Nikki is very proud of me for scoring that goal. I don't mention the nine against. Who cares for details? At the Arena over popcorn in the fourth quarter she makes a confession. She set up that call when I was offered an intimate massage. 93% of men fail the test, according to Antonia, she tells me. So I'm in the top 7% for faithfulness. Nikki denies Antonia put her up to it. I knew the woman didn't like me. I warn Nikki that she's trying to break us up, but Nikki laughs it off as a joke.

Sunday May 2

A blissful day, until Malik carries off my concubine 'to talk Saudi business'. I can tell he's still sore about being substitute. Tough — he'll be substitute again next week. And I won't even bring him on in the second half. That'll teach him.

Monday May 3

Redundancy cheque clears. Burn rubber in my Micra to Shopping Centre where I drool over this no-dustbag vac called a Dyson. It's a beautiful yellow. It works 'on the cyclone principle' the cardboard display says. It looks gorgeous. A gangly male sales assistant finishes eating the contents of his left nostril then asks me if I'm looking for the hi-fi section, Sir. I tell him no, and can he tell me more about this vac. He mumbles something about finding 'the girl who knows' and disappears. 'Girl who knows' sells me the Dyson and somehow manages to convince me I also need dustbags for my broken hoover.

Tuesday May 4

Sketch a new sculpture. On paper it looks promising: a rough cast, blackened aluminium figure of a tall, thin, black man holding a piece of moon in one raised hand; there are no recognisable human details until you reach the face and the splayed out hand holding the moon, giving it a symbolic, surreal vibe. I do several more sketches on the theme, each from a different perspective.

Ruby calls. I get my apron out. I'm not self-conscious about it when Ruby's around. She's happy that I'm getting on with her daughter again, she says. I deduce said daughter must have rung mum last night. Ruby goes on about how she and her husband had arguments. Mainly over his showering money on people like the Rich Man at the Gates of Heaven. Anybody who could work up a half decent sob-story had a chance with him, and yet he'd leave his own family no food on the table. We cook codfish fritters. I put my feet up and settle into a lager as Ruby steams into the washing up. I won't accept defeat with these pans, she says, they were once stainless steel, and I can get them there again with elbow grease. I make a mental note to look out for Elbow Grease at L-Mart. Eventually Ruby helps herself to a lager. I mention my upcoming stay at Blue Buffalo Camp. She wonders if travel agents do cruises to the West Indies for under a couple of hundred pounds. I promise I'll find out for her. Who knows, Saga may have a few rowboats bobbing across the Atlantic at that price.

Wednesday May 5

Debbie-Anne calls round to model but my head's in the new sculpture. Debbie's happy just to hang around. She goes through our video collection while I'm in the kitchen and shouts we are very sad people. So many boring art films. I explain it's Nikki who's collecting that stuff. She signed up for one of those mail order video clubs and can't cancel for another thousand years. Condemned to pay for unwatchable art movies for the rest of her life. I hear a triumphant "oh yeah?" and Debbie's waving something. It's the 'cooking' video. I try explaining it was a mistake but she smirks, then asks if she can borrow it for Malik. It could be very educational for him, she says. My turn to smirk — Malik forgotten what to do! Wait till I tell the football team! I cook me and Debbie chicken and rice in Red Stripe beer sauce, which she adores.

My last swimming lesson for two weeks. In the canteen afterwards, Siobhan is tearful. She's having a gruesome time with two posh brats and a giant grumpy dog she's looking after. She's only being allowed out one evening a week, the dog is fed better than she is and they pay her a tiny allowance later and later every time. She wants to go back to Stuttgart. If it weren't for Lola and me, she'd fly home, she says. I give her a consoling hug. Lola whispers she's acting up for my benefit.

Sex happens, late evening, slow spoons. I'm not sure we got the contraception sorted in time. Nikki asks me if I painted Debbie today. I say yes, because I think that's what she wants to hear. Nikki tells me her work at InterGlobe is going well. First time she's ever said that.

Thursday May 6

Blue Buffalo camp have cashed my cheque and sent a list of Do's and Don't on what to pack. The Don'ts include: no dogs, no alcohol, no drugs, no computer games, no recorded music devices, no mirrors, no mobile phones, no bleepers, no hairpieces, no radios, no knives other than the Swiss army type. The Do's are: waterproofs, waterproof watch, mosquito spray (where am I going — India or Essex?), a small axe, a compass, twenty pairs of hiking socks (twenty?!), broken-in hiking boots, bin liners, own tom-tom drum, pure sea salt, demerara sugar (why demerara?) spare pair of spectacles if you wear contacts or glasses, own toilet paper to last two weeks, fly sheet (why do we have to bring a sheet of flies?).

Roxanna and Edward call round to wish me luck. They used to go caravaning, they say. I show no interest whatsoever but they still give me this long tale about caravan aerodynamics, downhill braking, exploding gas cylinders, axe murderers, radiated sheep, water purification tablets, speed traps, aliens, a Nicaraguan jumping frog, how to cook crushed Spanish beetles with paraffin and time zone differences in the USA. I push them out of the door.

Friday May 7

Rush to buy water purification tablets. The only sensible item Edward came up with last night. Buy the small axe, fly paper, toilet paper etc. as per Blue Buffalo list. Can only find new, unbroken-in boots though, despite visit to Army Surplus Store. Things are bad in the Forces, no doubt. They're having to wear their kit for longer before it reaches civvy street.

Thoughts turn to Nikki. How will she cope while I'm gone? I tag all doors and machines in the house with stick-on labels explaining best way of preparation (food) and how to operate (machines), where stuff is etc. so she won't be totally lost without me. Malik comes round, to snigger mainly. He says why am I going on this white man's mission: "Rediscovering your masculinity — cha! The black man never lost it . . . Well, most of us." I could skewer him with the fish knife but I've just cleaned up in the kitchen and I don't want blood all over, so I ignore him and go rummage in the garage in search of my old woodcarving tools. Nikki and me go out. She thinks I'm brave. She herself would never stay in any accommodation lower than four star — it would be incompatible with her image and comfort levels, she declares. Nikki is a snob.

Saturday May 8

Ira rings. Before he asks, I tell him I am unavailable for two weeks on account of I have to go on this SAS training course. Ira sighs with disappointment. Malik's here so I hand him the phone to speak to Ira. I go back to checking I've packed everything.

10 a.m. Nikki drives me down to the train station with Malik in the back. They are both in high spirits about my leaving. Why? Nikki and I have a tearful goodbye scene. She hugs me and says she loves me and try not to bring back any creepy crawlies or bugs. Malik breaks us up. He hands me a shopping bag. Presents, he says — a box of Kleenex and a quiche. I nod sadly at Malik. My own personal growth threatens his ossified self. I try to hug him but Malik leaps back. He punches me on the shoulder and says "Good luck, bro". They both wave as I get on the train. Malik has a kleenex to his eye as he does so, taking the piss, no doubt.

12 p.m. Clanky train arrives at destination without problems. No one gets off at my stop but me. Have Ordnance Survey map ready, and, after a two mile romp in my new boots through drizzling rain along roads of cow manure, turn the map the right way up. It only takes me another half an hour to retrace my steps and head in the right direction. Countryside meant to be peaceful but am nearly mown down at bend by tractor pulling sawn-off horsebox full of wild yokels, with faces out of a Peter Greenaway art movie. My clothes splattered with cow manure. It's even on my lips — ugh!! Give them the wankers sign.

Cross a range of Essex mountains, tiptoe through various fields of filthy livestock, and finally reach Camp Blue Buffalo fields. Sign on gate says: "Druid High Trees welcomes you." In the mid-distance I see a straggly column of smoke. I climb gate and squelch over to the smoke. Spot the tractor and trailer. Pity I gave the wankers sign to them, but they won't recognise me: there must be hundreds of black men wandering the hills of Essex on any given day.

We are gathered around a tall, Druid-looking man who is addressing us in a strong, confident Cockney voice. The subject is accommodation. There are twenty-four of us, he booms. We will be based in three "tribal tents". He leads us in a stomp over to the tent zone. They are field green, and look suspiciously like World War Two army tents. There is a hole in the middle of each for smoke to escape. Then it's on to the latrines. We go over to some bushes. The Druid points to a pit. There are two benches over the pit, each bench composed of two planks with a gap in between for doing the business. We shit here, the Druid says. We can pee in the bushes. If we want to pee into the pit, there's no lid to lift, so we still have to sit on the planks. Everyone is gagging at the stench. The Druid smiles. These latrines are downwind from the tents he says. They were meant to have been sucked empty three days ago but there were no spare tractors at the time. There'll be one coming soon. I peek. The pit looks perilously full. We are given half an hour to unpack before dinner.

My survival instincts take over. I don't want to get left with a pitch by the tent flap. I duck under into my tent and bad news slaps me in the face. I'd forgotten I was last one to arrive. All the pitches are taken except the one at tent entry. Two hundred and sixty quid for this? I want back to Willesden fast. But the others pile in and I'm swept up in introductions. They seem a genuinely friendly lot. Finance Officer from Norwich, chief clerk from Nottinghamshire, an estate manager, two London graphic designers. The tent has a smell. Wood smoke and mould. One of them tells me they were waving to offer me a lift on the tractor. My traveller's code gave them a laugh and not to worry about it.

Dinner is served in a huge double tent with a long wooden table running the length of it and all these metal bowls which Jonty, the estate manager tells me are canteens. Dinner is lentil and mung bean broth. I am too hungry to care. I use the ladle to scoop some of the green gluck out of the cauldron and slap it into my metal canteen. I imagine Malik right now cackling. He was right about one thing. I am the only black man out here.

Druid High Trees recites the camp rules after dinner. Cooking will be done by rota. The menus and recipes are all taken care of. No punching, fighting, ripping or dissing is allowed on the camp. No shagging the sheep or other farm animals here. He is sorry to have to say this, but there was one incident last year. All valuables are on site at the owner's risk. Trust is an important part of the Buffalo experience. But there is a safe available if anyone wants to use it. There were some scurrilous rumours doing the rounds last year about him (Druid High Trees) using people's money to score dope. This rumour is untrue. We are to see him afterwards if we want to leave our wallets with him. As he talks, the Druid eats avidly, pawing his long, straw beard every now and again when a bean or pea becomes trapped there. There is a small river half a mile over the field where we can bathe. The river is also Nature's washing machine for our clothes. Only biodegradable soaps should be used. No women are allowed on camp. Anyone smuggling them in will be banished. Tonight's programme will be myth exploration and attuning the mind to nature's harmonies. It will take place round the big camp fire, weather permitting. Each man is to tell a story that tells something about himself.

The Druid is impervious to the smoke from the wood fire, and busy with the smoke from his hubba bubba pipe. When he has ashed half an ounce of hashish, he begins his story. He tells us he is a descendant of the ancient English wizard, Merlin, that he was rescued from the urban hellzone by King Arthur and that cosmic wave energy is heading to Earth for the second millennium and we have to be prepared. Unfortunately, at this point rain bursts upon us and we have to dash for our tents.

As our canvas is pummelled by hail, I get to know my tentmates. There's the serene Buddhist, Jack ("attachment is suffering") who works in advertising; the tense ex-con, Harold who has a strange way of rolling his shoulders and hanging out his tongue at the same time. He has the bed nearest the fire; the baby-faced computer geek, Pete Singh; Jonty "gold spoons", the Scottish landowner's estate manager, who knows Madame Butterfly by heart because his mum sang it to him when he was small; Ian of the Himalayan-Sherpa-tested mountain rescue gear; corduroy trousered Simon, who's just been divorced but doesn't want to talk about it; and Nikhil, the pirate-earringed jazz musician. We share out some secret rations, cold roast chicken, cheese sandwiches, Garibaldi biscuits and cashew nuts, and lament the rain.

The Druid looks in and says when we wake up in the morning we are each of us to pop our heads round the entry flap of the tent, and take a butchers. The first thing we see, to remember it because it will be our new name while we're at camp. He doesn't seem to notice all the contraband food. Maybe he's too stoned. Harold gets a fire going.

Sunday May 9

Woken by someone banging on what sounds like a huge tin lid. The reverberations take a full minute to stop inside my head. I am numb with cold. It takes me a minute to realise why. Water has flowed under the tent and into the dip in the ground by the tent entry. So I am lying in a small pool of water. When I shift I feel even colder so I just lie there for a while.

The tent air is heavy from wood smoke, stale socks and ten men farting all night. My feet are sore from the unbroken-in hiking boots, and my face scratchy. I realise I brought no shaving equipment. And there are no mirrors so I'd better get used to the scratchy face feeling. I ease out of the pit I'm lying in. My stomach feels lentilled. I'm shivering. I find my kitbag, pull out some dry clothes, and change right where I am. I'm too numb for modesty. The soles of my feet are wet and pink as L-Mart boiled ham. Nikhil comes into the tent and lets me know on account of the downpour last night breakfast is running thirty minutes late. I manage to dress myself . The dry clothes eventually raise my body temperature sufficiently for my teeth to steady. There's a churning noise outside. I pop my head out. A sewage tank is being hauled up to the latrines by a tractor. I realise I want a pee and head for the bushes.

Breakfast is porridge made with fifty percent water, forty percent porridge and ten percent milk. It tastes like milled chipboard. Everybody looks dead and ghoul-like, except Druid High Trees (and smug Ian, who looks very dry and content). Nobody talks. Shock most likely.

The first exercise after breakfast is the naming ceremony. My lodge (we are not called tents any more, we are lodges — a Native American Indian thing) goes first. We say what we saw when we first looked out of the tent this morning. This produces four Grey Skies, one Grey Clouds, one Leaping Antelope, one Sewage Tank, two Mud Fields, and one Cow's Face. High Trees says our choice of names shows how much the choking city has impoverished our imaginations. It is against the law (or did he mean the lore?) to change the names until the sun has risen and set again, but we are all to try again tomorrow morning, bar Leaping Antelope aka Ian, who looks unbelievably smug. He must have had some narcotic assistance in seeing a leaping antelope out here first thing in the morning.

Second exercise is roaring. Modern man has forgotten how to roar. High Trees stands and demonstrates. He throws his head back and lets loose a magnificent fifty decibel blast that's a cross between a Tarzan cry and someone who's just hit his thumb with a large mallet. We all have to stand up and roar in turn. Cell-hardened Harold can only manage a damp growl. Buddhist Jack fails to distinguish between an Omm and a roar. Pete has a painful, high-pitched whine. Jonty asks if he can sing the aria from Madame Butterfly instead. He can't. Simon sounds desperate. I come second closest to matching High Trees's bellow. But Ian shakes the trees. He roars like a lion on heat, and with a lion's smug ease. We are all sent off into the fields to practice roaring.

Afterwards, despite copious amounts of natural honey supplied by 'call me Leaping Antelope' Ian, my voice remains so hoarse I can only whisper. I am assigned to that day's evening meal crew. We're doing spaghetti.

We get a lot of smoke and a little fire going. A drop of paraffin helps. Dump spaghetti in cauldron of river water, then pop open four trays of tinned tomatoes and dump them in. High Trees comes over with some freshly plucked wild herbs to add. Later, everybody whispers (sore throats) how they love our cooking. I'm not a great fan of spaghetti, but the open air gives me an appetite and I gorge three platefuls.

Late night, we all sit around the open fire. Those with undamaged tonsils practice roaring, or tell the soul stories they've worked on in the afternoon. I get my sleeping bag out and lay it to dry by the fire. As the evening draws in and the sky reddens, the mood is mellow and fraternal. High Trees plays Bob Dylanesque songs on his guitar. Ian sings a few duets with him. I gargle the herbal laryngitis treatment that Leaping Antelope supplies me with.

Another night in the ditch. I wake up stiff as a deep frozen fish finger. Luckily, Leaping Antelope has lent me a spare ground sheet and so at least I'm not sodden.

Remembering last evening's instructions, I glance outside. At least I go to glance outside. In my frozen state I'm too clumsy and I butt my head against the centre tent pole hard enough to get momentary concussion. I see stars. This is convenient. This breakfast, I am renamed Morning Stars. Now we have bonded well, Druid High Trees tells us, we are ready to begin group discussions. This is to be a safe place for self-disclosure. There is no need to remind everyone of the basic house rules — no fighting, spitting or dissing. We must learn to support our brother man in a non-competitive way. The things said now will be deeply personal. Nobody is to snigger, or they will be banished from the tribe. Before he reveals the discussion topic, each must turn to the man to his left and pay him a compliment. I am complimented on my fine set of teeth. I compliment Harold on his manly appetite. The discussion is: what is masculinity? and we are each to talk about our relationship with our fathers in answering the question. High Trees will lead response to our stories. Two hours of gnashing, weeping and confessional later, I discover I have copied my father by choosing to work with metal. My strongest memories of him as a man are as a mechanic under a car, and now here I am in manhood working with metal as a sculptor. I have become my father. Masculinity for me means metal, motors. This is very common, the Druid proclaims. We hear sad stories of loss and estrangement and neglect. These greatly outnumber the tales of closeness and communion. Everyone lays it on the line, telling total strangers the most personal things. There is no judgment. Nobody laughs, at least not in a hostile way. By the end of the session we are all subdued by the weight of feeling. Until the Druid bursts out in a mad roar and leads us in a session of roaring that gets our spirits revived and our stomachs prepared for lunch.

Tuesday May 11

The options for the day are I either stink or jump in that stream. Only Leaping Antelope has taken the plunge so far. The rest of us prefer the thousand year old socks smell of men's stale sweat to the certain death of freezing water. Since I am already frozen I guess the cold will make no difference so I sneak my bar of soap (not sure it's biodegradable) into a carrier bag stuffed with fresh clothes, towel, sponge, back brush and shampoo. Realise I haven't brought any Dax to oil my hair with, so it is probably looking as dry as cactus fur. It feels as rough. Clamber down bank. The 'stream' is a fast flowing, small river, maybe four metres wide at its narrowest point and looking around a metre to two metres deep at its deepest. The shore is pebbly. I look back to the Camp. There is a distant wisp of smoke. If I drown in this, nobody will hear me scream. I undress, dip in a big toe, then a foot and so on until I'm submerged to my upper thighs. I shiver in anticipation of the next bit, take a big breath. I feel my testes swing upwards almost into my throat. The water doesn't feel so cold after a while. I soap up. Then surge fully into the water for a swim. I swim to the far bank, front crawl style. Then back just kicking my legs, backstroke style. Mad easy. I look up and the sun has come out. It's gonna be a fine day.

The afternoon sessions are about man's relationship with nature. Before, man was a hunter. He knew the wildlife. It wasn't wild. He appreciated it. Our lives depended on appreciating it. Are flowers a threat to masculinity? No! Wild man embraces flowers! We each have to present a flower to the person on our right who has to sniff it and say thank you. To my right is HammerCloud, the ex-con. HammerCloud's shoulders are rolling and his tongue is hanging out. I cheat. I hand him a blade of grass. He sniffs it, grunts, then sticks it in his mouth. Leaping Antelope hands me a small flower. He says it's from a rare family of naturally antibiotic-producing plants and if rubbed into the skin can provide protection against warts. It looks like a daisy to me. I thank him.

HammerCloud's crew serves beef stew "without the beef, as served at Her Majesty's Prison Risley." It's pretty good, but there again, I'm a very hungry man. Supper is "beef stew without the beef, as served at Her Majesty's Prison Risley". No-one dares complain. It's pretty good, even second time round.

Some kind of tiny bugs dine on me all night. I can't see them to kill them, despite turning my sleeping bag inside out. Heavenly Peace, the Buddhist, says I should become one with the pain, not be seduced by the yin of masculine desire to destroy little bugs.

Wonder how come the Druid gets to sleep in the log cabin by the edge of the trees, while we're in tents?

Wednesday May 12

The morning's session is drumming. The guest workshop leader is Brings Thunder. He looks like the Druid's nephew: yellow, locksed-up hair, Irish green eyes. He has a loping, lanky body, festooned with a Tibetan temple's weight of drums. He talks about drumming as the expression of spirit, the summoning of the gods (which ones he doesn't make clear), and the revival of our primitive selves. He looks at me on this last one as if for confirmation. I give him a 'don't ask me — I'm as thick as the rest of them' look. Then he lets us loose on his drums. If we're drumming hard enough, y'all, he says, our piss should be red today, from the blood we beat out of our hands. We have a session of pure noise in which it's every man and his drum to himself. I do my bit. Brings Thunder gets to play the boomingest drum.

Lunch is potato fritters with wild cabbage. The wild cabbage looks suspiciously like long-leaved grass. I wolf it anyway. It has a lemony tang. After lunch someone strikes a drum. Leaping Antelope begins dancing. It's a solid, flat foot dance with some smart spins and changes of height. HammerCloud joins him with moves that remind me of a dying buffalo, not that I've ever seen one. Finally Druid High Trees joins in, with a Mick Jagger-meets-the-Maori-warriors-at-a-Status Quo-concert jig. Soon there are more dancers than drummers. I stay sat on my butt. An exhausted Leaping Antelope flops by my side. His pupils are merrily dilated. Over the din he yells he wouldn't mind swapping places in the tent with me — he's finding conditions at his pitch too mild to test his survival equipment. I clinch the deal before he can draw another breath. Then drum madly with joy and get approving looks from both High Druid and nephew. I can see what they're thinking — "we just knew all blacks had rhythm". Later I piss and a stream of red liquid hits the bush leaves. This scares me. Brings Thunder wasn't kidding then.

Leaping Antelope and myself do the swap. I snuggle into my sleeping bag in its new position in the middle of the row. My feet are roasted by fire, my body squashed between two others so I can't roll or stretch. But I'm happy. I sleep as soundly as a bookmaker after the Grand National.

Thursday May 13

Awake with an unusual feeling throughout my body: warmth. Leaping Antelope must be mad to have swapped, I grin. I peel back the top of my sleeping bag and glance over at him. He is snoring the snore of the waterproofed: blissed as the Dalai Lama in heaven. I make a mental note to check all his labels. Whatever his equipment is, it's the business for this roughing-it stuff.

A tractor pulls up with a dozen canoes on a trailer and a dumper of lifejackets. High Trees jumps down off the tractor. We have to haul the canoes over the last two hundred metres to the river. At the bank of the river High Trees delivers a homily (man the hunter's ancient mastery of the elements . . . his being at one with water . . . the ancient joy in physical strength that's been forgotten in this dephysicalised, modern world . . . how his bad back ruled him out of hauling the canoes overland but he empathised with the expressions of intense pleasure on our faces as we pulled etc) before we enter the water in the canoes.

After the swimmers are separated from the non-swimmers, about half and half, and we've learnt the basic canoe strokes and how to right an overturned canoe, we're put in teams. I'm leader of a small flotilla of five on account of my Willesden Pool-honed swimming prowess (300 metres non-stop ranking me third best swimmer). We push off. The course is whitewater in places. There are a few cuts and grazes, but no-one drowns or even comes close. That is downstream. Making our way back takes four times as long. By the end of it there are huge red welts on my hands, gallons of water in the base of the canoe and my arms scream like someone's poured petrol over them and lit it. At lunch my hands are so raw I can barely hold my spoon to eat. Lunch is banana and wheatflake cereal — the cooks burnt all the eggs and sausages. People are too hungry to protest.

2 p.m. Brings Thunder gives his last workshop. 'Combining Music With Dance In A Celebration Of The Masculine'. We were ahead of him yesterday, he says. Men can dance. Dance is not a wimpish thing. And to dance with someone is not always to hope later to have sex with them. Men can dance with men. Dance can be about comradeship, about soul, about sharing.

Let the drums speak, he concludes. Those moved by the spirit of the drums are free to dance. For some reason nobody feels like dancing. I think we're all bushed from the canoeing. Brings Thunder doesn't push it. We drum intensely and well. Brings Thunder does his own dance thing. At the end, he embraces each one of us, then gathers his drums and heads for the wood lodge to collect his money from High Trees "before High Trees blows it on dope, ha ha".

Dinner is boiled potatoes, beans in tomato sauce on toast and wild herbs. Those wanting toast have to spear a piece of bread on a stick and hold it over the fire. The are some fierce mutterings. The cooks today aren't up to it. It's our turn tomorrow. Over dinner, Jonty approaches me for herbs. He says no, he's not thinking about the little wooden rack of fennel and coriander that I have back in Willesden. I say I can't help him then. He tugs my sleeve which I don't appreciate. He gives me this 'you must have some, you're black' look. I suggest he tries Leaping Antelope. He's not black but he's very resourceful. Jonty leaves for Leaping Antelope and I help myself to his plate of catering beans. A starving man does not turn his nose up at beans.

11 p.m. The air in the tent is heavy with bean farts. PS. I washed some clothes in the river and attempted to dry them by the fire. Result: damp and smoked clothes. Still, I have enough clean dry clothes to last another two days.

Friday May 14

Wake-up at 6am because I'm cooking. Breakfast is scrambled egg made from dried egg powder (BlueJay), bacon (HammerCloud) or quorn burgers (Nikhil), rice krispies in semi-skimmed milk, and fresh-baked oatmeal biscuits (my little flourish). Big smiles from breakfasters suggest it went down well. We wash up at the stand pipe then start preparing lunch.

As we're peeling potatoes and shelling onions and stuff, we compare notes on the week so far. BlueJay thinks he'll go Overland to the East next time. He was seeking something closer to enlightenment and he's heard nothing new here. Nikhil suggests maybe that's it. Maybe the enlightenment is that there is nothing new in the world. HammerCloud says he's discovered something new: you can be with a group of lads, twelve twenty four hours, even more, and by now he'd have had to smack someone, but he ain't done it here. Though he thinks his probation worker placed Jonty here just to test him. I have no pearls of wisdom to add so I keep my mouth shut and peel.

After lunch we get to join in the afternoon's activities for one hour. There's another workshop leader here called Spirit Man. He's a pie and chips Sunderland lad, about twenty five (years not bellies). He sings like the angel, Gabriel. Song is the sweat of the soul, he postulates. And to sing is as natural as to bathe. It cleanses the soul, and scrubs away the grime of tired emotions. Modern life causes blockages. We cannot sing in the city or we would be locked up and declared mentally ill. Someone points out you can Karaoke and you can get tight on a Friday night and sing your heart out on the streets of Bristol. Spirit Man waves these objections aside. That is not real singing. After a brief Do Ray Me warm up, we are told each to find a space in the vastness of these fields and begin singing. Sing for ourselves. And be watchful for when the Spirit of Song comes over and delivers inner peace. I sing. A herd of cows come mooing my way and stare in silence as I warble. One drops a cowpat. Then they leave. The smell of fresh cow pats reminds me I have to get back to the cooking. Two hours later Spirit Man sings speedily over to High Trees cabin. He's after his money "before High Trees blows it on dope, ha ha."

Saturday May 15

Constant drizzling rain. The coagulated spaghetti in sour tomato sauce for breakfast is revolting. We erect a huge teepee so the workshop programmes can continue. The rain drums on the tent as we Deconstruct Masculine Archetypes, with Crystal Lake, a twenty-something, shell-suited, moonlighting lecturer in Urban Anthropolgy. After lunch (overcooked spaghetti in a bolognese sauce that the people of Bologna would riot to avoid) I go down with the trots. High Trees is sympathetic. Did I bring my salt and sugar rations? Yes. Do I still have them? Yes. He shows me how to mix a diarrhoea cure from them. I spend two hours on the toilet slats under an umbrella but am cured by mid afternoon. It's still raining in the evening. Nobody from our tent can be bothered making the trek to the bushes for a pee in the rain. So they pee out of the front of the tent. I bet Leaping Antelope would swap places with me now.

Sunday May 16

I wake frozen as a Maxwell bank account. Sunday is 'a day for peaceful, non-specific, religious and contemplative practices'. I join the meditation peaceshop. It is either this or chopping wood duties. A beaming Timothy Leary figure sits cross-legged in the middle of our circle. He introduces himself as Shining Way. We can transcend the everyday hassles of life, he beams. We can cast off our negative vibespheres as easily as discarding an old coat. There are three stages. One. We call up all the images that are hassling our minds. Two. We consciously place them in an imaginary box called "not worth bothering about", thus unburdening ourselves, Three. We imagine love and blue skies.

I try stage one — things that bug me. Why do we have to be woken at 8am by an idiot clanging a dustbin lid? Why are the tents pitched on the field's watertable? Why does HammerCloud have to snore every night? Why doesn't Blue Jay ever bathe?

Why doesn't Nikhil squeeze the spot he's had on his nose all week, or else let someone else squeeze it? Why is Leaping Antelope so smug even when being pissed on? Why does Jonty not realise that his tuneless operatic humming drives me mad? Why am I sleeping like a tramp in a filthy, flea-ridden sleeping bag? Why am I eating crap food? Why am I wasting my life wallowing in the middle of a muddy field with umpteen quack gurus and loons for company? I look around. HammerCloud has reached the blue skies of sleep. He's snoring lightly. Grey Cloud Three is out with the skies and sheep as well. Meanwhile Shining Way's eyes shine chemically. Can we hear the bluebird of happiness singing? I hear rain pounding the teepee. When the session ends Shining Way unfolds his legs and smiles beatifically, then makes a beeline for High Trees's cabin. Dinner is vegetable pie with raw pastry.

In the evening there's a brawl in our tent. HammerCloud is trying to meditate when Jonty starts his opera hum. Without a word, HammerCloud stands up and flattens him with a right hook. Jonty is quickly on his feet and lays into HammerCloud. The whole tent shakes as everyone starts settling scores under the pretext of keeping the original two assailants apart. Then from nowhere, High Trees descends upon us, trailing clouds of hashish and patchouli oil. He wades into the ruck and stuns everyone by calmly knocking out HammerCloud with a haymaker punch. Peace is instantly restored. He places HammerCloud in the recovery position and leaves.

That night High Trees calls a tent meeting to try to resolve our differences. We agree we're all worn out and frayed and we should try not to get on each other's nerves for just another seven days. High Trees pulls out his multi-headed hubba bubba pipe and he, Leaping Antelope, Jonty and HammerCloud smoke a golf ball of hashish together. The four of them end the evening arms on one another's shoulders, chanting peace poems.

Monday May 17

Wake up frozen as a Hitchcock corpse. Everyone was too stoned last night to keep the tent fire going. Breakfast is a gruelly porridge. There's a rebellion of sorts afterwards. We insist on moving the tents. They've been pitched in the path of some natural stream and we're all (bar Leaping Antelope) tired of waking up soaked. High Trees advises against, but the democratic wish of the people who are having to live in the tents and not in the nice comfy log cabin High Trees pads about in, holds sway. Relocating the tents takes up the morning. Democracy is a dangerous thing. Once people start looking to change things it never stops. Laundry is next. Everybody bar Leaping Antelope is sick and tired of wearing damp, woodsmoked, filthy clothes. The river may be Nature's washing machine but it just doesn't compare to the 400rpm late 20th Century mechanical device, and it doesn't have a Dry cycle. A three-strong delegation strikes out for the nearest launderette with a dozen bin liners of dirty laundry. They don't return. Late afternoon, a farmer arrives with a written message:

Only one machine. Staying at Cottage b&b while laundry spins. Will rejoin Camp next day. Enjoying beds and crumpets!

-Laundry delegation

While they're getting their hands on crumpet (my mind runs wild at the thought) we, the wild men on the hill, are invited to "explore the wondrous calm of the night" A purple-robed, pagan priest takes us to a distant hill where we raise our heads and absorb the universal energy of stellar light. We return to find the tents have been trampled by cows. High Trees shrugs. We have planted the tents on this clover that the cows go mad for. That was what he was trying to tell us, but would we listen? No. The pagan priest sprinkles 'spiritual manna' around our new tent site to keep away the cows. I think it was pepper powder. High Trees stays inside his cabin all evening saying he needs to do some deep meditation. I hear a woman's laughter coming from that direction.

Tuesday May 18

I dream I am pressed between two milkmaids. They are rubbing themselves up against me and chasing their hands up and down me. I wake to the sight of HammerCloud and BlueJay snoring in unison. I am depressed.

After breakfast the laundry team shows up. They are scrubbed, shaved and towel-dried. They have the calmness that comes only from having slept on a sprung mattress. They have bags and rumour is, it's not all laundry. We pile into a tent and post a guard in case High Trees shows. Sure enough, the extra bags contain supplementary survival equipment: twenty four cans of Holstein Pils lager, a shank of boiled ham, one hundred Benson & Hedges, a bundle of newspapers, a shelf-load of tinned food, and twelve rolls of Andrex Ultrasoft to replace the IZAL High Trees supplies. We divide out the contraband.

The big thing today is a sweat lodge. It's been set up some five fields further South. The purpose of the sweat lodge is to bond while we sweat together. It is a Native American invention, High Trees tells us, and they used to smoke peace pipes in them. He has a small amount of medicinal herb to go in his pipe but he may have to make a detour into the village to pick up more supplies unless anybody objects. Nobody objects. A beaten up Transit van arrives by the Camp gates and we all cram in. The van breaks down in the middle of the village. The grinning village mechanic lifts the bonnet, wafts smoke, closes the bonnet, then shakes his head to High Trees the way mechanics around the world, city, town and country shake their heads. He says we need the carburettor cleaning out and a new camshaft drive belt and there's a radiator leak plus a fuel line clip missing and they don't have the parts in stock. High Trees has us pile out. In the circumstances, he announces, we shall have to retire to the local pub. But we are to remember our Buffalo vows and not consort with the local women. He will arrange taxis to get us back.

Wednesday May 19

High Trees calls an emergency meeting this morning. We cannot go bonking away at the drop of a hat and expect to get anything from this course, he admonishes. There were definitely women brought back to the tents last night and he won't allow it. He will ignore it this time, but it had better not happen again. His words would have had more power if he hadn't had that ruby red lipstick mark on his neck. But we humour him. In fact only two of us got laid and I wasn't one of them. Sex is becoming a distant memory.

I am swapped onto today's cooking detail with a brief to sort out a decent alternative menu using the smuggled food. For the short time High Trees eats with us, we serve coarse rice with corn, wild cabbage and lentil sauce. When he ups for his cabin (and his Aga, I suspect) we bring out the ham shank goulash and lemon pancakes with jam. Everyone burps their approval.

Tonight I am on cow watch duties. I eat tinned macaroni cheese by moonlight. Sublime! There are no cows, but there are sheep. They have this coy way of waggling their ears. One of them definitely winks at me. Would Nikki mind if I had an affair with a sheep?

Thursday May 20

Last day but one on camp. The sun peeps out. I spend the morning kayaking with Leaping Antelope and Smoke. We're the most competent and go off on our own.

2 p.m. A mythteller visits, a Rastaman called Jah Howling Grass. When it's my turn and I enter the myth tent, I see him start. His expression says, whoa! another black man! He listens to my life story. Then he tells me my myth. I am a son of Shango, the Yoruba god of fire and of metal, he tells me. I am Shango's son. I time-travelled to this western Babylon world to renew and replenish the African vibesphere which this Babylon is dying through lack of. I must sculpt more sculptures. I must worship at the temple of Shango. That's it. Before I leave his tent he thrusts me his card. He will do me a private consultation back in London for £35, discount rate.

Friday May 21

Last day on camp. I go kayaking again with Smoke and Leaping Antelope. I'm going to miss these two. In the evening, High Trees leads the final session. He says how we've all grown and learnt more about what it is to be a man, how truth is stronger than fiction, spirit stronger than sword, strength of mind stronger than strength of body, how the fish in the sea and the water in the rivers and the clouds in the sky know this to be the eternal truth, and we have only to decipher the signs to know the age of Aquarius is upon us, and men must be not old men or new men but whole men. It's a pretty good speech as rambling speeches go, and after it he leads us all in one last roaring session. I say my goodbyes to HammerCloud, Smoke and Leaping Antelope. Everyone wants to be remembered by their Buffalo names. I'll really miss being called Morning Stars. There are hugs, a few tears, exchanges of phone numbers, then we sup the rest of the cans and tell stories.

Saturday May 22

Back in Willesden, meet Malik at the station. He cries in mock horror, "It's the Yeti!" I tell him to modulate his negative energy field, and accept his offer of a lift. Nikki was up late with accounts, he says, and asked him to pick me up. He drops me off and goes. Nikki is at the door. We hug. I love the smell of her. We have sex on the sofa which leaves Nikki panting. She says Malik is right, I'm a wildman now. She draws me upstairs. The bed jumps about on its wheels. She kisses me to sleep.

Sunday May 23

Wake up, go down and find Nikki is on the phone to Malik. She blows me a kiss. For no reason at all, I wonder if she's been sleeping with Malik while I've been away. I say nothing, it's just a thought. From Malik I learn Ajax-Willesden crashed 5-0 yesterday, though he didn't play. Also Wilbert sold two more of my paintings and has a cheque waiting for me.

Monday May 24

Debbie is all over me with hugs and kisses. What was it like? Did I meet Robert de Niro who's in crisis and has gone AWOL during filming? Has Malik told me she's up for a lead role in a big East European film he's negotiating and she's going to be dubbed into Croat? My hands still feel stiff from the Buffalo campsite cold. I study her. She looks great. Her breasts are heavier and there's definitely a bulge at her stomach now as her pregnancy develops. I paint badly but with energy. Afterwards I cook her something. Gas is a doddle compared with an open fire. There's no wood smoke to dodge for a start.

Tuesday May 25

Get a shopping list together. Then sort laundry, which all smells of smoke, cow dung and grass. I miss the Buffalo fires. Life here's so dull compared to Camp.

Wednesday May 26

Sort through the last of my Buffalo things, the toothbrush and hiking boots and waterproofs. Remember Jah Howling Grass telling me I am a son of Shango. I've never taken much interest in African gods before, but make a trip to Willesden Green library and get a book out on him. Shango is God of Fire. But Ogun interests me more. Ogun, God of Iron and of Art. I try firing up the oxy equipment this early evening but it's too temperamental to work with. Some things don't change.

Thursday May 27

Flick through daytime TV: Plastic Surgery Victims Confront Their Surgeons. Do Martians Cause Dishwasher Breakdowns? Topless Skiing. Makes me want to go back to camp. HammerCloud is probably back in the East End, rearranging someone's features. Leaping Antelope is probably up a mountain in Tibet. Here I am, vaccing.

Friday May 28

Stand in the rain for nostalgia's sake and wonder whether you'd need a license to kayak the Thames. Probably. My forearms have developed all this paddling muscle, which is wasting away. Still, the bed is a big compensation. I've slept like a baby in swaddling ever since I returned to civilisation.

Saturday May 29

Ira doesn't ring. Malik calls me in the afternoon. He scored two goals and they won 3-0, he says, and can I put Nikki on the line for him? He and Nikki talk business for hours.

Sunday May 30

Malik drives off somewhere with Nikki in the early morning. Nikki makes up for it in the evening by taking me out to a five star hotel. There are fountains, statues, lush music. And that's just the car park. I am banqueted by candlelight. We have our own waiter on permanent hover. I almost ask him to pull up a chair but Nikki wouldn't approve. Nikki looks resplendent in a Versace gown. I am dressed in one of Malik's better dinner suits which he lent Nikki to lend me. We are the only black people here, though there are some wealthy looking Arabs. The night flows. We are dancing to sanitised live jazz. Nikki's the best looking woman in the hotel. At midnight, things get embarrassing on the dancefloor. All the men are doing Rudolph Valentino or Saturday Night Fever routines. Nikki tells me she's reserved a room.

The bedroom suite is all mirrors and china. The carpet's so deep you could lose a Chihuahua in it. The bed's a waterbed. Waterbeds are new to me and I'm all over the place. But Nikki proves very adept. Wonder where she gained her expertise. Make a note to raise this at an appropriate time.

Monday May 31

We check out next morning and they present me with the bill. Nikki revives me with a glass of water and says it's all on the company account and to stop causing a scene by lying there on the lobby carpet.

1 p.m. Check the freezer. It's chock full of freezer meals from Iceland. And there's a new 800 watt Panasonic grill-and-bake microwave gracing the kitchen. There's brie in the fridge and semi-skimmed milk and lettuce and vinaigrette salad dressing. And Australian wine. The kitchen curtains have been washed. Conclude my kitchen's been Nikki'd. I have to confess I'm disappointed. I was hoping she'd flounder without me. Debbie-Anne comes round, puts my hands on her stomach and asks can I feel the baby kicking, but I can't feel anything. She says the baby went still and only kicks for her mother.

Tuesday June 1

The joy of driving! I put my Micra through its paces up and down the High Street doing the shopping, visiting people. It drives like it's glad to have me back.

This evening I'm burning with ideas. Draw about twenty new sculpting sketches, all influenced by the African Gods books I've taken out from the library. I think I've found a new direction. These Gods have me spellbound.

Wednesday June 2

First day back at swimming class. I tell everyone about my exploits in the wild outback of Essex, shooting rapids, wrestling with huge waves, and surviving only thanks to my Willesden swimming class. Teresa asks me to put it in writing as next term's contract is being put out to competitive tender. In the canteen Siobhan presses a gift-wrapped present into my hand. I open it. It's a thin, gold necklace. She puts it around my neck. I thank her but why did she buy it? She smiles at me mysteriously. I explain I didn't bring anyone anything back from the camp because there wasn't much suitable.

Thursday June 3

Fire up the welding equipment. I'm going for a metre high black, male figure in blackened, rasped aluminium, who's stretching up to the sky to catch a piece of burnished aluminium moon. I get the basic profile of the figure done and I like it. It's etiolated, surreal, luminescent. I call it Moonshine.

Friday June 4

I blast and rasp until I get Moonshine as close as I can to how I want it. I watch the sun go down on it and think it's the best piece I've done. Nikki likes it.

Saturday June 5

Sun blazes joyously as I load sculptures into Micra and drive round some galleries. But they aren't interested. Malik calls round in the afternoon. There was a place for me on Ajax if I'd only showed up. I tell him what I've been doing. He says the problem is how I present myself and if he gets time he'll work on something with me. He then spends the next hour on the sofa with Nikki discussing "profit to risk capital ratios" while I pour them drinks. He keeps pawing Nikki's knee as he explains things. I notice, but Nikki doesn't seem to.

Sunday June 6

Leaping Antelope phones. He's setting off Tuesday for base camp of Everest. There's a party on tonight and I'm invited. Nikki doesn't want to go with me. She's setting up her laptop Internet connection software. So I ring Arnulfo the Bergmann's guitarist and he's all for it. I tell him I guess the dress code will be formal and I'll pick him up at Bergmann's. Formal dress for Arnulfo turns out to be his best psychedelic orange shirt, quarterlength cowboy boots and late period Elvis trousers. I'm in a blue suit, white shirt and plain tie. Arnulfo tells me I look like a cop. He drums on the Micra dash and wails glitter rock anthems all the way there. I think he's in his manic phase.

Leaping Antelope is all tuxed and bowtied but doesn't bat an eyelid at Arnulfo. It's all a bit stiff. The music is classical. Or was, until Arnulfo gets bored and finds the sound system. He bangs in some guitar band CD and boosts the volume. The mountaineers look lost, but Tom (Leaping Antelope's real name) yells he loves the stuff, or else why would he have the CD on his rack? Suddenly The Young Guitar Murderers is fine with everyone. I dance with a tipsy woman mountaineer. She says she wishes I was a mountain so she could climb all over me. I can see Arnulfo chewing some pretty little thing's ear over by the coats. I stay teetotal while everyone around me gets tight on the huge bowl of punch. Tom comes over and gives me a hug. He's going for the big one, he says. Many don't make it back, that's why everyone's turned out to see him off.

My first impression was wrong. Mountaineers know how to party. By the end of it, everyone is thoroughly wasted and yet there's been not one brawl. I drive Arnulfo home in the dead of the night. It's muggy warm. Arnulfo's dead drunk, and sleepy with aftersex hormones. He had a bit of posh, tonight, he says. A Sloane. He lied to her he was Blur's drummer. She wore green silk knickers, with a lace edge. They did it in the bathroom, the Bombay roll. She was very proficient. He drifts off to sleep. I wonder what a Bombay Roll is.

Monday June 7

A monk calls round — the hippy monastery and all that — I'd forgotten! I usher him in. He has the classic brown robes and cropped haircut. He's no older than me. He introduces himself as Brother Robert and says he used to be a chainstore buyer. He speaks with a Geordie accent. We're in the middle of this conversation about modern life and personal sacrifice when Debbie rings the bell. She gives me a quick hug, says don't mind me and disappears upstairs. The monk seems in no hurry to leave. When Debbie shouts down that she's taken all her clothes off now and I can come up when I'm ready, he's in even less of a hurry to leave. I try to explain I'm painting. He says can he stay and observe. I shoo him out. Monks ain't what they used to be.

After the day's sketching I tell Debbie I want to concentrate on sculpting for a while. The galleries keep rejecting my sculptures, even though they take the paintings, so I want to work on getting the sculptures the best they can be. Debbie is disappointed. She likes modelling; she likes being admired. Malik doesn't even look at her, now that she's pregnant. I tell her I think she's beautiful and she can always come round. I'd love for her to keep coming round every Monday, whether or not I'm sketching her. She's happy then, and stays for lunch.

Tuesday June 8
The streets are Tandoori-hot. Driving along High Street my eyes feast on a sight not seen since all of last Summer: the breasts of London, finally free of winter smotherings, and displaying their smoothlicious selves to the world again. Some breasts flaunt, some are shy, all are appreciated. I buy supplies: chisels, some acid for etching, goggles. On the way home I buy a bag of smooth-skinned peaches from a market stall.

Wednesday June 9
Gillian pops round. She says she feels no shame doing Betterware parties and the like. Everyone on the Estate is mortgaged up to their eyeballs, and at least she and her husband are doing something about it. Her husband sells driveways. He's won two company awards so far, a battery powered puppy that yaps when you approach it and, just recently, a week's holiday for two in Tunisia. He's away a lot, though he phones every day. Organising the parties keep her occupied. She likes my Moonshine sculpture and says I have talent. I tell her it's nothing compared with the sales talent she and her husband have — I'm useless at selling. The Betterware party's next week. She's going to keep me back something special.

Thursday June 10
Sculpt like mad in the morning. Then I go to check out Debbie's latest show. This time it's at House of Munro and she's showing a bread-baking machine. 'Perfect ciabatta every time. Only 399.' (That's pounds — if you shop at House of Munro you can afford it). There are two or three takers in each

of the three demonstrations Debbie does. She's good, better than with the Multiblender. I calculate on say, ten percent, she's making £300 in an afternoon. Nikki home from InterGlobe and boasts of her record sales performance. She's increased margins by 6.5 percent. I applaud her. How come everyone can sell except me?

Friday June 11

A sculptor must sculpt. I blaze away in the blazing heat all morning. I'm soaked in sweat by the end of it, but the piece looks good. I sink three cans of lager, then shower.

HammerCloud rings! He's been invited into a little get-rich-quick scheme, a security van holdup. He's trying to say no, but the others are questioning his manhood. He can't talk to his probation worker, she's straight from the X-Files. He wants to know: what should he do? Would I stand in for him? I'd be using a sawn-off and they'd pay reasonable expenses but I'd have to provide my own balaclava. I tell him I'm sorry but it's not my area of expertise. Add does he not remember what High Trees said?: "Millennium Man has evolved beyond brute force. True masculinity is harnessing the yin force of the male in a positive way". HammerCloud says he'll sound an idiot talking about harnessing yin forces to his mates. He'd rather just say he's going to do a job in Tenerife. Whatever works, I tell him, whatever works. Turns out Debbie is paid just eight rotten pounds an hour for her ciabatta demos.

Saturday June 12

Ira asks how the SAS training course went. We're playing the Seventh Street Animals. For once I'm not keen, but I can't let him down. Our team warms up by touching our toes. The Animals kick a tailor's dummy's head around. At least I think it's a tailor's dummy. They all look like they're on steroids and they grunt and growl at us at the kick-off. Ira's playing as

Captain at the back. We hold firm and win 5-1, though half of us need dental work afterwards. Malik is the hero. He scores two and trips up their huge central defender who turns out to be soft as a parish priest's loan. I have to bear Malik retelling each of his goals in the pub and all the way home.

Sunday June 13

Nikki spends all evening talking about what she's going to do with her £5K bonus. It's either a small swimming pool out the back, or a bigger engined car, or else more Pacific Basin shares. A new electric tin opener would be very useful, I think to myself. The manual one we've got doesn't actually open tins, just polishes the rims. But I don't interrupt Nikki's flow. She's having a financial wet dream. Then she's on the phone to Malik to share it.

Monday June 14

Make a few welds to get the basic structure of the second 'African Gods' inspired sculpture. It's going to be a flying mass of pitted aluminium, representing lost spirits. Debbie calls round later than usual. She doesn't understand why I've dropped the paintings when they were selling. Let's just say I'm irrational, I tell her. What would the world be like if everyone went around being rational? Squarer, says Debbie. With labels on everything. She lets me cook her lunch, then we head off for Gillian's Betterware party. We're both Betterware virgins. I buy a set of bowls and Debbie buys a bunch of twigs, tied with string and sold as a whisk. The whisk looks mildly erotic. I mention this to Debbie. She says she's off to flog some egg whites unless I want her to put me across her knee and flog me instead. Little does she know she's fingered my ultimate fantasy.

Tuesday June 15

Ring round the galleries again. Same shit, nobody wants to know my sculptures. Maybe Debbie's right. Maybe I should get commercial. Do something outrageous, like make a plaster cast of my wedding tackle. That would sell. In a temper, I rip open a bag of plaster of Paris, dump the powder into a bowl of water, mix, then strip and smear on the plaster goo. The plaster sets rock hard. Temper over, I try to ease the cast off and realise maybe I missed out a step because it won't budge. I can't call the fire brigade, I'd die of embarrassment. So I use a chisel and mallet, very carefully. These tools and a copious amount of 15W/30 engine oil eventually do the trick.

Tonight, Nikki gets amorous. Great timing! I feign a headache. Nikki sulks. Have hidden my bruised genitals under baggy Y fronts.

Wednesday June 16

Did L-Mart miss me? It's my first visit since Camp Buffalo. They've moved the long life milk out of the third aisle and into the refrigerated section, dropped the price of the own label baked beans, jacked up the prices of all cheeses except Parmesan and withdrawn the Little Cuckoo brand of frozen chicken. Apart from that, everything is as was: still too many idle shelf fillers and too few check-out operators, the Muzack is as naff as ever. I feel like crying out, I'm home! my people! My supermarket! The friendly L-Mart undercover detective (there's a uniformed one as well) tails me as I wander round. I ask him to push the trolley while I load, it'll be easier for both of us. Get back, cook. Aren't birthdays a wonderful thing? I say to Nikki (mine's in two day's time) over yoghurt desert. I think she gets the hint, though she doesn't actually ask me what I want.

Thursday June 17

Sculpt all morning and to hell with the galleries. Find out from Sappho I should have shaved my pubes, then oiled them before applying the plaster of Paris. Art-wise it's old hat though, Sappho says. It's been done since the Dadaists. I thank her for her encouragement. Go out and buy some candles and a birthday card for myself. I don't trust Nikki to remember.

Wondering aloud how old I'll be on my next birthday (27 — aagh!) Nikki's head is wedged in her laptop, 'internetting consumer resistance curve data' she says. Whatever. Later, she pops out with Malik 'to go over some figures'.

Friday June 18

My birthday! I tiptoe downstairs to see if Nikki's left a present. Nothing. No cards on mat either. OK, Dad's dead, so he's got an excuse, and Mum's eloped to Brazil with a short order chef. Still . . . I'm inconsolable. My sculptures look glumly back at me. I put a blanket over them and sulk. Nikki's mother arrives. She tries to get me into the kitchen to learn how to prepare fish, but I'm not interested. We end up on the sofa drinking lager. I tell her it's my birthday. She says isn't it a bit childish to be celebrating birthdays at my age? I agree, glumly.

Doorbell goes. It's a Gorilla-Gram! The Gorilla comes in and leaps around the furniture while playing a Happy Birthday To You tape. I applaud. The gorilla bows and plucks its rubber head off to reveal a gorgeous Naomi Campbell look-alike. One shimmy and she sheds her gorilla suit to reveal a comic Twenties swimming costume. She says happy birthday, then gives me a peck on the cheek and a card. It reads:
To my handsome partner, Harvey. Happy Birthday! Put your tongue back in — mum is there to make sure you don't get up to any hanky-panky with the Gorilla-Girl! I'll be back early with another surprise.
Yours adoringly, Nikki XXXXX

I get the Gorilla-Girl a glass of water. She's thirsty from all the grunting. Her name's Dion and she's from Lewisham and is paying her way through college. She stays for a quick bite of lunch (salad), and then her pager buzzes and she's got to go.

8 p.m. Nikki home with a book on African art for me and a tub of Tom & Jerry's frozen, low-cal strawberry fool. She undresses, spreads the strawberry fool all over herself and I get to lick it off. Phew — what a birthday!

Saturday June 19

Ira rings. It's the last match of the season. Honour is at stake. If we lose today's match we'll be bottom of the league, lower even than the Geriatric Bartenders XI. The Geriatric Bartenders XI have not won a match in three seasons in the league. I am called off the bench with only fifteen minutes to go. We are 1-0 down. Big Bird feeds me the ball in the semicircle. I jig past the fat man with the inhaler. I dummy left, then go right past the zimmerless one. Malik is screaming, as only Malik can scream, for the ball on the edge of the penalty area. I calculate he's in an offside position and astutely hold the ball from him. I rampage past two defenders. Just the goalie to beat. The goalie adjusts his bifocals. I let loose a lethally angled half volley. By some fluke he stops it. By another fluke he throws it accurately all the way to their centre forward, who buries it in the back of our net. Malik chases me and grabs me by the throat. There is a short struggle. The ref sends us both off. We lose 4-0. In the dressing room Ira rips up both our registration cards and eats them. Neither of us is playing for Ajax-Willesden next season, he decrees. Then he starts crying. The team leaves him alone so he can salvage his dignity.

Sunday June 20

Get a telephone call from Foxy Lady. Her CB radio antenna has been twitching and a certain person has said

"Someone ought to tell Harvey that Malik's been shagging his Nikki for God knows how long," and she's just passing this information on. I ask how this certain person got this information. Foxy Lady tells me Malik's mobile phone is not 100% tight, security wise, on account of his buying from somebody in the renumbering business, and this person -the snoop, not the seller, she points out — heard some extremely revealing conversations between Malik and Nikki using her handheld scanner. This certain person is even willing out of the generosity of her soul and to promote the cause of truth within relationships as Oprah said you have to, to part with the tapes this certain person has made for a small administrative fee of fifty pounds. I tell Foxy Lady to tell this certain person to fox off. But am concerned.

Monday June 21

Visit Bergmann's and beef about the galleries fobbing me off. Sappho takes me to Ade's. He works in phone banking by night but by day builds his art collection, she says. It takes Ade three minutes to open up, he's got that many locks on his front door. I like Ade instantly. He's a Yoruba, a short, intense, worried looking man in his mid forties. He has a brickie's crunching handshake. He hurries us in and operates all the door locks again. The house is chockful of African sculptures. It's spooky; you can feel the spirits inside and it makes you tiptoe. Ade shows us through to a room with a two-seater settee. He fetches us kola nuts and coffee, then stands without talking while we sit. Sappho doesn't find this unusual and we two sit in silence. I look around the room. One mask in particular stares directly back at me. There! shouts Ade, startling me. He offers me the mask. But it's such a powerful mask, and I have nothing to give him in return, I protest. He says to bring round one of my sculptures sometime and he'll contemplate it. If it's good enough he'll accept it in exchange.

Get back and Nikki has left a message on the answering machine: can I cook lamb ragout tonight? A request from Nikki is unusual. I cook her the best lamb ragout she'll ever taste. She loves it. It's exactly right, she says. I take a humble bow. Maybe I should set up in the chef business.

Tuesday June 22

More disappointments with galleries. Feel like getting a skip and piling all my stuff in it and trading it all in at Alucan Recycling like so much waste metal. I'd earn more money collecting cans off the street. Debbie suggests painting more but I don't want to. I'm a sculptor if I'm anything.

7 p.m. Nikki is kind about my stuff not selling. She describes it as an 'adverse take-up scenario posing a turnaround challenge', and offers her body as consolation. Afterwards, her pillow talk is all about this next big deal she's going for. It's reached a crucial stage; she just has to win round one key opinion former, and it'll be signed, sealed and incentivised.

Wednesday June 23

Go swimming. It's good relaxation. I glide like an otter. A splashy otter, Teresa says, but an otter, none the less. Siobhan pairs up with me for advanced life-saving. She brings me out of the water, no problem, and lays me out in the correct resuscitation position. We're meant to maintain oral hygiene but Siobhan says she'll take a chance with me, and makes a perfect seal of her lips on mine. Her tongue darts into my mouth and before I know it her tongue is cleaning my tonsils. When she is finished I feel very revived.

Get back and there's a set of messages from Nikki, each one

more frantic than the last. I must have Lamb Ragout for four ready for when she returns at seven. We are having very important guests. Nikki turns up at six and removes all black culture stuff from the walls, including Ade's mask which I've just put up. She tidies away my sketches and swaps my Dizzy Gillepsie for some tinkly piano music. She doesn't want her guests scared, she says. They are an important business associate and his partner. Well, I proclaim, I have done my duty and the lamb ragout is ready on time.

7 p.m. The guests arrive promptly. A young tyro exec and his modelly partner. They love my ragout. Nikki tells them I'm a sculptor. I have a studio in East London, she says, which is news to me, and I have been boycotting the Turner Prize "on principle" otherwise I would probably have won it. After making some brave attempts at discussing art, mostly price tags, they all three talk market adjustments and strategic repositioning. He is relaxed enough to fart in my kitchen. They leave glowing with wine and Nikki's witticisms. Nikki says thank you, I was great, then kicks off her strap shoes and collapses on the sofa. She thinks they liked her. She's happy.

Thursday June 24

Spend morning going from gallery to gallery. Arrive back hungry and impoverished. Not one sale. My face don't fit, I conclude. My art don't fit. The owners are all racist philistines and to hell with them. Maybe I should become a busker instead. I spend the afternoon trying to find my old blues harmonica but can't. I make do with some vintage vintage vinyl blues and a four pack of lager. Nikki blows in and says to stop moping around and go fishing or something. Harvey Robinson has never fished.

Friday June 25

Watch old videos, Ice T in a gangsta movie, then Poitier in something noble. Am struck by the contrast in the physiognomy of the traditional black hero in contrast to that of the modern anti-hero. My thesis is as follows; Sidney Poitier, Denzel Washington Will Smith etc. are the traditional black male heroes, perfectly manicured, groomed, slim, conservatively dressed, with short and neat, afro-d hair. Eddie Murphy, the joker, is allowed a 'tache as well. The black male gangsta anti-hero on the other hand, has a rough, razor-bumped face, facial hair, is often squat and enters his first scene with gun drawn. I'd bet all my sculptures (for what they're worth) that no traditional black male film hero ever had a gold front tooth. I look in the mirror and try to guess where I fit in, in this traditional hero/modern anti-hero spectrum. I am definitely the anti-hero, I think gloomily. Malik rings and confirms,yes, I am ugly, he won't lie to me, but he'll take me out tomorrow to cheer me up. We'll do whatever I want to do.

Saturday June 26

Go canoeing with Malik. He is protesting even as I wedge him into the canoe: "Where's the steering wheel?" I hand him a paddle, push him off and tell him to shut up yelling. Push myself off. Malik is blubbing with fear. I tell him how easy it would be for me to drown him and no-one would know. Everyone would think it was just an unfortunate accident. He says he never meant to say I was ugly. It was a joke. I mention Foxy. He says don't believe Foxy, he's never had sex with Nikki. Heavy petting — once, long ago — but no sex. Their flirting's innocent. And as for his hands on Nikki's knee that time, he's just a touchy-feely person. I should know that — he can't help it — and I should remember that he's trusting me with Debs. The truth is the same as he told me before. He and

Nikki are working on a Middle East deal. It involves temperature regulation units, souped up air-conditioning. It's hush-hush, a grey area, not illegal. Her company wouldn't like her working on it, so he's helping her. I'm to go easy on him because he, Malik, is extremely incompatible with water. Malik carries on blubbing for the next two miles until I take pity on him and nudge his canoe to shore.

Sunday June 27
Nikki flies to Scotland on a takeover deal. It looks a dead cert, she says. A Scottish media company in trouble. She's flying to Edinburgh with Mr. Lamb Ragout to dot the i's. They'll be locking in key personnel with golden handcuffs. I tell her she'll make a beautiful jailer.

Monday June 28
Debbie calls round. Malik's with her. He's come to help with my problem selling sculptures. I hate to admit it, but his plan is clever. Artefact-robbing has always been the British art establishment's main line of trade, he explains. So, if a Nigerian arrives on a Gallery's doorstep, with stuff allegedly from the local population in a diplomatic bag, then they might just be tempted. Like all Malik's plans, it leaves me a little uneasy. Malik says legally we're watertight. I think his subconscious is still being affected by our little canoe trip.

Assume Nikki is still in Edinburgh. She hasn't rung. Why not? For a moment I get nervous about Mr Lamb Ragout. Are they booked into separate rooms?

Tuesday June 29
6 p.m. Nikki back, furious. I won't believe this, she says. The entire Scottish management can go eat haggis. She was stitched. The Scots got hold of all her bid figures in advance somehow, went behind her back and found venture capital

backing. The venture capitalists persuaded the Scots management to swallow a massive poison pill. Nikki has heard of levered buy-ins with floating collateral before but this one took the biscuit. It's in the hands of InterGlobe's lawyers now. She thinks Mr Lamb Ragout had a hand in it all because he was behaving strangely. Whatever, there goes her incentive bonus. She bursts into tears. I wonder whether to ask her what a levered buy-in with floating collateral is but decide it's not the right moment for forensic curiosity. And how did your day go? she sobs. I set about pampering her with food and attention. She is so gorgeous when she's crying, though she hates it and says she only ever lets me see her in this state, 'never those bastards at the office'. By her third cup of milky cocoa she's smiling sweetly and speaking revenge.

Wednesday June 30

Siobhan wants to go over last week's lesson, the resuscitation bit. Lola rescues me. It's backcrawl today and I spend most of the session contemplating the Victorian swimming bath roof. Teresa breaks bad news. She's not had her contract renewed. The Council can't afford it. The mood is defiant: we're going to continue meeting every week in protest.

Nikki home, cursing. Mr Lamb Ragout had blamed her for the collapse of the deal. She should have gone straight back to the office, Tuesday. It was his feeble presentation to the Scots that fireballed it all anyway. The MD had her file on his desk when he called her in to express the company's disappointment that the deal was off. The file didn't have a pink sheet on the first page so she thinks she's survived. Which means Mr Lamb Ragout's on his way out. I don't try to understand this logic, I'm just glad for Nikki. As for Mr Lamb Ragout, he deserves all he gets. Never trust a guest who farts in your kitchen.

Thursday July 1

Nikki returns, beaming. Mr. Lamb Ragout was fired today. She uncorks a bottle of Australian to celebrate. To Mr. Two-Faced Lamb Ragout's demise, she toasts. Wake up in the middle of the night. A bald truth confronts me. I haven't sculpted anything all week. I have artist's block. It's incurable.

Friday July 2

Suspect the L-Mart manager is a frustrated installation artist. He has created an auditory-olfactory experience out of the cold meats section. Piped, mooing music, a waft of roast beef, and the upright freezers sighing, 'Mmm' when you put your hand in them. I ease out a four slice pack of garlic sausage and one Edam cheese, to two moos and a sigh.

Saturday July 3

11 a.m. Go to inspect sculptures in garage. Find Malik pressing up against Nikki there. Again. He jumps off her, says he was only congratulating her on surviving the week's backstabbing frenzy at InterGlobe. I light my blowtorch and point it in Malik's direction. He blubbers something about an urgent appointment, scoots to his car and burns rubber. Nikki storms off, nose high, saying I always misinterpret things and there's nothing going on between them. Am unconvinced.

Sunday July 4

Must get Malik off my mind. Try roaring, but Edward pops his head over the fence and offers me Colonel Bristle's Cough Linctus, so I do deep breathing instead, then smoke some stuff Filo's slipped me. I make a pipe out of a piece of copper tube and a bit of gauze. Then tote. I find myself wondering if Leaping Antelope's up that mountain yet.

Nikki wanders onto the patio and smokes a pipe with me. She says Malik is important to her, part of her support network. And, working in that bastion of white male privilege called InterGlobe plc, she needs all the support she can get. I cook her her favourite, grilled lemon sole in Chinese leaves. Nikki wanders away after lunch to phone Malik. I smoke another pipe.The Lebanese Gold resin levitates me to the astral plane and I finally understand. Malik was put on this earth to torment me.

Monday July 5

Debbie-Anne comes round. I pick up my paint brushes again just for her. She wants a series of portraits of herself up to full term. She's big now. We work out a reclining pose that she's comfortable with. I still can't feel the baby's kicks but Debbie's stomach feels pillow soft. I turn the radiator on full. She sits for an hour as I sketch. Then I cook her lunch. She demands sweet and sour pork, with the pork fried, not battered, and lashings of pineapple ("Baby likes pineapple"). I rustle it up fast and watch her eat. She burps after she's licked her plate and declares baby satisfied. The two of them fall asleep on the sofa.

Tuesday July 6

L-Mart's free magazine, The L-Mart Shopping News. Headline is cute: "Alien gave me monster orgasm!" I pop one in my basket. Nikki and I so rarely have sex aliens may soon be my only hope. There's an influx of summer stock on the shelves, charcoal briquettes, baby marigold plants, fruity condoms etc.

Back home am lost in L-Mart Shopping News. I have never read journalism like this before.

Navel Gazing — The New Craze Sweeping America! This is the decade in which the full beauty of the navel has finally been recognised. Midriff baring is It. The navel is the new heart, the lotus blossom, the desert flower, the titillating corona, the kingpin of the body! Pierced, tattooed, garlanded, women are flaunting it, men are decorating it with abdominals hard enough to pluck a tune on.

There are twenty photos of celebrity belly buttons, and one advert for a liposuctioning plastic surgeon. I pull off my shirt and take a glance in the mirror. Maybe I should do some sit ups. I cook myself baked beans on toast, then have a siesta. Dream about Debbie-Anne's navel. Am woken by doorbell. It's Gillian. She's bored and not in a selling mood. I get her to explain to her telesales technique and she promises to help me develop some patter of my own. For some daft reason we plan a barbecue at my place tomorrow.

Nikki returns and collapses with laughter. The MD nearly died today. Mr Lamb Ragout has pulled a skank on InterGlobe plc. He's become a partner of the Scots Management Buy Out team of the company they were trying to take over. Word is he was a sleeping partner all the time and leaked all our plans to them. You have to admire his bottle. I don't understand why this tickles Nikki but I laugh along.

Wednesday July 7

Gillian jumps in the Micra and comes swimming with me. She was the best swimmer at her school and made it to Central League Intermediates Individual Medley Finals. There are no lessons and the pool is open to the general public. We pay our money and go in. The pool's not so full and I easily spot Siobhan and Lola, and Edwin and Kushil. We swim over and I introduce Gillian. Siobhan immediately challenges her to a race. Gillian compliments Siobhan on her costume and the challenge is forgotten. Lucky for Siobhan. Gillian swims like a dolphin.

Afterwards we all jump in my Micra and cruise along, sunroof open, windows down, stereo blasting. It's not a beach buggy but it's fun. Siobhan sits up front, Gillian and Lola in the back. We pick up pizza, and pistachio nut ice cream. The three of them slurp beer while I drive. Micra breaks down. Luckily we're not far from a garage and we all four push it in. I bribe mechanic a fiver to lift up the bonnet and shout something about the carburettor being sorted now before he puts petrol into the tank.

Back at my place, I cook some side dishes while Lola gets the barbecue going. We spend a hazy afternoon discussing lipsticks, moisturiser and bratwurst. Edward and Roxanna join us, which means we're soon all out of beer. Ruby turns up as well. Uncanny how many people can scent a barbecue from five miles. Siobhan corners me and snogs me in the kitchen. Doesn't even disguise it as resuscitation practice. I offer feeble resistance. No one sees us.

Nikki back late. She notices all the paper plates and other junk scattered about and I mention that, oh yeah, there was a barbecue party going. She mutters something about some of us having to work to keep this country going while everyone else lazes around. I say it's very patriotic of her. We have a shouting match. I'm a lazy, do-nothing, drunken, failed artist, is the gist of it. I call her a workaholic. She hits the Australian chardonnay and offers me a glass. We agree a truce — we're both merely alcoholics.

Thursday July 8

Gillian and Debbie round. I teach them five card poker. The stakes are Betterware bowls (Gillian sold Debbie-Anne a set yesterday). Gillian wins all her Betterware back, but in a magnanimous gesture, lets me and Debbie keep what we lost. Next time it's for keeps though, she warns. Debbie-Anne says baby wants me to cook Sweet and Sour Pork again. Luckily for baby there's enough pork left over from yesterday. Debbie shows me the scan picture. They can't tell the sex yet.

Friday July 9

Malik takes charge of my sculptures. He gets me to sign a piece of paper that says he gets 20% of net profits from any sold. Loretta, an old girlfriend, rings. She's in town. Do I want to do lunch with her? We do lunch in town. Are men and women essentially incompatible? she asks. She's about to split up with her latest beau, Derek. He lasted three months which is above the average for her. The quality of the men, and not just the quality of their sperm, is declining nowadays she says. Should she keep on holding out for better? Why don't men come with a six month's guarantee like everything else? Maybe she should join a dating agency I suggest. We talk dating agencies.

Saturday July 10

We're celebrating, official. Something to do with Nikki's office. She's taking me to the very swank Carib Sum restaurant, where she'll tell all. Nikki dresses me in a mud brown Moschino suit, white Brooks shirt, and brown brogues. Everything fits perfectly. She wears one of her Pierre Cardin suits. She takes embossed calling cards. The Lexus has been waxed up.

The Michelangelo-style frieze on the ceiling of the Carib Sum is stunning. All the demigod figures are dark skinned instead of the usual white. There is a tuxed jazz combo playing softly. Nikki tugs my sleeve. The famous chat show host, Nightingale Summers is here, she whispers, at the best table on the platform by the mirrors, there — air kissing a couple of rich black media moguls, if she's not mistaken. A waiter brings a menu. I notice everyone gets a big silver platter that holds around twelve tiny dishes, each dish containing about two dim sum sized spoonfuls of food. There are chillis and condiments in the centre of the platter. I read the menu. Plantain sauté, chicken breast à la jerk, etc. It's all 'oil-free', dry as a bone. Nikki eats two mouthfuls then ups and makes a beeline for

Nightingale Summers. When she returns she reveals what this dinner's in honour of. The MD's hand-picked her to work on InterGlobe's biggest deal ever. We celebrate with champagne.

Sunday July 11

Nikki's head in InterGlobe reports all day. I go to Bergmann's. Everyone's smashed. There was a party thrown by a Virgin talent scout last night. Nobody got an offer though they've all got his number. They laugh at me when I copy the number down ('the last time I Karaoke'd at Bergmann's the audience booed me off — if none of them could break in how could I?' etc.). I refuse to respond to their pettiness.

Monday July 12

Nikki's office is dizzy. The entire department's wages for the next twelve months is riding on this deal she's working on, she says. The signals are overwhelmingly good. But she's nervous. The ratios she's looked at are very wide of the norm. But the MD's happy with it. Big margins mean big profits, he's told her. He's pushing her to wrap it. But she has this funny feeling it could go pear-shaped. It could be a gift horse, she says. She wants to look right into the mouth of the numbers. I think she's been scared by the last deal collapsing.

Tuesday July 13

I finish the Moonshine sculpture. Then I immediately have this idea for a series of spirit masks made from old, chrome, car wheel trims. It means finding a scrapyard with 70's Cortinas and Anglias, Minis and Chevettes, the kind of cars that had metal hub caps. I dash off a whole series of possible hub masks in one go. Then I can't find my Yellow Pages. Call on Gillian for hers. Gillian says it's a good week for another barbecue, am I doing one, or should she? I tell her go ahead and throw one, I'm busy. She asks to borrow some briquettes and lighter fuel, and oh yes, my portable barbecue as well. By the time I've wheeled it all over, it's too late for the scrapyards.

8 p.m. Nikki comes home. Why haven't I cooked anything yet and why is the place a mess and what's that trail of black dust across the carpet? I shove something in the microwave for her, then take off for Bergmann's. It's closed. I knew this even as I drove there. Drive aimlessly round town.

Wednesday July 14

I ring that Virgin talent scout and offer to enhance the creative ambience of his apartment quickly, easily and with a minimum of mess. (Gillian's recommended patter). He tells me to send round three sculptures and he'll bike a cheque to me by return if he likes them. By twelve noon I am nine hundred pounds richer. Amazing! The same spiel you use to sell plastic containers can be used to shift sculptures!

The barbecue at Gillian's goes fine. I tell her that her patter worked on the Virgin talent-scout. She smiles and says to get networking: each visitor in this garden here is a potential customer. I introduce myself to all and sundry. Nikki's pillow talk is that at the barbecue all the women were singing my praises. She mimics them. 'I've never known a man like him!' 'He has time for me!' 'He listens!' 'He's ever so sympathetic!' I didn't know she was at Gillian's barbecue. I promise to be more obnoxious. This pleases her. We have ten minutes of slow sex.

Thursday July 15

I need those hubcaps. But Ruby calls, just passing by. I bundle her into the Micra and chase down to Arnold's Breakers. As I cold-eye the cars, Ruby gets all soft-focus, dabbing back tears and and sniffling. This was the car her husband used to trundle around in, she says, pointing. That was the car they went to their wedding in. I try to hush her because the scrap dealer's by our shoulder and she's bidding the prices up prattling on like this, but she won't be hushed. The scrapyard dealer is an old geezer with a chimney pot head and thick grey bristles on his chin, the kind you used to get on backyard brooms before they went plastic. His name is Randolph, he claims. He was in the army, he tells Ruby. When he was demobbed he drove one of these. On his first release from prison, he drove one of these . . . The two of them go off around the yard on a nostalgia fest. I hear Brushhead say "you can't put a price on memories." I make my pitch fast, and his answer stuns me: since I'm with this nice young lady (i.e Ruby) I can take as many as I want. For free. He then wanders off with Ruby. I think Ruby, I love you, then zig-zag the Micra round the potholes, flip the boot open and load up with chrome hubcaps. Parting Ruby from Brushhead takes ages. I suppose I should be grateful to her for wangling me some free metal.

Friday July 16

Spend the day polishing hubcaps. My oxy equipment has packed in totally. Nikki comes home irritable, which makes two of us.

Saturday July 17

Nikki vanishes with Antonia all day. Malik comes round. Why don't I go back to the paints? he asks. "Artistic integrity, something you wouldn't know about,Malik," I answer, and explain my sculptures are as good as my paintings. Malik ripostes the market doesn't think so — he's tried and they won't sell — and the market is God. I tell him the market can kiss my arse. He says he's heard that one before — at the Bankruptcy Courts. I reveal that I've sold three sculptures this week. The great sales guru is humbled for a second. Then claims a twenty per cent cut since I signed over exclusive dealership rights to him. I suggest he finds a lake and jumps in it. He settles for a vodka and coke, and waits for Nikki. He's fast asleep by the time she returns, alone. She's looking okay but tired. Malik is whistling in his sleep. We let him lie there on the sofa. I phone Debs to let her know where he is.

Sunday July 18

Let slip at Bergmann's that I cut a deal with the Virgin scout. Sappho says that all she can say is — I must keep my talent hidden deep down inside myself because last time she heard me singing I was worse than a St Bernard with appendicitis. Three rounds on me later, they're all singing my praises. I forget to explain the deal was for sculpture, and not a recording contract.

Monday July 19

Debbie's latest fad is auctions. She drags me along to one. It's of Railtrack Lost Property and Goods from Other Bespoke Sources. Debbie bids for fishing rods, bicycles, mobile phones and umbrellas and manages not to buy anything at all. I keep my hands pressed to my sides until Lot 46, a high power welding/oxy kit with associated tools. The strange things people lose on trains. I need a new kit. I bid. An over-muscled, shaven headed, white guy who looks like a dull-witted garage hand is the only one bidding against me. We go from five to thirty quickly. There's whispering among the crowd and they gawp at me like I'm doing something amazing. They obviously don't know the value of a good oxy kit. My opponent bows out at fifty-five, muttering. The kit is duly mine. Me and Debbie just about manage to get it into the Micra.

9 p.m. Nikki back. Her big deal is building. The MD is pushing her to say yes and wrap it.

Tuesday July 20

Debbie round again. We go to the local pub, The Last Drop. I am approached by the guy I bid against at the auction. His name is Tommo. He says no hard feelings about the kit, I bid for it fair and square and that it used to be his but they lost it when a security guard interrupted a certain job they were doing on a certain supermarket safe. The police put it into the auction when Tommo's mates failed to claim it back as lost property. Tommo says people don't usually bid against them, on account of their reputation for grievous bodily harm, but he says I can keep it. He admires me for working alone, it's much safer — no-one can grass you up and I've done well to keep my nose so clean that even he, Tommo, hasn't heard of me before. I choke on my Heineken. Tommo ends by offering me a nice little earner as look-out on a bank job coming up next week and I won't even have to carry a shooter. I try to decline graciously but he tells me to think about it and everyone knows it's smart to be on the right side of Tommo and his gang. You get looked after then, otherwise accidents can happen, things can go bump in the night.

I spend the night imagining things going bump.

Wednesday July 21

The temperature is 85 degrees. Willesden Pool is closed for repairs, so we all head for the Willesden Lido. Caligula would have been at home at the Lido. It's an open-air heaving mass of near naked bodies — . There are deckchairs, bikinis, wave machines and lilos. And breasts and bums everywhere. Everything wiggles. Siobhan and Lola gasp at two people having sex in the water — either that or he's tying her bikini top and she's ticklish and wriggling like mad. We jump in and play shark, and they both go underwater and attack my swimming shorts. 100% fun.

9 p.m. Nikki is still unconvinced about the merits of the big deal and wants an independent audit before they buy, she says. I nod off daydreaming of group sex at the Lido with Gillian, Siobhan and Lola.

Thursday July 22

Get a phone call from the PA to Charlotte Hawkins, a big shot in the London art-buying world. She asks if Charlotte can visit my studio tomorrow. She saw some of my sculptures at the Virgin Music Executive's place and was interested. I say sure, she can come over. Then panic. I phone Malik: what should I do? Malik says buy a smock, have lots of empty wine bottles and traditional African art scattered around, the full Picasso set. Decide not to follow his advice.

Friday July 23

Charlotte Hawkins calls round. She hates my paintings. But she loves my sculptures. *Nirvana*. She leaves with a promise to make me a proposal. Nikki returns. She's not in a talking mood. She stays up late scrolling through spreadsheets.

Saturday July 24

Half the neighbourhood's at Gillian's BBQ, all clutching Betterware brochures. Some of the local hubbies make snide comments about my being a househusband, and warn me away from their wives. Strange people. I shrug them off.

Sunday July 25

Nikki says she knows the numbers don't add up but the MD has threatened to sideline her unless she closes the deal fast. He keeps saying the Scottish one got away due to delay, which Nikki thinks is unfair because that was Mr Lamb Ragout's doing. The deal just doesn't stack up, Nikki says. It's not what's there, it's what's not there. She's been trying to plug the holes all last week. She spends the day on the phone. I try out the new kit. It welds like a dream, and cuts like a starved barracuda.

Monday July 26

I head out to The Last Drop hoping to catch Tommo. I'm tired of worrying about things going bump in the night. I find him there. Look there's been a misunderstanding, I explain abjectly. I'm just an artist — a sculptor — I had no idea — if he wants the equipment back . . . Tommo puts an arm around my shoulder. He's not riff-raff like the rest of them here. He knows his Modernists from his Mannerists. He wants a private viewing of my sculptures. He might take one or two as an investment. I try to fob him off, but his Audi A6 tailgates my Micra home. He chooses two of my five latest steel sculptures. All that work for nothing! I am about to kiss them goodbye when Tommo pulls out his wallet and peels off two thousand in Scottish fifty pound notes: will that do? Yes, I reply, swallowing. Tommo leaves. I have two double whiskies. I can just picture the headline: Harvey Robinson, Artist To The Criminal Classes. What do I do with two thousand pounds in hot Scottish fifties? I stuff the money in a vase.

9 p.m. Latest from Nikki is Personnel insist she take a holiday. Part of the mission to change company culture. Nikki says she'll fight, because the bastards will drop the ball while she's away and she'll have to carry the can for it. I think they're right, she should take a holiday. I keep my mouth shut.

Tuesday July 27

"Am I a workaholic?" Nikki demands when she comes home. Before I can answer, her mobile trills. When she's done on her mobile, she flicks open her laptop and demonstrates, with the aid of a full colour line graph, how her seventy-six hours a week average is 5% below the company average work hours for her salary level. The day Gorbachev went on holiday, she intones, the Russian coup happened and he never made it back. The day Thatcher swanned off to Europe, she was shafted by the men in grey suits. Caesar invaded England in the holiday season. She spells it out plain. Things happen when you're on holiday, desks get reassigned, P45's go out. I tell her not to panic. She won't die of a holiday. After fettuccine and stuffed aubergine in a chestnut sauce Nikki dives back into her laptop. She's been won over by my arguments. And since holidays are compulsory at InterGlobe, she says, she must make sure she gets the best dates!

Wednesday July 28

Skip swimming for a walk with Debbs. She's starting to feel the baby's weight but doesn't want to sit around getting fatter and fatter. They've decided not to ask the sex, though she thinks it's a girl from the way it's lying. She wants to be as close as possible to her. Debbie herself was adopted, she tells me. She stops at the newsagents for lemon fizz bombs. She emerges with a quarter pound of lemon sherbert. We walk back and I rustle up lunch. Just before we eat, Debbie screams with delight, grabs my hand and places it on her lower stomach. This time I feel the baby kicking, two big healthy whacks. Suddenly wish the baby was mine not Malik's.

8 p.m. Nikki back. She's booked two weeks in Biarritz. She apologises that she couldn't get Guyana or anywhere tropical. We're leaving next week. Wednesday at 6 a.m.

Thursday July 29

Weld a giant chrome mask. It looks regal and defiant. After lunch, I dash across to the newsagents' and borrow his counterfeit pen. Tommo's money passes the test. It's all real!

Guess I should have a business card made:

Harvey Robinson sculptures, paintings, money-laundering.

There's not much time to prepare for the holiday. Get a spare set of keys cut, hand them to Roxanna and ask her to keep an eye on the house when we're away. Demonstrate to her how to switch off the house alarm if she has to get in. Then whizz down the High Street and use Tommo's dosh to splurge on holiday stuff: three pairs of sunglasses, coconut oil sunscreen, sandals, three pairs of Bermuda shorts and assorted Hawaii shirts, a new toothbrush, dental floss. Nikki back very late from tying up loose ends at the office.

Friday July 30

Decide I need to brush up on my school French. Recall my crush on Ms Hughes, my first form French teacher. How proud she would have been of me now, twelve years on, still dedicated to learning la langue française. I buy a dictionary and a phrasebook. Flick through it. *Je voudrais une glace* — I'd like an ice cream. *Voulez vous coucher avec moi?* — Will you sleep with me? Phrase Books have changed since I last flicked through one. Wonder how you say "would you lick me all over please?" and look it up, word by word. Rent an Elvis Presley in Hawaii movie but Nikki refuses to watch. I can tell she's still fretting about her stupid deal. I wish I was going with Debbie — me and Debs'd have fun.

Saturday July 31

Malik and Debbie round. Malik claims he's got morning sickness just like Debbie. What a prat. Nikki gets a call from Antonia. Debbie wanders into the back garden with me. She's going to miss me, she declares, stroking my cheek affectionately, even though it's only a fortnight. And me, I'll miss her, I confess. And she'll miss my cooking, she says, a bit sharply. I cook her a couple of meals for freezing.

Nikki has a talk session with Malik in the garage. I spy on them. She has her laptop in there and they're both bathed in its green-blue glow. I see her scrolling a spreadsheet. At one point she gets agitated and Malik puts an arm around her and kisses the back of her neck, which calms her down, but riles me. Later, we all four head for the basketball arena. Nikki drives, Malik rides in the passenger seat and me and Debbie ride in the back. Nikki's happier after talking to Malik. She doesn't mention business once, all the way there and all the way back. Got to admit Malik and she click. He calms her somehow in a way I can't. Malik tries to invite himself with us on holiday. I insist no, not unless Debbie comes too. He says Debbie is too fragile to be crossing the Channel. Debbie glares she's not. Nikki puts an end to it by saying there are just two tickets and just two people going, me and her. We get down slowly to the honey'n'base sounds of Luther Vandross. Kitsch but nice.

Sunday August 1

10 a.m. Nikki watches European stock movements on Ceefax. Claims she can figure out the latest plotting on her deal from the ups and downs of the London Stock Exchange. Thought the stock exchanges closed on Sundays. She's simulating, she explains. She's practising so when she's on holiday she'll know how to read the movements. I think it's a bizarre way to spend a holiday, but say nothing.

Early afternoon, I head out to Bergmann's. They all egg me on to take the mike. I've been boasting about my Virgin scout deal. Obligingly, I get up, close my eyes and do *Unforgettable*, Nat King Cole style. There is this hush when I finish. Then James intones: "And that bullfrog got a deal with Virgin? Nah, I don't believe it!" Sören, the owner, comes over. He hands me a free double rum, then says I'm banned for life from going anywhere near the mike again unless I book the entire place for a private function. I thank him for his compliment.

Monday August 2

Cherryville Estate is a burglars' paradise, the newsagent tells me as I'm cancelling the newspaper delivery. So I buy a gizmo off him that will switch things on and off automatically. It's programmable. I spend all morning experimenting with it, hooking it up to the Multiblender and having it puree plum tomatoes. Twelve jugs of pureed tomatoes later, I think I've got the hang of it. I presume we are taking the Lexus to the airport and leaving it in Long Stay. Which means I can park the Micra in the garage and lock it up. All my sculptures will be safe there as well. I dig out all the window-lock keys and check they work, then hide all my bank books and stuff in an old suitcase under the bed. Nikki gets back. She hasn't started packing yet. But I find out she's got fresh batteries in her laptop and mobile.

Tuesday August 3

Expect Nikki to come home all irritable and sour, but she breezes in with a smile. If you've got to holiday, you've got to holiday, she says cheerfully. After dinner she packs. I watch her wedge clothes into one suitcase, mostly casuals though I notice one business suit, also: an electric toothbrush, eye brow pluckers, lash curlers, nail clippers, emery boards, six nail polishes, blusher, lip gloss, sunscreen. On top of this she plonks some books: The One Minute Manager, Only Losers Blink, The Business SuperAmazon, How To Close That Deal. On top of the books she places a sheet of paper with row upon row of mysterious numbers. My own holiday packing is: a portable iron, continental plug adaptors, a Walkman, Farrar's Complete French Grammar, Pascal's Pensees (Ms Hughes, you'd be proud!), The Biography of CLR James, 100 Continental Chat-Up Lines, Beachwatching for Beginners, charcoal sticks and a drawing pad.

Antonia rings. Nikki laughs through a half hour conversation with her then rings off saying she'll send her a postcard. Damn. All those people I want to make obscenely jealous by sending them a postcard from swanky Biarritz, and I don't have their addresses!

Wednesday August 4

We're in British Airways Business Class. Nikki's laptop is talking to her mobile phone which is talking to InterGlobe HQ's On-Line Enquiry System, Password Level Five. I know this because I'm leaning over her shoulder watching. I nudge her. A last minute foray, she pleads. We 'broker an agreement'. Clause One: The moment the plane touches down on French soil, she will abandon work, put her business tools in storage and adopt a seriously frivolous holiday mood. Clause Two: All talk of work is henceforth banned for the duration of the holiday. After her last quick fix, Nikki packs the gizmos away and we snooze in each other's arms for the rest of the flight.

Unpack at palatial hotel, marble floors, pillars, spotless cream furnishings. Nikki is disappointed she can't fill even half the wardrobes with her clothes. The remote that opens the curtains to a view of the bay and the sea with the white blobs of little yachts on it. Biarritz used to be a fishing village.

It's hot, but not sweltering, thanks to the sea breeze. The clientele are mainly high society French. We dine off silver on gourmet food. I thought we'd do something in the evening but Nikki, after choosing a dress plus accessories, promptly falls asleep, so I leave a note and pass the time at the indoor pool and sauna. When I return Nikki's still snoring. I move her over to undress her, and find her laptop hidden under a pillow.

Thursday August 5

Nikki tries to rescue her mobile and laptop from the hotel safe where I deposited them last night but I hold her to our agreement. They're in my name so she can't get them out herself. She pleads. She calls me cruel. Eventually she gives in and tries on this Seventies style, cream and white itsy bitsy bikini that I've been looking forward to her wearing. But when she gets to the beach she panics. The fashion here is Fifties retro, those awful all in one girdles that cover everything from the elbows to the knees. I tell her she looks great in the itsy bitsy, but she dashes off and comes back with a yellow and red all-in-one. Groan.

Lie back and watch lots of joyously bare breasts and neat bums. Am I a bum man or a breast man? It's a tough choice, but the bums win. Slumber in the sun, dreaming of the women of Biarritz all flocking to me and running their hands all over me, rubbing their bums in my face. I wake up and Nikki's rubbing oil in my back. Aaaah . . .

At the first club we go to, the DJ plays a mixture of classic disco, funked up techno and French ballads. People dance for fun, not to pose. We get a few stares because we're the only blacks here other than the waiters. Nikki lets herself go on the dancefloor. I let go at the bar. She steers me home at 2 a.m. The linen blankets are delicious.

Friday August 6

Frst genuine French hang-over. We walk hand in hand, window shopping. Nikki falls in love with a dress and just has to try it on. A pastel green chiffon halter-neck by Galliano. I admit she looks superb in it. The 10,000 franc price tag doesn't matter to her. She's happy, I'm happy. Her plastic's happy.

We dine al freso. I have steak frites, she has ham-stuffed crêpes. It's 86 Fahrenheit. 30 Celsius. Some nubile young women are playing petanque in square opposite where we're eating. Nikki tells me to blink now and then and shoves food in my mouth because I'm gawping.

Back at the hotel Nikki puts on the Seventies kit and does a little belly dance. We do it on the lambswool carpet with the French windows open so the surge of the sea and cries of the seagulls mingle with our pants and grunts. After fifteen minutes Nikki still isn't satiated and I have to glug some iced water from the minibar to get my energy back.

Saturday August 7

The colours here are clearer than in England. Biarritz is Mediterranean, deep blues and sharp yellows. It's as if some film of dirt has been wiped away from my eyes.

Late p.m. We find another club. There must be a Eurowarehouse of doormen, all bristleheaded, dumb-brained and overmuscled. This lot mistake us for musicians and let us in for free. It all happens in French and Nikki doesn't understand. The music's low key jazz and the vibes are sweet. Black people lend any club authenticity, I muse, among the smoke and sweat and kissing. We are the originators of jazz, music's prime innovators. The club owner comes up and invites us to step up to the mike. We decline politely. Twice. The club owner get impatient and waves over a bouncer. My wife is ill, but I'm more than happy to oblige, I explain. I am escorted to the mike. Someone gives me a short intro I don't catch. In the audience nobody much is paying attention but the musicians, who all look Sudanese, are waiting. I start my Nat King Cole number . . . Nikki finds my being tossed out onto the Biarritz pavement very funny. I don't. At the hotel bar, Nikki gets drunk and sings Whitney Houston's *I Will Always Love You* to rapt bar staff and my sozzled self. If she had only got up instead of me, we might still be in that jazz club.

Sunday August 8

Nikki says do I know they play nude boules in the Village Square here every Sunday? I tell her the only body that interests me is hers. Later I get a town map and purely out of curiosity and a desire to learn more about the customs of a strange land, drop by the Square. Nikki wasn't lying. They are nude. They are playing petanque. But they are all village elders. She is waiting in the foyer with an amused grin splat over her face when I return.

Sunday's quiet. We take a walk. Nikki tries to sweet-talk me into letting her see her e-mail. I am resolute. Non, non, non! In the evening in our chambre, Nikki pulls out a surprise package. A saucy French maid's outfit. She promises to wear it if I let her use her mobile once for no longer than five minutes. I cave in. Nikki returns with a gleam in her eye. I guess her big deal is going the way she wanted it to go. She slips into the bathroom and emerges as a French maid. (Since all the maids here are Algerian she looks closer to the real thing than you'd expect, except the maids here don't wear the timeless French maid uniforms. They wear white overalls and pink rubber gloves and swear in Arabic.) By amazing coincidence Premiership football is on TV here and I catch up with the scores. Nikki sulks under the covers. She refuses to watch the replays of Ferdinand's swerving overhead kick.

Monday August 9

Over lunch Nikki tells me she's met someone called René. René Mazarin. He has offered her not only his hand in marriage, but a business partnership in his metals company. She says it's a very attractive offer. I am jealous for a second. But René is a preposterous name, I reason, so she's probably made him up. Poor Nikki. I smile at her indulgently.

Hang around hotel pool. Nearly fall off my lounger when Nikki appears in her itsy bitsy, exchanging pleasantries with some walrus of a man trotting by her side. She spots me, places a soft hand on Mr Walrus's shoulder and points me out, then leads him over. He gives an extravagant bow, says he is René Mazarin and is pleased to have met my wife and I am a very lucky man. He holds out his hand. He is charming, I have to concede, in that old-style chivalrous way. I decline to join them in the pool and watch from behind Le Monde as Nikki cavorts in the water with him.

Tuesday August 10

René has left for a business meeting in Marseilles. We take to the beach. Nikki goes topless. I position myself on my front so I can take in a good view of the beach without showing my erection. The breasts of Biarritz are out in force. Nikki asks me to rub oil on her buttocks. It's the first time I've seen her bare bum in this Mediterranean light. I smooth half the bottle on it before she says she thinks that's enough. Late evening, we stroll along the beach again. Nikki shakes out a towel, drops it and we have sex in the setting sun. Sand gets into my shorts, up my nose, into my hair! Next time I'll take a swimcap, plus kneepads.

Returning to the hotel, we are stopped in the foyer by (white) Security and accused of being hooker and pimp. I manage to persuade them to check the residents' list. Instead of an apology we are reprimanded for not carrying ID. I've never seen any white people being asked for ID in all the time we've been here. It sours the evening and we both get sour drunk. Nikki curses the hotel staff then moves on to cursing InterGlobe. I curse hotel staff and then all the galleries in all the world. We stumble up to bed drunk and cursing.

Wednesday August 11
Find René playing tennis with Nikki on the hotel tennis court. She waves me over and begs me to watch. René wobbles and whacks the ball very effectively. Nikki loses and doesn't mind. She hates losing when I play her. René insists we all have a drink. He's married and his wife's here somewhere, he says. He tells rather good risqué jokes and might actually be serious about offering Nikki a job. René says he can learn more about someone from one game of tennis than from a month of boardroom meetings. I can see Nikki likes him, more as a father figure than anything else.

Thursday 12 August
Nikki goes shopping. That list of numbers she packed is a set of conversions for dress and shoe sizes from English to French. I spend day on the beach while Nikki melts plastic in the shops. Meet up with her later. She's hired a car. A top of the range Mazda.

Friday August 13
The Mazda is a smart move. We zoom off to St Jean de Luz down the coast. It's a picture book fishing village only just opening up to tourists. They serve us huge portions of Ttoro

(Basque fish soup) for lunch. On the way back we hit car problems. Nikki manages to crawl it to a garage in second gear. What is 4 Star Super Unleaded in French? she asks me, as the petrol pump attendant smirks by the pump. I wobble around with my French and the attendant manages to smirk and sneer at the same time, which is quite a feat. Nikki gets a result from the English-French Translator gizmo she fishes out of her bag. She watches the still smirking and sneering attendant fill the car up. Then she tries starting the engine. There's a clatter then nothing. The attendant nods for us to get out. He looks and says we need a new starter motor Nikkis gets out and asks what the problem is. I tell her what he's said. While Nikki converses with him via her machine I whip down a tool set from the garage wall and unscrew the four spark plugs. The attendant protests that I can't touch his tools but I'm much bigger than he is. I clean the sparks, then try starting the engine. Nothing doing. Maybe he's right. Nikki laughs. This is a hire car, she says. We just pick up the phone and they'll send another one straight away. And it happens! We pull away in the replacement Mazda. In the rearview mirror the attendant is giving me the left-hand-over-right-biceps international 'have a nice day' code.

Saturday August 14

We go to the beach, flop and ooze. René joins us with his wife, Gisou. She looks like Brigitte Bardot's cousin. She and Nikki go topless. I bury my head in a book. The threesome start playing beachball: René throws to Nikki. Nikki throws to Gisou. Gisou throws to René etc. Not very complicated but are they enjoying it — René especially! After some cajoling from Nikki, I join in.

Realise there's a colour bar at this hotel. Front of house employees are white, behind the scenes chambermaiding, carpentry and stuff is done by either Sudanese or Algerians.

Sunday August 15

Nikki writes a postcard to Malik over breakfast. I read it surreptitiously:

Briefing On Biarritz: Temperature is 31 degrees C — optimal for leisure activities. Enjoyment levels are high. I am advantaging strong networking opportunities with promising continental niche players. Will update you further on return. Harvey sends his regards.
XXX Nikki

I write a postcard to Debbie-Anne:

Well Debbs, here I am in bonny Biarritz. Hope you are both bottoms-up!! Life here is a tough regime of sand, sun, sex and shopping. Loving it. Wishing you were in the room next door.
Love Harvey X

The cuisine at the hotel is so amazing I've just got to meet the head chef. The mâitre d'hotel escorts me on a tour of the kitchens. It is a chef's paradise of organised chaos. Steam, fire, steel and Gallic yells. The washer-uppers and vegetable preparers are mostly blacks. Then I am introduced. The head chef is, a pony-tailed Englishman called Tom!

Monday August 16

Tennis in the early morning. I win. Nikki shrugs and laughs. Over lunch she giggles. I've never seen her look so radiant. What's more, René is nowhere in sight! Gonna be a fine day. We take to the beach. I apply sunblock to her back and watch her discreetly eyeing the hunks on the beach. My own biceps are not exactly bulging. I wonder if they sell t-shirts with built-in padding around the biceps region?

After le repas, we take to the beach again. As the sun sinks, madness seizes us. We ditch our clothes, run straight into the sea and try to make love in the sea waters. We fail miserably. I know now why octopuses have suckers.

Late night pillowtalk: Nikki tells me she had forgotten the simple pleasure of doing things like swimming and tennis and stuff, and what a fool she has been to drive herself so hard in her job. It's only a job.

Tuesday August 17

Last day. Nikki goes on one last shopping expedition and manages to reach the dizzy heights of her credit card limit. Frankly I didn't know she had one. I blow the rest of Tommo's money on a couple of suits.

We pack. I go to fetch Nikki her laptop and phone. When I get back René is there pitching a job to Nikki. She says if she ever does consider changing jobs, she'll contact him. René hangs around. Nikki logs on to her laptop, then gasps. InterGlobe's shares have been looping the loop. René says to remember the big stockbrokers are all on holiday, it's the junior staff running the markets now and the juniors are more excitable, that's why there's turbulence. Nikki's impressed with the analysis, but unconvinced. She can only just stop herself from phoning HQ. She wants to get to the airport straight away. We're packed and ready. René is in tears. The two of them hug and kiss for ages, swap endearments and promises to phone. When they finish weeping on each other's shoulders we're on our way.

London. Heathrow Airport Hotel is a come down after Biarritz, but neither of us feels like driving in the dark and rain. Yes rain, that wet stuff that falls out of the sky.

Wednesday August 18

Nikki abandons me at the kerbside of 57 Cherryville. She has to get to work. I walk up the driveway. There are a thousand copies of the Willesden Advertiser wedged in the letter box.

Open door to another wedge of mail. Find burglar alarm box ripped from hall wall. Have head in hands thinking we've been burgled when doorbell rings. It's Roxanna . . . The police 'disconnected' the alarm she tells me, and hands me a bill to prove it. She says it was her fault. She went in because she saw a light come on in the middle of the night and then couldn't remember how to deactivate the alarm. She was very brave to go in, I say, through gritted teeth. Realise I forgot to tell her about the automatic light switch device I got from the newsagent. More bad news in kitchen. Fridge has failed and everything inside it is either whiffy, sprouting or yukky. Apart from that, everything is as we left it. I've just about sorted out the mail and dusted stuff down and unpacked for us both when Nikki gets back. She's very quiet all evening and mainly stares at the kitchen walls. Guess she's missing Biarritz like me.

Thursday August 19

Sort the fridge (just a blown fuse in the plug). Gillian comes round and helps me clean up. I promise to show her our holiday snaps. Am concerned about Nikki. She says she should never have gone away, and spends night getting high on coffee going through photocopied reports and accounts.

Friday August 20

Get letter saying that an Assessor is about to visit me on behalf of the Destitute Artists Benevolent Fund. I must have applied to them during that mad, form-filling week with Sappho. Dash to Bergmann's and ask Sappho what to do and say. After three hours coaching I return home with a basic knowledge of 'grantspeak' — the language of funders.

Nikki's subdued. She's had an ultimatum from her MD: decide on the deal. Yes, *that* deal — it's still dragging on. Monday's she's got a face-to-face with him, when she's got to say yes or no, and he expects her to say yes.

Saturday August 21

Nikki off to see Antonia. Malik calls round. He has worked a miracle, he declares, sold three of my sculptures while I was away to conscious brothers and sisters who appreciate fine art. He hands me a roll of bills, of a colour I don't recognise. They're English £50 notes. What's more, he says, the Willesden Star wants to do a feature on me next week. They're going to phone. I count out the money — nearly a thousand pounds. I grovel at Malik's feet and he lets me. He hangs around for a while emptying my fridge while waiting for Nikki, but Nikki doesn't show till almost midnight and looks wobbly. Antonia drops her off. Malik for once does the decent thing and excuses himself.

Sunday August 22

Nikki visits her mum. Says she wants to get closer now her mum is old and might die. Strange. Ruby looks as strong as a sherpa.

Monday August 23

Debbie phones, peeved. Why have I not called her since I got back? The meals I prepared ran out at least five days ago and she needs more. I apologise. Baby is very angry, she says. I cook her stir-fried prawn chow mein for lunch. Later, she apologises for having become addicted to my cooking. She'll try to wean baby and herself off. I say it's no problem. She has started to waddle slightly. Only three months before the birth.

Nikki returns and tells me she's resigned from InterGlobe! She refused to capitulate to the MD's ultimatum. She told him the deal didn't stack up and anybody who went through the accounts properly could see that. They were buying into a debt mountain and a set of intangible, overpriced assets and it just wasn't in InterGlobe shareholders' interests. The MD's going ahead with it anyway and wanted her out of the way, so she resigned. She says she suspects he's got his nose in the trough like Mr Lamb Ragout had, it's the only rational explanation.

Tuesday August 24

Nikki goes in to work to clear her desk. She's found out what's going on and it is as she suspected: massive handshake share options all round. She's not joining and mark her words, it'll all end in tears. I admire her for sticking to her principles. It's not about principles, she scolds, it's about economics. The deal makes bad economics. It'll wreck InterGlobe's share price. Then their handshake options'll be confetti. I realise I'm over my head and retreat to the kitchen and the durum wheat spaghetti.

Wednesday August 25

Willesden baths seems pokey after the Hotel du Palais pool, but the old friends are there. Lola's heading back to Germany next week. Her grandfather's died. Siobhan said she'd go with her but Lola wants to go alone. Lola says it's no big deal, she hardly knew him, but I can tell she's wobbly. Siobhan gives Lola a big hug. She cries a little.

4 p.m. Nikki has found out from the Internet that the deal has gone through. What's more, far from going belly-up, InterGlobe shares have risen. She is calm about this. Once the facts have been digested the shares won't look so good, she's certain. InterGlobe Personnel ring and say no hard feelings, the door is still open, they're holding her job for her. She says something rude back and puts the phone down on them.

Thursday August 26

Finish the hubcap project: five masks, two gallery wall size, and three public space size (i.e big). They sulk in the garage but come alive in direct sunlight, bouncing and flashing fire and rage, like the god, Shango, himself. Nikki is 'considering her options' regarding future employment. I suggest the Job Centre. People of her status do not visit Job Centres, she informs me. The positions worthy of her status and skills are not the kind advertised in your run-of-the-mill Job Centre.

Friday August 27

Nikki reads about InterGlobe's deal on their Internet site. There's a tribute to Nikki's role in brokering it. She says someone's 'taking the piss'. In the evening she gets through one and a half bottles of Chardonnay. Clearing up around her when she's nodded off, I notice a scrap of paper with InterGlobe's number on it. Is Nikki about to eat humble pie?

Saturday August 28

Ralph and Antonia visit. I eavesdrop on Antonia in the bedroom telling Nikki, "Crying's OK, crying's organic." Nikki bawls, "It's not right." Antonia says, "I know a great outplacement specialist". They sound like a bad soap script. This is a callous thought and I'm ashamed of it. Before she leaves, I corner Antonia and ask her if there's anything I should be doing. She says just act normal, be patient and cook chicken soup. What has chicken soup got to do with this, I ponder. Act normal. Normally I would watch Italian football on TV. So, following Antonia's advice, that is what I do. Nikki blazes away at me for ignoring her and says I don't care. Thanks for the advice, Antonia, I mumble. Nikki hears it and asks what I've been saying to Antonia. This leads into argument number two. I slam off down to The Last Drop and smoke off a vending pack of cigarettes before I remember I don't smoke.

Sunday August 29

Sore head from The Last Drop's Real Yorkshireman's Muddy Chestnut Ale. Apologise to Nikki about yesterday. She apologises to me and we argue over who needs to apologise most. Ruby calls round, sinks the last half of Red and decides to stay the evening. Great. All I need now is Malik. He duly arrives. Nikki perks up, apologises for her apology, and drives off with him 'to discuss business'. Ruby wakes and asks why I don't have Sky TV and I've used too much pepper in this day-old chicken dip I've served her so she'll have to have some milk with it now. I fetch her a glass of milk, muttering next time it won't be pepper, it'll be arsenic. Ruby overhears and chuckles what a joker I am. Hmm. When Nikki gets back she's thoughtful. She compliments my chicken soup. All evening she gazes out of the window with empty chicken soup bowl in lap. She sleeps there in the Tuthankamen position: legs together, arms folded over chest, empty chicken soup bowl.

Monday August 30

Notting Hill Carnival day. Nikki doesn't want to go. Debbie has left already with Malik. I hang around some Sound System for a while in my best Jamaican tailoring and RayBans to boost my street cred. A thousand and one people I haven't seen since, well, last Carnival, go by. Filo is there exhibiting himself. We team up and get drunk on cans and he takes me to this party at some house up the Hill. You have to wear a mask to get in. They have them at the door, little Pierrot masks. I don mine and soon lose touch with Filo. The house is jammed and rocking, hot and smoky, a frotteurs delight. I wriggle my way around a bit, sample the punch, and find myself pinned to this superbabe in a glitter mask. She's wearing silver lipstick and a pink silk dress with a wayward front zip. The zip is caught in one of the button holes of my natty threads. We wriggle upstairs together to find some space to untangle ourselves and we can't and she has to remove the dress. Well, we've come this far, so we get down to it. Someone shouts can we hurry up in there because there's a queue. Filo. I swear him to secrecy. He just grins and pushes past. The babe in the silver mask disappears while I'm talking to Filo. I'm starving and blow my last dollars on dry patties. Crawl home from a blues at 3 a.m.

Tuesday August 31

Wake up. It's 4 p.m. Nikki delivers me breakfast in bed! I don't know what I've done to deserve this but I ride my luck. Nikki asks how Carnival went. I say same as usual. I spent most of the time at a University friend's house discussing Minimalism and Ancient Egyptian crop irrigation systems. Nikki laughs and says I should write fiction. When I reach the bathroom and look in the mirror I see why. My face is a glitterball of silver lipstick. Nikki traps me coming out and I mumble something about yes, I did take precautions. Keep a low profile for the rest of the day mucking about in the garage. In the evening, Nikki tells me InterGlobe phoned today. They're offering her fifteen thousand in severance pay linked to a gagging clause so she can't talk about the deal. She's going to reject it. I remind her of her credit card debts.

Wednesday September 1

Nikki has decided to take InterGlobe's money, but not the paltry offer they've made her. No, she's going to take them for every ECU they've got, she declares. I'm right behind her. She phones them and demands twenty thousand k. as a combined severance payment and fee. Around 6 p.m InterGlobe phones and caves in. Twenty thousand to keep her mouth shut. One costly gag.

Thursday September 2

The Willesden Evening Star phones me. They're sending round a journalist to do a 'local boy makes good' feature. A trainee just out of school arrives on my doorstep with a camera slung round his neck. I primp and preen through the interview and insist he photographs my left (best) side. Two hours later I dash to the newsagent. Scan the Star cover to cover but don't see my picture anywhere. Sulk home. Nikki returns from 'networking' for a new job. She's had a few offers, 'but nothing commensurate with my skills and experience'.

Friday September 3

Nikki works the phone all day. She's going to call in a few favours she's owed. She's looking for something in the fifty k range. She deserves a rise after all she's put herself through. I go to Sainsbury's. Thoughts: Why is decaffeinated coffee more expensive than caffeinated? After all, they're taking something out, not giving you something extra. What happens to all the caffeine they take out? Is there a caffeine mountain somewhere? Harvey Robinson would like to know. Pick up the Willesden Evening Star on the way back. Flick through it. Am stunned. My photo's on page five. It's a glowing write-up apart from the last line. The proof checker must have forgotten to edit it out: "To Ed — here's the article on that local sculptor-wanker you wanted."

Saturday September 4

Tour breakers' yards looking for a left wing mirror — mine was torn off sometime last night. Get no joy from Willesden Jap Breakers. The Rhodesian ridgeback guard dogs there go ape. While the dogs're going ape, this dumpy white dealer sits in his Portacabin grinning and makes no attempt to call them off. He must have high-loaded life insurance because I could be somebody else. Somebody who might not like being threatened by rabid canines. I just stop myself from reversing into a ridgeback and splattering it.

The guy at the other scrapyard wants to know why Ruby's not returning his calls. I let him weep on my shoulder while I unscrew a wing mirror from a D reg Micra. A pale sun is out and the gleam of something catches my eye. Chrome grilles. There's a stack of chrome-grilled Sunbeams at the rear of his yard. Realise this place is a gold mine for metal sculptors. He says I can take what I like. He's going out of business soon so it's no skin off his nose — liquidator's going to give it all to the banks. I load up as much car chrome as I can get in the Micra, 3 grilles, five tubes and some bits and pieces, and insist on giving him a tenner for the stuff I'm carting away, plus another five for the wing mirror. The pot holes driving out of his yard are big enough to swallow a Jeep without burping. Why do Breakers' Yards never have concreted roads? — Harvey Robinson would like to know.

What am I going to do with a load of iron junk, Nikki sneers when I arrive back. Say I don't see junk, I see psychedelic fun sculptures. She snorts. There are times when I think Nikki is just so square. Later she drives off in her Lexus 'to do some thinking'. I go into the garage and gaze at the beauty of all that pre-owned, pre-cast chrome.

Sunday September 5

Begin work on 'psychedelica' sculptures using Tommo's kit. Half an hour into the work it strikes me.I should do these ones stoned. I'd get inside the spirit of the metal more. So I make my way down to The Last Drop. Who should be there but Tommo. He asks me how things are going. I say just fine and thanks for the gear, it's really high quality both the cutter and the welder. Tommo nods sagely. Safebreakers only use quality tools, he informs me. It's a false economy to use cheap. Time is like gold dust and the best kit saves you time. If you're going for big money and you're cutting, then the best kit is what you want. Of course there's more than one way to crack a safe, though all that film stuff about listening to the clicks of a combination lock is bollocks — you just whack the lock with a big hammer so the spindle shoots into the case then you can turn the handle easy as an off-licence job. I nod sagely. Against my will, I'm becoming an expert in safecracking. After the third pint, Tommo lets me go with a friendly maul of my hand. I find The Last Drop's resident cannabis dealer and manage to score. Back home, I'm zonked and buzzing. I fire up the equipment and blaze away in a fierce rhythm. Then gaze at the result. I put my ear to the sculpture and listen to its murmurings. It wants to be juiced, jumbie-joyed, zummer-zocked with colour. So I get all the car paints down off the garage shelf and crack them open. When I eventually finish, smear the paint off my watch face and look, it's 1 a.m.

Monday September 6

Debbie-Anne phones. When will those meals be arriving? I promise to get on it. Stop off at Bergmann's. Everyone greets me as 'that sculptor wanker'. I tell them they're jealous I got the publicity. Filo asks for his own gagging payment not to tell Nikki what he saw me getting up to at that Blues. When I refuse and tell him she knows already, he says he has the number of the silver masked babe I bonked. He waves this piece of paper in front of me. I'm not interested. He waves it under my nose. I snatch for it. He whips it away. Yeah, he's full of beans today, is Filo. I lunge for it, the table goes sprawling. Sören throws us both out. The ball of paper Filo gives me has no number on it. Filo guffaws away as only Filo can. We walk the High Street, just talking. For all his clowning he's actually quite low. He's been playing and recording for eight years now, he says. His hair's turning grey at the sides. And he's never had even the sniff of a record deal yet. He's thinking of giving it all up, going to college and studying computer science. He was at University once. Dropped out to play guitar. It's either that or become a gigolo. I look up at him and he's wearing that mad jester smile of his. He puzzles me, Filo. I ask him a favour and he agrees to come back with me to see the new sculpture. He loves it.

Tuesday September 7

Debbie-Anne rings. I drive her to L-Mart so she can pick out the ingredients herself. She's got that clear, glowing complexion that non-pregnant women empty rainforests to acquire. The seat belt only just goes round her belly now. We work our way through the aisles. On the way out, I'm steadying her when an L-Mart shelf stacker photographs us. It seems they only hire eccentrics at L Mart. We get back and she sees my latest sculpture. She says it's amazing, the most wonderful thing she's ever seen. I don my chef's hat. Nikki returns just as I'm driving Debbie back with a boot full of cooked meals in Betterware containers. We wink headlights at each other. Get back to find Nikki is concerned about something but she won't say what. She spends the evening looking at old photographs of herself.

Wednesday September 8

Go swimming. Siobhan's there. Strange but, without Lola around, Siobhan isn't so all over me. We talk about Lola and how she's coping. Siobhan had a phone call from her last week. She's staying on longer at her parents' place. Lola was tearful on the phone. Siobhan's writing to her. I ask Siobhan to say I'm thinking about her in her time of sorrow. I hope it sounds better in German.

6 p.m. Nikki's livid. InterGlobe rang her. They're trying to hold back ten k. from the twenty k. deal for two year's until the gagging clause lapses. Ruby arrives — 'to see her daughter'. I mention Randy the scrap man is pining for her. She corrects me — 'his name is Randolph' — then hands me my coat: she wants to talk to Nikki alone.

I wander the mean streets of Willesden on foot, contemplating the signs of Autumn: Christmas sales stuff going up in shop windows, car owners jump-leading their cars, winter-tan shop owners grinning and glowing. Ruby's still there when I wander back in. The atmosphere is thick as congealed porridge. I ask if everyone's happy, and, if sour looks could revive the dead, half Willesden cemetery just woke up. I make myself scarce. What's bugging those two?

Thursday September 9

Malik shows his face on my doorstep, always a bad omen. He's come to give 'financial counselling' to Nikki, he announces. Coming from someone who's seen more red ink in his bank statements than a Maoist calligrapher in his quill, that's rich. I warn him not to upset Nikki. He ignores me and swaggers into my living room with a "Nikki my love!" Nikki's face lights up. She's got no ready money, so I guess Malik can't do her too much financial damage. I take off to the backyard and my sculpting.

Midnight Pillow talk: Malik wants Nikki to join him in a 'little venture', namely buying up old Ladas in the UK and shipping them to Eastern Europe where they're worth triple the price. Nikki says he's got all the documentation to prove it and she only needs make an initial investment of five thousand k. that will convert to twenty thousand on successful completion of the plan. He's letting her in as a friend because this one's the scheme that's going to make him rich. He already has advance orders for the first hundred cars. A five thousand investment would still leave her enough to pay off the credit cards for six months, job or no job. She could work with him on the project while she's suing InterGlobe. Nikki asks me what I think. I say Ladas to East Europe sounds like snow to Eskimos, that it's a crazy speculative venture — you might as well stand on Willesden High Street handing out tenners. She snorts, turns her back on me and hogs the quilt. Harvey's Third Law of Relationships: If someone asks what you think, never tell them what you actually think: they are merely asking to have their own opinion confirmed.

Friday September 10

Letter from The Destitute Artists' Benevolent Fund. They want to visit on 24th September to see if I qualify for assistance, whether my art is the sort they want to support and 'within the ambit of the Trust's objects' whatever that means. I ring to say Friday 24th is fine. The administrative assistant says he'll pass it on. The only clue he's giving as to what these trustees are looking for is 'integrity in its formal sense'. I um and ah sagely, ring off and scramble down to Bergmann's. Sappho says I will have to wax on about the overarching coherence of my oeuvre, the underlying artistic concepts etc. I drive back chanting the phrase "overarching coherence of my oeuvre".

Nikki's faxed a counter-offer to InterGlobe. She's prepared to accept a fifteen thousand straight settlement .

Saturday September 11

Malik phones. He's still trying to push Nikki into coming in with him on the Lada deal. He wants her to meet him at his place to go over any concerns she has. It sounds like pressure selling to me but this time I keep my mouth shut. Nikki decides to go. There's no petrol in the Lexus, so she siphons mine! Very resourceful when she wants to be, our Nikk.

Ira rings. The Ajax -Willesden season is starting. He tells me to bring twenty pounds subs and a ten pound bond against fines. What is he running, a football team or a small business? We win. I score: a powerful volley after taking a sharp angled through-ball on my chest, reminiscent in many ways of Pele's superb 1958 strike against England. Ira alleges I mishit it and got lucky. Real jokes, our Ira.

Sunday September 12

Nikki spends the day number-crunching Malik's proposal. It really does add up, she says, if the figures he's given her are all halal. She really must be thrown by this InterGlobe thing if she thinks any figures Malik proffers are halal. Unlike myself, Malik knows how to tell people only what they want to hear. I keep my mouth shut however, even make vaguely approving noises to Nikki . That way she doesn't mind my watching Italian football on TV. The season's only three games gone and AC Milan are already top of the table. Arrivaderecci!

Monday September 13

Nikki goes chasing promising leads in the executive employment market. Debbie and I visit L-Mart. The poster over Aisle Five has us gasping: a ten metre wide photo of me and Debbie, looking like shoppaholic lovers. Below it the caption "Love & Shopping at L-Mart: the ideal match!" When I complain the Manager says go ahead and sue him, make his day. I storm off. Debbie stays, flutters her eyelids, bursts out crying. Three minutes later we emerge with the poster under her arm. A Hollywood class performance, I tell her. She grins. PS. must remember it's Debbie's birthday next week Thursday.

Tuesday September 14

Nikki shell-shocked. InterGlobe Personnel have a whispering campaign along the lines that she's not trustworthy, and one month pregnant so there's no sense in appointing her. How low can they go? she fumes. She takes the Micra and shoots off like a Pope out of Stringfellows, for I don't know where.

Drag myself to The Last Drop. Tommo's maudlin. He can't raise a safe gang. He holds forth on his theme: robbery was once an honourable profession. Nowadays it's ugly, with all this semi-automatics and GBH. There's no craft in that. The Sixties were the glory days. They even had apprenticeship schemes then. You'd start off on the little house safes and work your way up to safe deposit boxes. It's all gone now, the craft, the expertise, he moans. We should be given a Lottery grant like clog dancers because it's an art, an English tradition, is safebreaking, part of the national heritage. He gets more and more stroppy sinking pint after pint. I scarper sharpish when he heads for the toilet before he ropes me into some shotgun robbery revival society.

Nikki is very Lady Macbeth tonight: "There's blood in the water," she murmurs mysteriously, "and InterGlobe thinks it's hers, but it isn't." I check the taps. London's murky yellow stuff continues to trickle out.

Wednesday September 15

Swimming. Siobhan's already in the water. She whooshes up all excited. Lola's coming back this Saturday. She didn't want to, but she has to finish off her PhD. Isn't that great? It is. I didn't mean to but I think I kissed Siobhan at this point. Not a sexual kiss, just an affectionate peck on the cheek, one that says, 'I'm happy that you're happy'. How the lifeguard managed to make it out as heavy petting I don't know. Anyway, he threw us out. In the café Siobhan says we should organise a party for when Lola returns. I wonder if she'll be in the mood for a party, so soon after her grandfather's funeral. Siobhan says of course she will, it'll take her mind off things.

7 p.m. Nikki eats a bowl of King Prawn Curry from the fridge. At midnight she's tossing, turning and farting. She wakes me up in the small hours in a cold, dreamy panic, but she can't remember what she was dreaming. I lull her back to sleep by asking her to tell me again about her greatest spreadsheet ever.

Thursday September 16

Nikki home all day listening to Vinyl and CDs. Her playlist is:
I Will Survive (G.Gaynor)
O, Superman (???)
Blue (B. Holiday)
I Have Nothing (W Houston)
Sweet Honey On The Rocks (???)
When The Going Gets Tough (T Turner)
Me Myself & I (J Armatrading)
Where Does My Heart Beat Now? (Celine Dion)
Another Sad Love Song (Toni Braxton)
Just Give Me Money (The Beatles)

Friday September 17

Invite Bergmann crowd over to view my mini exhibition. Everyone agrees that this last work is brilliant. I urge them to write this down in my Comments Book using their own and assorted false, but real-sounding, names. Sappho points out I'll need to hire a crane to get my sculpture out of the backyard if I ever want to move it. I tell her it's a minor problem.

10 p.m. Nikki comes back gleaming malevolently. She's started her own whispering campaign against InterGlobe. She spends the rest of the evening on the phone to Antonia, plotting InterGlobe's downfall.

Saturday September 18

Phone Ira and tell him Ajax Willesden can go hang. Take Nikki to basketball instead. She whoops and screams like her old self. On the drive back she suddenly talks torrents, a sort of sermon on business and chat show confessional rolled into one.

Nikki's aria: (Forte Piano)
"InterGlobe used to be fun, playing like a team, everyone doing Assists, winning together. All right it wasn't the Garden of Eden. But we were a team. Then. (Dramatic Pause) For some reason, we turned on each other. The industry went into a downturn. No more easy pickings. We got ruthless. For example we would have sacked half the staff in Scotland if we'd won that takeover. Not straight away — that's bad PR after a decent interval when the whole thing had died down in the press. (Second Dramatic Pause). One night, in Edinburgh, something happened. I couldn't wield the knife on them, the Scots workers. God, I had incentive enough. I would have got a three year's salary more. But three thousand people would have collected their P45's and I couldn't do it. (Third And Final Dramatic Pause) Now I'm a changed woman. I've lost the bloodlust. They know it. I'm corporate carrion and they're moving in for the kill. In the last month I've been stabbed more times than a voodoo doll. Harvey, Harvey, I don't think I can hack it any more."

We cry together in the car, pull over, scoff a bowl of Pistachio nut ice cream each at Whitegates Beefeater, and wail again.

Sunday September 19

An average, regular Sunday. Washing machine croaks, kitchen flooded. Somebody's car-squashed cat dies on our lawn. Nikki spends day reading 'The Zen of Winning: Your Enemies Are Your Best Friends'.

Monday September 20

Full set of bills fall through letterbox. Place them on the kitchen table for Nikki. Nikki spends three and a quarter hours in the bath. When she emerges, in a huge, new, pink bath sheet she says she wants us to move up North where 'the people are kinder'. We sit by the fire all day getting drunk on Wray and Nephew's white rum.

Tuesday September 21

I hint to Nikki that perhaps she might think about paying some bills. She unleashes a tirade the gist of which is: I've been living off her so long, it's about time I started to pay them. I guess she's right. Later, Nikki wants "to find her centre". I suggest she locates her belly button. She wants me to teach her the meditation stuff I learnt on the Iron John weekend. I take her through some deep breathing exercises. Then we move on to yogic sex. When I ask her afterwards if the earth moved for her she answers maybe what she really needs is a new hairstyle.

Wednesday September 22

Nikki goes out 'to spread vicious rumours about InterGlobe'. Machiavelli would have been proud of her. I go swimming. Lola's there, feeling blue. What has theoretical mathematics got to do with life? she asks. We live, we die. Where does theoretical mathematics fit in? Since I wouldn't know theoretical mathematics from a pound of pork sausages, I'm not much use here. Neither is Siobhan. We buy more doughnuts instead. Siobhan says she's given up au pairing. She's got a job in an Enterprise Agency providing German-English information and translations. What's more she's got her own flat above a shop. As soon as she's decorated she's going to have a house-warming party. Good to see Lola and Siobhan together again.

11 p.m. Nikki declares she wants a baby and she's coming off the pill. It's late. Rather than argue I just go to bed. She tries to seduce me in bed but can't get me aroused. This annoys her and she advises me to see a doctor about it. Later when she's asleep I arouse myself just to check it's all working properly. It is.

Thursday September 23

Debbie-Anne rings. It's her birthday! She wants us both to call round. Nikki goes into Great Garbo mode ("I want to be left alone.") Malik comes on the line. I pass Nikki the phone. Upshot is, Malik's calling round here, and I'm visiting Debbie. Debbie tells me to bring my stir-fry ingredients with me. I feel like a travelling chef.

Debbie is glowing, hot, flushed and hungry, but mostly hungry. After scoffing my sweet and sour pork with extra ginger and garlic, she smacks her lips and says Malik is hopeless in the . . . kitchen. Really? I say. So she tells it. He's hopeless in the sack as well, at least recently. He thinks she's too fragile for sex. A woman likes to be loved, even if it is just now and then, Debbie says. Her foot is rubbing my calf under the table. We have a quick kiss. Well, not that quick. She says I must come and cook for her again.

Drive back and find Malik squashed up with Nikki on the sofa. His hand's crawling up her thigh and that stupid new moustache of his is wiggling over her nose. Nikki's giggling. They jump apart when I walk in. Malik adjusts his tie and says

"So that's the ultimate destination of the first Lada shipment."
I guess he wants me to believe Nikki's thigh was the map and
he was showing her the shipping route. He tells Nikki he has
to go now, and does. Nikki goes back to her Greta Garbo
routine.

Friday September 24

The Art Wallahs visit. They ask for my accounts. I tell them
they're with my accountant who uses a full year to year
rotation spread and audits for liquidity ratios as a matter of
course. They make vague approving noises about my
sculpture, tick some boxes on their clipboard sheets and let
themselves out. The whole thing lasts about ten minutes. No
heated debates about the deconstruction of space and light. I
never even got the chance to explain 'the overarching
coherence of my oeuvre'. Don't think I'll get any money out of
them.

Saturday September 25

Nikki didn't want to tell me yesterday because of my visitors
but she surrendered to InterGlobe and the lousy fourteen
thousand pounds severance they offered her. I tell her if
fourteen thousand is a surrender, find me someone I can
surrender to fast. Nikki takes offence at this and drives off to
Antonia's. I doodle. She comes back later looking fresher than
when she left and is all sweetness with me. We watch a
continental film from the sofa. It's full of long, subtitled
conversations, extravagant family dinners, close-ups of
intertwined fingers, and bonks. We try to copy what the two
lead characters get up to. Nikki crys F*** me! f*** me! f*** me!
I do and try to speak bad French poetry to her at the same time.
She falls asleep on the sofa in the middle of the act.

Sunday September 26

Nikki's question: can a woman ever make it in the male-dominated world of business? Tell Nikki, Anita Roddick is a success. Nikki says Anita's exceptional, she, Nikki is not. Do I look twenty eight? she asks. Or do I look thirty? Or thirty five? Tell me the truth. She looks twenty four, I tell her. (In fact she looks twenty-eight, which is how old she is). She wants to be a housewife, she's had enough of business, she declares. She insists we go to Sainsbury's. She sees a tin labelled 'refried beans'. Who fried them the first time? she asks. Why have they been fried again? Then it's Extra Virgin Oil: How can you improve on virginity? she quizzes, either you have it or you don't. I tell her we're talking olives here, not schoolgirls, which, she says, is a sexist comment. At the frozen food aisle she oozes, ooh, I never knew they could make cauliflower taste like chocolate. Why do they do that? But she's fidgeting and getting bored. We can't find bleach. She starts dragging stuff into the trolley indiscriminately. This pisses me off and we're soon arguing so badly some saddo security man comes over to tell us to cool it. We drive back in heavy silence. I'm relieved when she rushes off to Antonia's again.

Monday September 27

Nikki's off with Malik 'on the East European run'. They sound like drug smugglers in a Gene Hackman movie. I hope Nikki knows what she's getting into. At least she's busy doing something. She's hell when she's bored. Sketch Debbie-Anne again. Ask her what she thinks of Malik's latest scheme. Debbie says she's heard it all before with Malik and got the matching earrings: from 'non-returning boomerangs' to 'direct-mail pets'. She knows he's actually very smart and no doubt one of his ideas will eventually make him a lot of money, but until then there'll be a lot of upset.

Nikki back late. The shipment's on its way to Gdansk now.

They watched their containers being swung into the belly of the ship. The sun was just beginning to set and the water rippled in this adorable red-gold light as the ship eased its way graciously forward. The ship is called The Albatross. I winkle out of her that it's registered in Panama, that the Captain's Russian, the crew's Malaysian, the North Sea was heaving and the cargo's totally uninsured. Wonder how much money is going to sink with The Albatross.

Tuesday September 28

The Destitute Artists' Fund leave a message on my answering machine. 'They are saying 'no' to my application but they are forwarding my name to some Lottery Agencies because blah blah blah.' It sounds gloomy but when I get the blah blah blah translated by Sappho it turns out they've recommended me for a major commission funded by National Lottery money, so that's all right then!

Nikki spends the night with her head pressed to a speaker. The radio's tuned to The Shipping News.

Wednesday September 29

Surprise surprise-Malik's Lada deal fouls up. Import duties have not been paid, Nikki reports. The buyers are adamant it's for the senders to pay, since delivery was to be made by the sellers to the buyers' warehouse. Meanwhile, the goods are at Gdansk harbour and clocking up US$300 a day in storage fees and will be sold after seven days by the harbour authorities who now have a lien, a legally enforceable charge, on the goods. The import duty is fifteen hundred US dollars. After melting the handset with expletives, Nikki wires Malik the money to spring the goods.

Lola phones. She's moving in with Siobhan.

Thursday September 30

Ladas still in storage in Gdansk! Port authorities want another thousand US dollars to waive import regulations viz. car registration documents — Malik can't supply log books. Nikki is livid. And suspicious. She searches the EuroNet using her laptop and discovers the private company controlling Gdansk harbour is a subsidiary of the so-called 'buyers' of the Lada shipment. They're being conned, fleeced, suckered. She calls Malik and tells him to bail out, cut our losses. Malik says she's being rash. This is eastern Europe, you have to expect hitches. Nikki pulls out. Malik stays with it and promises her two thousand back of the three thousand five hundred sterling she invested. He can't give her any more because she's leaving him to bear all the risk. Nikki swears at him down the phone. I laugh up my sleeve. At last their cosy relationship is falling apart!

Friday October 1

Malik rings Nikki to say he'll be wiring her the money shortly. Nikki yells he'd better, then goes out on a job search. I do some burning in on a sculpture.

3 p.m. Nikki returns despondent. I say has she tried René — the guy we met in Biarritz — he promised her a job didn't he? She calls. His answering service tells her in French to leave a message, which she does. She waits all day, but he doesn't return her call. We get drunk on the sofa listening to the Shipping News even though this time we've got no cargo on the High Seas. The Shipping News is strangely calming.

Saturday October 2

Ira rings me. I do him a favour and turn out. He tells me in front of everybody in the dressing room that my subs cheque bounced, and do I need to pay by instalments? Big Bird leads the sniggering. We play uphill first half, then into the wind second half and lose 14-3. I tell Ira don't blame me. The two own goals I scored were gentle back passes that the new goalie was too hung over to pick out, and what's more not even Maradona could have got this bunch of stiffs, shysters and stumblers he's dragged from Willesden's massage parlours and cut-throat pubs and called a football team to come alive; and what's more Big Bird in particular was pathetic and should be got rid of: whoever heard of a striker with a goals — attempted to goals -scored ratio of a hundred to one? (All that in one breath). Big Bird punches me in the face. For once he's on target, though the punch is too feeble to break my nose. Am about to launch into him when Ira breaks it up. He fines Big Bird a fiver for indiscipline and me a tenner for giving him lip. Is this justice? Harvey Robinson would like to know.

Ira drives me back in my Micra because my right eye has sealed thanks to Big Bird. He says Big Bird doesn't work, that's why he fined him less. I say what about me, I can't work now. I can't weld my sculptures with one eye. Get back and lie on the sofa with an ice pack thinking, the things I do for that lousy team, and wondering where Nikki is. Experiment trying to grab things with my new, monoscopic vision. Nikki comes back from wherever and is so self-absorbed she doesn't notice my huge facial injury. Peeved, I stamp up stairs to bed.

Sunday October 3

Nikki wakes me up, 4 a.m. What happened to my face? I struggle to the bathroom and take a look in the mirror. The upper and lower lids of my right eye have ballooned overnight. The skin of the closed eyelid has gone a colour that I've not seen in the oil paints catalogue but that comes close to iridescent lime. I look like a Cyclops, or some Saturday night lager lout. I swagger back to the bedroom like Robert de Niro in Raging Bull. Proudly tell Nikki it was a clash of heads during the match. She is very attentive, dabbing it with Dettol and fetching me a weak cup of sweet tea. I switch tactics in the morning, ditching the warrior bit, and by timing my groans right I manage to spend the day in bed being waited on by Nikki.

Monday October 4

Debbie-Anne comes round. I can't cook because with only one eye I can't gauge distance to chop vegetables and stuff, so we go down the High Street and grab some fried chicken from Allen's. Debbie's nervous about her pregnancy. Will she make it to full term? Will she have to have a Caesarean? Has the scan missed something and she's carrying triplets? She's due in eight weeks and sparkles with health.

Tuesday October 5

11 a.m. The news from Nikki's mole at InterGlobe is bleak. InterGlobe's PR team is about to character-assassinate her. Personnel is responding to enquiries from Nikki's potential employers by giving the bare legal minimum 'satisfactory' rating to her performance. She gets upset telling me this. Then hits the bottle.

9 p.m. Nikki asks if there are more pluses than minuses to our relationship. I tell her our relationship's definitely in credit. She's not reassured. Am I (Nikki) still attractive? Are my breasts beginning to sag? etc. etc. This InterGlobe battle is ruining her confidence. I just hope she accepts a job, any job, soon.

Wednesday October 6

Toil all day to perfect this Italian sauce. Nikki gets back and the fax immediately starts spluttering. It's a garbled message from Malik in Gdansk, Poland. The only words legible are 'need more money' and 'else bankruptcy'. Nikki says in reference to Malik that "That good for nothing briefcase hustler's getting no more of my money."

My finest fettuccine is delivered to the table. Nikki toys with it, and finally says what is this muck? Enough. I take up the fettuccine and dump it in the kitchen swing bin. Me, she can insult. Nobody insults my fettuccine. Big row ensues. Every wrong I ever did her is brought up including the new-to-me fact that I annoy her the way I suck my teeth when I'm thinking, which fortunately is rarely. I exit house — slamming doors.

2 a.m. Come back from The Last Drop. Kip on the sofa. Fall asleep thinking, (1) given that so many people end up sleeping the night on sofas why can't they make them so you can get at least half comfortable? (2) Nikki is becoming impossible to live with. I'd need a Transit van and about ten tea chests to move out. Maybe we need a break from each other.

Thursday October 7

Nikki's burst into the boardroom at InterGlobe and was on the Chief Executive before they could stop her. He claimed he didn't know she'd been fired, and hadn't ordered his PR people to rubbish her. She said she was broke with a mortgage to pay and threatened to spread InterGlobe's dirty laundry all over the financial press for a thousand days and nights. The Chief Exec promised to look into her case. Then she was escorted out by Security. I think she feels better for having had the confrontation. She's totally calm later when all her calls to Malik mysteriously fail to connect. Maybe he's been murdered by the Russian Mafia, Nikki speculates, without an ounce of pity. I love it. Still, I try ringing him myself later with no luck. And the Gdansk Port Authorities state (in perfect English) that they have no knowledge of a consignment of Ladas arriving in the last fortnight.

Friday October 8

Still no news of the Ladas, or Malik. Nikki thinking of flying out with an interpreter to look for the Ladas. Malik will have to look after himself, she declares.

Saturday October 9

Ira rings and asks am I still seeing double and it's the only way Ajax-Willesden are going to see double figures on their side of the score sheet. His sad idea of a joke. I hear BIg Bird with him at the other end of the phone, laughing. I tell Ira I'm OK but I'm not playing this week. Ira says fine. But he wants me back only when I'm fully recovered. Me and Nikki go see Manchester

Giants get trashed by Sheffield Sharks. Nikki blubs into her popcorn. Debbie rings. Have we seen Malik? She's had no word of him since Wednesday evening. I lie that he rang Friday.

6 p.m. Nikki gets a call from Commerce On Sunday about the InterGlobe thing. They're going to run a story. They want her side of it. Also they want to know is she photogenic and does she mind them taking some relaxed shots of her, suitable for midshelf magazines? Nikki puts the phone down politely.

Sunday October 10

That Sunday paper rings again. They held over the InterGlobe story because of the Maxwell Footprints Found In Devon splash they ran, but they're definitely going to run it next Sunday. It's in her best interests to cooperate, they'll even pay her a decent fee. Nikki says she'll think about it. I suggest she gets hold of celebrity spin-doctor Max Clifford.

I get calls today from three ex-girlfriends. They have all read the 'sculptor wanker' article in the paper, as they all describe it. I'm expecting the usual wisecracks but they're all impressed that I've got my act together. Susan even volunteers to take her clothes off for me if I want to paint her. It's too much, too late, I tell her over the phone. Still, I take her phone number. Spend the rest of the evening hidden in the garage looking through my old little red book remembering all the girls and all the times I had in the halcyon days when I was the Romeo of Willesden. There are almost a hundred names and numbers. And funny little squiggles after each girl's name to indicate how far I got with them. Actually I can't remember even half these names. I couldn't have made them up, could I?

Monday October 11

Debbie wants the Polish police to dredge the River Vistula Malik may have fallen in. More likely pushed, Nikki mutters. I tell Debbie not to panic but she is inconsolable. Why don't we do something? She's so upset she looks like she'll give birth right here on the sofa. Nikki says she'll fly out. When? insists Debbie. Nikki says tomorrow. Get a charming letter from the Inland Revenue. They too have read the article on Willesden's sculptor wanker. They want to know all about me so can I please fill in the enclosed self employed tax form?

Evening finds the three of us sitting on sofa. Me groaning with the tax forms, Debbie moaning for Malik and Nikki gnashing about her pay-off money. Debbie sleeps over, in the main bedroom. Me and Nikki kip down on the living room floor.

Tuesday October 12

Nikki is packed and at the door when who should walk in but Malik! Debbie hugs him, all tears, then kicks him in the shins for not phoning. Nikki troops back and dumps her bags down. I serve him black coffee. He looks jet lagged. Turns out, far from drowning, Malik has resurfaced with a fish in his mouth. He's sold the Ladas, he exclaims, all of them! He's soon holding forth on how he 'cut the deal' by making sure certain people were taken care of, financially and otherwise. It sounds very sinister the way he says it, but I laugh along. A rich man's jokes are always funny. He writes a cheque for Nikki, magnanimously giving her all her capital back despite her pulling out midway. What's a thousand to him? He's fifteen thousand pounds sterling up from one shipment. Who'd have thought of selling Ladas to Poland? he says in his smarty-pants way, and prophesieses he'll be the UK's first Lada millionaire. I plump cushion for him and ease his shoes off.

Wednesday October 13

Nikki is first in queue at Hong Kong & China Mutual to bank Malik's cheque. She comes back with broadsheet newspapers and is livid. The gossip columnists have already started on her. She reads aloud: "A certain minor league Superwoman Found To Be Not Such A Superwoman After All". etc. She flies off in a squeal of rubber to have it out with InterGlobe's PR department.

Go swimming. Lola and Siobhan say I'm getting rusty and help me sharpen up my strokes. We go back to their flat afterwards even though Siobhan says it's still not ready. It's beautiful: chintzy and yet airy, flowery and yet uncluttered. I notice there's only one bedroom with one (double) bed in it. Are Lola and Siobhan . . . ? They do get on extremely well.

Five Turkish coffees later I'm back home. Nikki's mum phones. Will I allow her daughter to ring her tonight? Yes ma'am, I reply, I'll untie her and take the gag off straight away. Why does she always think it's me who's stopping her daughter ringing her? Her daughter is a free woman.

The free woman comes back drunk in a taxi. InterGlobe Security stopped her at Reception and threw her out, physically threw her down the steps Nikki says. She's never felt so humiliated. She called the police to have them arrested and they cautioned her instead. Her Lexus is in some police pound or other. She wants the number of that journalist. Luckily she can't find it. I forget to tell her her mother called. Her mother comes round in person but Nikki ushers her back out and says she'll call round tomorrow. Her mother rings me later and says she's never felt so humiliated etc.

Thursday October 14

Drive Nikki to her Mum's. She has me wait for her outside. She wants quality time alone with her mum. Three hours later she emerges. She's worried. Her mother is a little confused or something, she tells me on the way back. She's wearing a strange, flowery perfume that just isn't her style, new jewellry, a new wig, she's changed all the furniture around, and even got a new hi-fi system. She spends all her time rambling on about moving on in life. Is she going senile? Nikki asks. These could be signs. Or maybe she's faking going senile to get attention. She wouldn't put it past her. To cap it all, her mum told her she wants grandchildren, fast. She was instructed to pass the message on to me. She says we should marry but keep our own names. I say yes, maybe she is going senile, but Nikki likes the idea of babies. I remind her we vowed not to, for at least five years, we want to live first, right? Nikki sulks for the rest of the journey and all through the evening.

Friday October 15

Nikki retrieves Lexus from police pound. Journalist rings again while she's out. I put the phone down on him and tell Nikki when she gets back. Nikki rings Antonia who comes round. Nikki's still not actually speaking to me so she doesn't tell me where they're going, but Antonia gives me a reassuring smile as they leave and whispers 'tactics meeting'.

Bergmann's is quiet. The booked band haven't turned up. There's a jazz session going. A trumpeter from out of town blows everyone off. Even Filo admits, 'that white dude can play'. Get back late to no Nikki, and no message.

Saturday October 16

Early a.m. Grope around in sheets. Nikki not in bed. Not downstairs either. Phone Antonia. Antonia not in. Forget them, roll some skunk I picked up last night, drag some metal into the back yard and get into sculpting. Come back in at 11 a.m. to find Ira's left an irate message for me. No message from Nikki. Smile at Ira's voice. Worry about Nikki. But since Antonia's missing too, decide no need to panic. Get drunk, watch that corner shop video again, munch Nachos. A good night in.

Sunday October 17

Wake up with hangover, check answering machine. Antonia's left a message. They're at the Sheraton Hotel. Nikki's been interviewing with the financial press to set the record straight on InterGlobe. She's in fine shape. They'll be back Monday.

Cure hangover with quality sensi. Attack sculpture. A timewarp later, I've finished another chrome and car paint masterpiece. I drag it in from the yard and contemplate it from sofa. Spend rest of day at Bergmann's watching Filo doing his Jimi Hendrix's ghost schtick with an African American woman keyboardist. Seems he hit all the right notes because they're practically inside each other's pants when I leave.

Monday October 18

Nikki materialises, late a.m. Did I read the Sunday papers? she preens. Plead total ignorance. She drops half a tree onto coffee table and shows me she's in every one, including Commerce on Sunday with photo (fully clothed, Armani) The copy reads good: "Intelligent . . . fragrant . . . bright . . . mature . . . cool headed . . . rising star of the City." Just some of the epithets. The business world are smelling a rat in the InterGlobe merger deal now, Nikki informs me, and the smart money's already leaving. Things are moving her way. InterGlobe's goose is cooked, she declares. We celebrate with some Liebfraumilch. Later we hear InterGlobe PR Dept. bluster away on the answering machine. They want her to get in touch. Pathetic. We blow them raspberries and carry on glugging.

1 p.m. Nikki gets on the phone again. She isn't through with InterGlobe yet. She and Antonia are going to grind InterGlobe's PR machine into the dust. Attagirl! I keep her fuelled with coffee.

Ira calls. Ajax-W won 3-0 yesterday. My replacement, Malik, scored two. There's a training session Tuesday evening at the Moon. Anyone not turning up won't play. "I'm starting a tough new approach," Ira warns. "Slackers and fly boys are out". I ask him can he feel me trembling?

Tuesday October 19

Nikki leaves in Armani to carry out her 'second wave press campaign'. She's going to leak further 'facts analysis' of the merger deal. InterGlobe will not be able to deny the figures. And she'll prepare the journalists for any reverse spin InterGlobe tries. She says she's getting the hang of this public relations thing.

Maybe I've smoked too much skunk recently, but my mind goes a complete blank whenever I pick up my tools. Have a panic: has my gift gone forever? Will I have to go back to rat-catching? Debbie-Anne phones, bored. I tell her come over, and we can be bored together. I cook her Chinese fried rice. She eats hesitantly. Will she be able to lose all this weight after the birth? Course, I tell her. She scoffs two bowls of rice and doesn't bother asking if I want the extra pork chop, just spears it, carves it and swallows it. Then she pecks me on the cheek and rushes off. She's late for her ante-natal class.

Malik calls in the middle of the night. Nikki answers the phone. She ums and ahs a bit then nudges me and says, Debbie's 'craving for some!' I take the phone and tell Malik that, much as I'm his friend, I draw the line at providing a sexual service to his wife and can't he get it up himself? Malik says we're talking Chinese fried rice here, not shagging. She's in the kitchen now banging pans, making a total mess. Can I help them out? I don't believe it. Then Debbie comes on whimpering she can't sleep without it. I get out of bed, make them Chinese fried rice in our kitchen, and drive it over to their place. Malik is hugely grateful. I tell him he owes me big. Very big.

Wednesday October 20

Watch Lola and Siobhan perform a comic synchronised swimming routine they've worked out specially for me. I applaud vigorously.

Back at their flat the drinks flow. Lola plays some acid jazz and she and Siobhan skip around the room together in a sort of waltz then disappear into the kitchen. A lot of giggling takes place there. When they re-emerge they sit me down because they have something to tell me. I tell them I know already. I noticed the bed, just the one, and lesbians are alright with me, I'm broad minded and quite familiar with their lifestyles. I've watched videos. Lola says I'm a twit and I'm sitting on the other bed. Notice for the first time the sofa is a sofa-bed. Look for a hole to swallow me up. What they wanted to tell me was they're throwing their house-warming party next Wednesday evening and it's going to be fancy dress. I have to come, and in costume.

Thursday October 21

Nikki is glued to her mobile watching InterGlobe shares plummet on Ceefax. Malik stops off in the morning wearing a Savile Row suit. Has quick conference with Nikki before flying British Airways Club Class to Gdansk to meet his next shipment of Ladas. He's hired twice the containers he used last time and expects to double his profits. He's back late Friday. I'm to take care of Debbie, and he'll see me right, he says. He gives me his mobile number in case of emergency. Like what, I ask, aliens landing in Willesden? Like Debbie's waters break, is his answer. Daddy wants to be at the birth, he says cloyingly. I kick him out. Even babies wouldn't listen to such drivel. I suppose I'd better buy a present for it for when it's born. Enjoy myself imagining Malik trying to change a nappy.

Friday October 22

Ceefax loves Nikki. Nikki loves Ceefax. She tells me InterGlobe shares are continuing their graceful slide. Spend time in garage. It's a chrome Klondike and I get dizzy just looking at all the metal.

Malik phones at 2am — he's back. Another deal delivered, another 20 k. in the bank. He just had to ring so he could boast to someone about it. Him and his money. He makes me puke.

Saturday October 23

Ira rings 10 a.m. I missed training Tuesday so I'm not playing. Do I not realise there's competition for places now? Coolly, I call in my favour from Malik. Malik moans. I got up in the middle of the night to cook rice for him, so he can fetch his butt over here to clear a game for me. Malik shuffles round, rings Ira and says he can't play because he's damaged ligaments lifting weights, but Harvey's the one you want anyway — he's had his eyes sorted with contacts and he's been road-training with boxers so he's fit as a mule. Ira duly phones, apologetic, and asks me to play.

11 a.m. I play. Ajax win 12-5. I score two. Should have been awarded Man of the Match but Big Bird needs the cudos of these awards more than me, so I tell Ira that I understand.

Sunday October 24

Malik round to see Nikki. The two of them are locked together for hours boasting about who's made the most money fastest. Since Nikki doesn't actually have a bean at the moment she's not going to win this one but she argues anyway just for arguing's sake. She switches on Ceefax and shows Malik InterGlobe's share price has halved — that's all my doing! she said proudly. Eight million pounds worth of damage. What happens if she's sued? Malik says. I panic.

Monday October 25

Nurse hangover from trying to keep up, pint for pint, with Tommo last night as we (or more like he, I merely nodded along) discussed the irrelevance of the post-modernist movement to working-class artists. Realise I could break safes with this man, just to further my education.

InterGlobe shares are bumping along the bottom, Nikki declares gleefully. But doesn't she have some shares? I ask. The blood drains from her face. Seems there's a slight flaw in her plan. She rushes out, wailing in deep funk.

Gillian calls. She's dropped Betterware for Welsh timeshares. She has also swapped her flowing locks for a beehive look. I stifle yawns as she tells me the advantages of being in on the Welsh Timeshare Dream. 'Welsh Timeshares — an exceptional real estate opportunity' she says. Consider Welsh Timeshares the most unreal estate opportunity you could ask for. The world has gone mad. Gillian gives up on me for the day.

Pillowtalk. Nikki's chastened. She has £6K of shares tied up in InterGlobe. They used to be worth 18K. She should have sold them before opening her big mouth to the press. Whatever happens now, she loses. She'll just have to bluff it.

Tuesday October 26

Washing machine hose springs leak. Scrape together enough coins from under settee, behind back of fridge and Micra glove compartment to buy new hose. Micra's radiator blows as I drive to collect washing machine hose. Nurse Micra home.

6 p.m. Nikki resurfaces. She's been offered full twenty k all-bonuses severance deal in exchange for her media silence. She turns them down. It's the principle that matters, not the money, she tells me. I fully support her. They ring her back: how much to buy out her principles as well? Nikki laughs and says she'll call them back 'just to give them a ball park figure'. She eventually rings back and says her principles plus the original deal equal 60K. It's a big ballpark, she smiles down the phone at them. They say they'll think on it. Selling her principles! Can Capitalism buy anything?

Wednesday October 27

Go to Lola and Siobhan's housewarming party as D'Artagnon, of The Three Musketeers. Got the outfit from Filo, hell knows where he got it from. Micra lunges like a true musketeer all the way. Arrive late and find I'm the only black person there. What's more, for a male, I'm overdressed. Most of the guys haven't bothered at all. The girls have at least either stuck on a mole, or are wafting Elizabethan fans. Siobhan comes over, takes my cloak, and gives me a big welcoming kiss which makes me feel better. She introduces me to a few people. Mostly students. It's a young crowd. Some Chinese, quite a few German speakers. A couple of hours after I arrive, a troupe of actors bursts in, in full eighteen century dress and full operatic voices. They're fresh from a student production of Figaro and half-tanked already. The party takes off. Drunken carousing, open fornication, fights and tears, in at least three languages. I get drunker. Siobhan feeds me vol au vents in the kitchen then snogs me in a way I can't resist. Lola walks in later when I'm alone and we snog fleetingly. The Countess flutters in, bursts into a short aria then clasps my face. We snog operatically. Five hours later, I'm exhausted with all this. I wave good bye to Siobhan and stagger outside. Lola calls me back, plies me with coffee and orders me a taxi. Sensible Lola. The coffee is out of this world. Fresh ground, percolated. I decide that from this day on I can't live without a proper coffee percolator like the one they've got.

Pillowtalk: Nikki tells me she's accepted 40k. Which means she's sold her principles for 20k. Sad. Business is amoral.

Thursday October 28

The InterGlobe picture's changing fast. The takeover deal Nikki has been paid off to keep mum about has begun to unravel of its own accord. Nikki's the epitome of glee. Apparently, all the things they hadn't nailed down in the deal have started to drift up: hidden bad debts are surfacing, artificially inflated profits collapsing, huge forward discounts from suppliers have been revealed. The stock market's aghast. The shares are aquaplaning. Nikki sits tight. Sure enough, she gets a call from Head Office begging her to help with the rescue. They blanch at Nikki's consultancy fee rates. Nikki says if they want her advice they can bloody well pay for it. She's not their employee any more, remember? They ring off. I leave Nikki la-dee-dah-ing.

Go to Bergmann's. Josie says she's going to pose naked in the park to protest against (1) racism, (2) the tyranny of fashion and (3) the arbitrariness of gender assignment. I will do my duty and turn out as a witness, I tell her. Filo looks at me haughtily. He will do no such thing. Nubile as Josie is, Filo is above such juvenile and debauched activities, he says. He, Filo, is getting married. He's met a heiress and she wants him to marry her. She's very respectable so I mustn't ring him any more, he adds. I apologise to Filo for existing. He says that's all right, so long as I don't ring him.

Friday October 29

My stars must be all lined up. Letter arrives from MegaWatt Electric. They want me to build a piece they can stick outside their new administrative building in the heart of London. £20K plus any reasonable amount necessary for materials, staff costs etc. When can I start? Staying ice-cool, I put off calling them right away and instead get as lethally drunk as possible on the fridge's entire stock of L-Mart 2% lager.

Saturday October 30

10 a.m. Malik wants his place back in Ajax's midfield. While we wait by the phone for Ira to call, Malik launches into A Thousand Things You Didn't Know About Ladas. In desperation I try calling Ira myself. He's not in. Malik Ladas on. Consider hanging myself, but worry Malik would follow suit and pursue me to the netherlands still talking Ladas. Only when I tell him about my Electric deal does his jaw stop. He reminds me he's my agent. Ira finally rings. I let Malik play.

Sunday October 31

We visit Nikki's mum. Nikki's brave-faced, driving there. It's just too bad her mum's got Alzheimer's. She's still her mum and Nikki will stick by her, enjoying the good times to come, remembering all the love they've shared. If she has to go into a home, so be it, but it will definitely be a last resort. Meantime, we must keep her mum busy, Nikki says, keep her stimulated. Sounds like Nikki's been reading a book on the subject.

Turns out Ruby has found a pretty good way of fending off senility herself. She's got a fancy man, namely, Randolph the scrap metal merchant. Nikki can't stop laughing all the way home. The signs were all there and she didn't read them, she proclaims. The perfume, the new clothes, the new hair. Nikki keeps repeating like she's going gaga herself:

"She's gone and got herself a fancy man, and a sugar daddy at that!"

Malik rings. Ajax-Willesden won 3-0 yesterday. Ira only used Malik as a substitute because he didn't turn up for training on Tuesday. So Ira's serious about this training lark. Washing machine floods kitchen. Sloshing water blows freezer motor. Dead Machine Count today: Washing machine. Freezer. Tin opener. Weirder than the X-Files.

Monday November 1

Visit MegaWatt people. First time I've visited them other than to pay the bill / plead for time in paying the bill. Am greeted by a bunch of suits. The money is coming from the Millennium Commission, they explain. Should have known they wouldn't be spending their own. They want something that symbolises the positives aspects of electricity. Something abstract, symbolic, monumental. With clean lines. If I could work their logo into the piece so much the better. I'm to send them basic sketches by end of November plus a breakdown of costs. They want it in place in two months if possible, ready for filming their new TV commercial. I ask for a thousand up front. They write a cheque there and then. Drive home kicking myself, which is very difficult to do while driving, thinking, I should have asked for more. Bank cheque. Sun shines. Still dizzy with this sudden commission.

Nikki home late. She's been negotiating with an InterGlobe intermediary. They want her back in full time employment with them, to sort out the mess. She told them she'd rather bathe in cold baked beans than work for them again.

Tuesday November 2

Force myself to go training at the Moon. Arrive there to find Ira and the others standing around cursing. There's a bonfire piled up in the middle of the pitch: pallets, somebody's settee, couple of burnt out cars, rotting mattress, dead cat, half a washing machine — the usual bonfire. We try to take it apart but a gang of kids hurl half bricks at us and we beat a tactical retreat to the pub. All the new recruits suck up to Ira as he holds forth on The Role of Wing Backs in Diamond Formation Midfields.

Wednesday November 3

Rendez-vous at Willesden Baths. Lola's "erschopft" — German for exhausted — after the swim session, but she looks relaxed, the happiest I've seen her since the funeral. Siobhan's eager to tell me about her new boyfriend. She met him at the party, she says. He's drop dead gorgeous. I feel a pang of jealousy. Why? There's supposed to be nothing between us. Her hunk is called Jake. He's twenty two and works in a theme restaurant. Lola tells me afterwards she thinks Jake's all right but a bit shallow. She prefers the more educated type, one who would not feel uncomfortable with a Maths PhD for a partner. She says such a man is rare. I guess she's right.

7 p.m. Sky ablaze with fireworks. Huge thunderbursts. I go sketch-crazy. Dash off twelve chrome spectaculars.

Thursday November 4

Another surreal day. Early morning, one of InterGlobe's young suits calls at our house in person, kneels on his patent leather suitcase and begs Nikki to come back. Nikki smiles, calls him a bright kid and tells him to vamoose. Debbie rings. She's bored. Can she start modelling for me again?

Friday November 5

2 p.m. Go inside and find InterGlobe go-between with feet under my table. His name's Anthony. I think Nikki fancies him because her voice goes all soft and purry and she strokes his hand at least five times over the Sainsbury's Microwave Lasagne. They babble numbers after dinner. I leave them to it.

10 p.m. Nikki and I drive to a Bonfire Night Show at the Lakes. Anthony rides with us in the back. The Show's been paid for by a Chinese-backed Conglomerate that's a rival to InterGlobe. Somehow Nikki's got tickets. Everyone's in fat jumpers because it's minus 7. The Conglomerate bunch are OK people. One has even heard of my sculpture and names the Gallery he saw it at. The firework display is cosmic. But then, the Chinese invented gunpowder, didn't they? Nikki spends midnight surrounded three deep by Conglomerate people. Anthony talks to me about the vastness of the Universe and how we are all alone. We console ourselves with Nacho dips.

Late night thought. Subject: The 'Catherine' Wheel. Who was Catherine? Why did she have a firework named after her? Late night thought Number 2: Subject: Me. I need a studio. The garage is too crowded. And Nikki being around all day disrupts my concentration. Thought Number Three. When am I ever going to start that Commission piece?

Saturday November 6

Ira leaves a message. We're playing at Mars. Takes me an hour to get to the ground and find I'm not on team sheet. Ira says Ferdinand, Zola and Shearer have been left on the bench recently, so why's it such a big deal for Harvey Robinson? I notice he never leaves himself on the bench. We win 7 — 3. I refuse to celebrate. It would have been 9 if I'd played.

Sunday November 7

Last night I dreamt up a sublime sculpture for the Commission, but my mind went blank by the time I'd padded across the bedroom to my drawing pad. Spend all day trying to recall but it's gone. Move drawing pad, sticks of charcoal and torch to side of bed so I don't get caught out next time.

Monday November 8

Cursed by a vanishing Commission Sculpture dream again last night. As soon as I grabbed a sketchpad, the dream vanished. Go Willesden Library and dig out book on aborigine dreampictures. I want to find out how to stay with the dream.

Great pics, but no advice. Stop off at Bergmann's and Sappho tries psychoanalysis. Am I afraid of the doing the Commission work on a subconscious level? Does it represent joining the Establishment? Am I afraid of success?

Debbie-Anne comes round. I can't stop the Nudes project yet, without the last paintings showing her gloriously pregnant the series would be incomplete. I paint inspiredly. She eats a bowl of coleslaw afterwards, then three raw carrots. Just manage to stop her chomping through my charcoal sticks. She's lost her Demonstrator's job. They sacked her because she's pregnant. Isn't that sexual discrimination? I ask. She shrugs and says she was only a temporary worker and had no rights. She puts my hands on her stomach. The baby kicks likes Ian Wright in a bad mood.

Tuesday November 9
The Commission work must be started. But my heart doesn't want to abandon my beloved chrome, and I blaze away trying to weld and jigsaw four last sculptures.

Wednesday November 10
Splash around with Lola and Siobhan. Lola has an aristocratic body: sleek thighs that go on and on, perfectly formed, small feet, long neck, long nose, light arms. She carries herself with the old world serenity of the European Upper Classes. Siobhan is more robustly figured. Her thighs have the muscular energy of the lower bourgeoisie. She walks with a healthy spring in her step. Her feet are bigger than Lola's and surer. I'd like to paint them both as nudes.

1 p.m. Get back with shopping, dry cleaning etc. Nikki's not in. No note either. Work on the beginnings of the firework sculpture series that I've sketched. Feel guilty doing this, since still haven't started Commission work.

7 p.m. Nikki returns. She's been at InterGlobe HQ speaking to Directors! They need her back more than she needs to go back, so she's holding out for all she's worth. Sounds good to me.

Thursday November 11

Ask Debbie to stay away. Turn my back on chrome. Think hard about Commission. Still can't produce a half decent sketch. Go Bergmann's, get drunk. Doesn't help, but drunk is better than sober. Nikki out at another rendezvous with InterGlobe.

Friday November 12

Filo phones. Says he's suicidal. His heiress has only gone and run off with a bloody heir, he says. He loved her for herself not her assets. Funny thing is, I believe him. Anybody else I wouldn't. I drive over, pick him up and we motor aimlessly around town as he pours out his heart. Lose concentration and end up on M25 orbital. Run out of petrol. Pull over on hard shoulder and use roadside phone. Emergency garage insists on towing me off motorway before pouring thimbleful of petrol into tank and charging me £75 plus VAT for the privilege. Next time Filo has a wounded heart, we'll wander by bus.

8 p.m. Nikki's been talking with InterGlobe's Renumeration Committee. Don't want to display ignorance by asking what a Renumeration Committee is, so nod sagely and grind more pepper onto her steak. Nikki looks happy. She might not have a job yet, but she's got the wind in her sails.

Saturday November 13

Make it onto the subs bench. With five minutes to go I'm on. We're leading five-one. Team do not respond to my intelligent reading of the game and we drop a couple of goals, but still win five four. I realise now I think too fast for the simpletons Ira has assembled into a team. I'm playing chess out there, while they're all playing draughts. Big Bird isn't even up to the draughts level. OK, he scored three goals, but they were all flukes. PS Malik scored one. He's now equalled his total for last season.

Sunday November 14

Malik round. He might have to go to Gdansk. Goods have gone missing; no record of them being unloaded from ship. Insurance won't cover the full loss and anyway it would take years to get them to pay out. He wrings his hands a lot but finally makes his mind up. Gdansk it is. He wants Nikki along but, sensibly, Nikki refuses to go with him.

Monday November 15

Washing machine breaks down. I call Honest Al, my washing machine repairman out, ask him how's the wife, how's the kids, and did he take the plunge and do that Access course he was talking about last time round, etc. He offers to get rid of washer for me. There must be a scrapyard somewhere composed entirely of my old washing machines.

Tuesday November 16

Huge bill from MegaWatt. Get magnifying glass, and read it includes cost of a new meter. I didn't ask for one! Customer Services doesn't answer phone. Decide to ignore bill.

7 p.m. Train at the Cemetery. Five a side. I notice for first time that Big Bird's left footed, so I play the ball to his left foot. He wallops the goals in. We win. In pub afterwards, he mimics Ira shouting out his garbled orders from touchline. Whole team agrees that Ira doesn't understand the modern game. BB's got a job now, in the glazing industry as a sales advisor. I'm happy for him. A year of earnings will pay off his debts and buy some physiotherapy for his kid. His son's got sticky lungs, he says.

Wednesday November 17

Siobhan's boyfriend turns up at the poolside. A real Mr Universe, he doesn't actually swim, but parades around in his Speedo swimming trunks, striking poses and wiggling his ample biceps. I think he has a shuttlecock down the front of his trunks because I've heard bodybuilders' bits are meant to be small. Maybe he's just permanently aroused.

Mr Universe is even worse in the canteen. He sits three tables away and glowers at me. I wave him over. He sits with Siobhan, putting his arm around her possessively. "This is my girl," he declares, beaming. "No, you are my boy!" Siobhan corrects him. He looks at her confused. She kisses him. "See?" he beams at me. The conversation is a bit stilted after this and we break up soon after. I don't think Jake and Siobhan are going to last. Lola says you never know.

Thursday November 18

Malik back. His Lada shipment is still lost in transit. He's going back to Gdansk as soon as he can sort out an interpreter, which is why he wants to get hold of Nikki. I tell him to try InterGlobe's Privileges Committee, which is where she was headed this morning. He leaves to track her down, but not before he arranges free studio space for me with one call of his mobile, a six month rent-free trial in a warehouse conversion. Sometimes I almost like Malik.

Late evening Nikki and Malik arrive together. For a man about to lose thirty thousand sterling he looks very relaxed. Nikki says she's got something to tell me. I say what — that you and Malik are eloping? She says don't be silly. What then? I ask. But she's highly offended by my remark and won't say. Malik vamooses. I watch Star Wars till early a.m. Alone.

Friday November 19

10 a.m. Corn flakes are chewy-soft. I spit them out. How about some cheese? Everything is sprouting merrily in the fridge. Next time, if L-Mart can't tin it, I won't buy it. Besides, after I've eaten the contents I can flatten the tins and use them as panelling in my chrome sculptures. Easy, huh? Yet I'm still blocked on the damn Commission thing. Call studio space estate agents. The keys to my studio will be ready Monday next. Can't wait.

Nikki roars home in a spanking new Merc. It only just fits on the drive. She's signed back with InterGlobe! The Merc is her company car from InterGlobe's Privileges Committee, she says. They've also doubled her salary, courtesy of the Renumeration Committee, and given her a twenty thousand share option, courtesy the Board itself. She's in Materialist heaven. She's throwing a party tomorrow and I can invite all my friends.

Saturday November 20

10 p.m. The suits mingle efficiently. The artists hang around the punch bowl. Anthony is here, hero-worshipping Nikki. He tells me Nikki's promoted him already so he can work in her Division. and all the suits here are the ones who fought her corner. The other faction's been routed and are out tramping the streets looking for positions. There's been a lot of bloodshed, he says. Careers, reputations put through the shredder. Nikki is chief of the new Young Turks running InterGlobe.

The punch runs out and my artist friends begin to notice each other. I wish they hadn't. Filo and Siobhan hit it off, which gets Jake upset and there's a scuffle in the hallway. When I get there, Jake is floundering under a heap of coats and Filo is poised over him holding an umbrella, picador style. I disarm Filo and help Jake up. He leaves, cursing me and ordering

Siobhan to follow him. She declines. Jake by now is on the driveway and whacks the Merc in frustration which sets the alarm off. I rush for Nikki and find her half drunk, snogging Anthony in the airing cupboard. I pull her away and get her to zap the Merc alarm off. Notice Siobhan gazing adoringly at Filo as I hunt that creep, Anthony. I think to have it out with him. I find him collapsed in the same airing cupboard, face down in towels, without a pulse. Seriously. He's not breathing. I open his airway and start mouth to mouth. Nikki opens the airing cupboard door, gasps and asks me why I didn't tell her before, we and we can talk about it. At this moment Anthony jerks to life and doesn't know what's going on. I go off to fetch him a glass of water. When I get back he's passed out again but this time he's breathing. Nikki helps me lay him out on the upstairs bed. We have to ask Siobhan and Filo to screw somewhere else to do this.

Get down. Debbie is throwing up in the kitchen. Antonia and Ralph say they have an announcement; they're getting married. Druid High Trees and Leaping Antelope, the only ones apart from me listening, applaud. High Trees gets drumming and Leaping Antelope does a warrior celebration dance. For some reason the new Young Turks find this fascinating and someone takes the music off while Leaping Antelope begins leaping around like Nijinsky. Soon all Nikki's Young Turks are at it. I make a mental note to ask Nikki what she put in that punch. Lola looks lonely. I comfort her with a friendly kiss and introduce her to Sappho. Big Bird joins them.

Sunday November 21

Stay in bed. Somebody is out there scything grass with a combine harvester. Someone else is composing a doorbanging concerto (Bang bang. Bang. Bang bang. Bang bang. Bang bang bang). Resolve to dig out that Monastery video brochure again.

Bladder forces me up at 4 p.m. I venture downstairs and

look around. Kitchen table has three neat lines of what looks like cocaine. I use a toothbrush to sweep them into an egg cup then hide the egg cup on top of a cabinet. Never know, I might need it one day. There's a Young Turk sleeping in the dirty laundry. I leave her there. Look out of kitchen window and see High Trees has set up in the back garden. His teepee's on the patch of grass out there. Wood smoke's drifting from the top of it. I can see two silhouettes but can't figure out who's in the tent with High Trees. Guess it's Leaping Antelope. I don't bother going out and asking is there's anything they need. They're survivalists.

Inside, find five used condoms and several sets of underwear in the bathroom. Plus two stray mobile phones, four sets of keys, three coats, one wallet (with approx £500 in £50 notes in it), one left foot court shoe (size 5), four rolled, unsmoked spliffs and a scattering of wine glasses. Carpet looks ill. Make coffee. Take Nikki some in bed. Give some to Young Turk who has started to stir. Go back to bed.

Monday November 22

9 a.m. Answering machine crammed with requests to search house for lost keys, wallets, coats, contact lenses, irreplaceable sticks of lipstick. Two apologies to Nikki from unknown persons for obscene behaviour on the landing (voice 1) and lawn (voice 2).

Debbie-Anne round. Baby is about to pop and she's upset that Malik not even in the country. What's more she saw the interpreter he took with him and she was a stunning, leggy blonde and she just knows they're staying at the same hotel. She has the number. I try phoning the Gdansk Hilton but the lines are all down. Malik's mobile is still switched off. I cook her a sumptuous chow mein with what's left of the fresh vegetables and she's a bit calmer. I paint her, capturing the sad beauty of her face. Then we drive down to the High Street and go window-shopping. She can't wait to get back to wearing regular clothes instead of tents.

3 p.m. We try Malik's numbers again, but no luck. Debbie falls asleep on the sofa. I put a quilt over her and she's still sleeping when Nikki gets back. Nikki doesn't know Malik's whereabouts, anymore than I do, but tells Debbie not to worry. Pillowtalk: InterGlobe's share price has rallied, Nikki tells me.

Tuesday November 23

Debbie's asleep on the sofa again. Malik still hasn't rung her. We agree he's a complete shit. Privately, what I can't understand is, he was looking forward so much to being a Daddy and told me last time to ring him in case of emergency. This is what makes me think maybe he is in some trouble. Hide this thought from Debbie.

7 p.m. Go training. They lost 3-1 last Saturday, and Ira's in a foul mood. He has us doing push-ups, then one touch five a side. Team up again with Big Bird. Our side beats everyone. Ira's impressed.

Wednesday November 24

Swimming. Siobhan is smitten with Filo, thanks to me and my party. I groan. I was hoping it was just a punch-fuelled one night fling. I hate it when my best friends start pairing up. You end up as referee, confessor and messenger all in one. As soon as they have their first row, I'll be the one who's blamed. But Siobhan's so happy about it in the canteen, I resign myself. Lola's glad for Siobhan that she's finished with Jake, but makes no comment on Filo. Pick Debbie-Anne up on way back and cook her something. She comments on smelliness of the clothes pile. Says rats will nest in it.

Nikki has left note on the table, with a cheque for five hundred on top. I snaffle cheque, then read note:

My Beautiful Concubine,

You must try to keep on top of the housework. I notice a gap in the kitchen where the washer once was. Please use this cheque to buy new appliance. Try to make a start on the dishes too, they've been there since the party. PS. Anthony lost his filigree gold navel ring at the party. Could you check the vac to ensure you haven't accidentally sucked it up. He's quite distraught — it's a heirloom passed down to him from his late aunt.

Your everlasting amour, Nikki.

Filigree gold navel ring? Hmmph! I'm not spilling the guts of a vac for that. I buy reconditioned Hotpoint from Honest Al's Appliances for £150 and give the rest of the money a home in my wallet. Then call at Debbie-Anne's and she comes back with me. She says baby's head's engaged and he wants to be born, but she's trying to hold him in until Malik gets back. She falls asleep on sofa with legs crossed. As Debbie-Anne sleeps, I hoover vigorously everywhere Antony might have been, to make sure he never gets hold of his filigree gold navel ring again. Heirloom my foot. What was his aunt, a travelling, Greek belly dancer?

3 p.m. Honest Al calls and installs the new(ish) washing machine. Debbie still sleeping when Nikki gets back. We argue in whispers about why she's always round here. Nikki is annoyed (jealous?) at all the attention I lavish on her. I promise I'll take Nikki out this weekend, wherever she wants. Nikki sends a message for Malik through to the Gdansk Hotel via her laptop and the Internet, saying re his baby that the head's engaged, so he'd better fetch back quick.

Friday November 26

Meet Filo at Bergmann's. He's in romantic raptures about Siobhan. The heiress is history, he snorts. He loves Siobhan's accent, the way she moves, her body, the way she laughs, the way she makes love. He's never met anyone like her. This is the big one. How can he thank me for bringing them together? etc. I sigh and tell him to thank me with a beer.

8 p.m. Malik shows! Debbie rings Bergmann's to tell us. She puts him on. He sounds really subdued. Things are fouling up bad in Gdansk and he's just got to go back. There's too much at stake. I must look after Debbie for him. Can she move in at our place? Get home to talk this over with Nikki who vetoes Debbie stopping here, but says she'll visit Debbie herself daily. I promise her I'll always be on the end of a phone. Malik gives me his mobile phone, complete with charger. He says I'm to keep it with me all the time, even at night, so Debbie can always reach me. I enquire what the problem in Gdansk is. He mutters something about the Polish mafia, then he's off. No sign of his blonde interpreter all the while.

Saturday November 27

Ajax-Willesden victorious 2-0. We're tenth from top in the league. Highest we've ever been. Big Bird banged in two, both from my superlative passes. I played entire game with mobile phone in my hand. Everyone thinks I'm a sad poser. After the game reckon Malik won't mind me making a few calls, so I cold-call a few galleries, then a few old friends, then anybody else whose number I can remember. It's a handy gadget. I could get to like it.

Sunday November 28

1 p.m. Debbie round. She and Nikki chat about buggies and baby clothes. Well, Debbie chats, Nikki attempts to listen politely. Read in Willesden Courier that MegaWatt is pushing up local electricity prices by ten percent due to the rising cost of maintaining the local infrastructure. Robbers.

6 p.m. Accompany Nikki to her Mum's. We knock forever before Ruby opens. Nikki talks loudly to her Mum because maybe she's going deaf now. Ruby says she waited half an hour on our doorstep last Sunday, and we never opened at all, that's why she made us wait. Randolph, the scrap metal man, is in her sitting room, and occupying the cosiest chair by the fire with his shoes off. Ruby says she's moved him in. They might as well be lonely together! Nikki hardly talks for the rest of the visit, but in car revives her senility theory and worries that her mum'll get hurt.

Monday November 29

Loan companies literature pours through our door, the first sign Christmas is on its way. Debbie round. Go for a walk over to her place. She says the baby is sitting so low now, she's sure he's going to be born tonight, Malik or no Malik, and can I stop over? I tell her not to panic, I'll be by the phone all night. She gives me a spare key to the apartment in case she can't get down to the door after she rings.

Sleep fitfully but mobile's quiet all night. Pillow thoughts: this was to have been my first day at new studio doing the Commission work. Have done absolutely nothing all week. Not even thought about doing anything.

Tuesday November 30

9 a.m. Debbie rings, convinced she's about to give birth. She managed to hold things up last night, she declares. But the baby won't wait any longer. I ask her if she's getting contractions yet. She says no.

1 p.m. Debbie arrives by taxi. I tell her off for panicking, then go back to washing dishes. Two minutes later, she screams my name. I rush in. She's on the floor, puffing. Big contractions! she yells. The baby's coming! I dash for the phone but she tells me it's too late, she can feel the head's nearly out, I'm going to have to deliver it. I panic, then get down there. I catch the head. Debbie gives another yelling shove and I ease the shoulders out. Another two seconds and he's born. It's a boy, I tell her, and the little fella saves himself from being slapped by giving a little cry. The baby's fine. It's the other bits I don't know what to do with. Like the cord. Notice it's tangled round not only his legs, but his neck. Am just unravelling it when the doorbell goes. Someone shouts through the letterbox. "I'm the midwife!" Finish untangling cord, then pop baby up into Debbie's arms and dash for door. Midwife is a big, doughty Asian woman and radiates calm. What's baby's name then? she asks as she cuts cord. Debbie's in shock and rapture and just mumbles, Harvey! Harvey! Midwife takes that for the baby's name and mistakes me for the proud father. I go along with it. Go with Debbie to hospital when ambulance arrives. They take my blood for sickle cell tests. Everyone thinks I'm the father.

7 p.m. Debbie rings me from hospital bedside. She sounds dreamy. I must visit her tomorrow morning, she says. I'm to bring flowers and a card saying, 'from your loving husband', else all the other mothers will think she doesn't have a man, or he doesn't care.

Wednesday December 1

Drive through blizzarding snow to hospital. Meet Malik at Debbie's bedside. He snatches flowers and card from me, presents them to Debbie himself. Nurses are all calling the baby Harvey, and midwife still thinks I'm the father. Malik apoplectic when he realises. He mutters baby is too light skinned to be his and doesn't have any of his features. Debbie bursts into tears. Malik rolls giant spliff in waiting room to calm himself despite the No Smoking signs. Nikki phones me on mobile. I tell of confusion over baby's name . She finds it hilarious. Malik snatches his mobile back off me. Debbie says tearfully she'll arrange blood tests to settle paternity if that's what he wants. He says yes, that's what he wants, and storms off. Baby sleeps beatifically through all this. Black ice on roads all way back. Micra slithers and slides. Shattered by the time I get home.

Thursday December 2

Malik has calmed down. Accepts baby his. Hospital has renamed him Steve Harvey. Birth hasn't been registered yet — so everything's OK. Malik apologises to me for his behaviour yesterday, says he's grateful for my delivering baby Steve and being around before the birth and all that, and is there's anything he can do. I tell him just relax. Tells me he's managed to extricate himself from his Polish Lada nightmare. It means paying ten percent of his profits over to the Polish mafia and having an agent on the ground there to watch over things, but it's worth it. He's lost twenty k. on the last shipment. The mafia's took the entire shipment as a "tax" on his previous deals. He can't fight them. They're too big and it isn't home territory. Besides, there'll be no hitches from now on with the mafia on side, so he's happy. The way he says it though, it sounds as if there'll be hitches all the way from now on. Pillowtalk: Nikki thinks the mafia have got Malik over a barrel and he should pull out. Also, she wants a baby, like Debbie.

Friday December 3

Debbie held over in hospital because of excessive bleeding. The afterbirth didn't detach fully. Malik's practically sleeping at the hospital and Debbie's so proud of him for this. Nikki's up for yet another promotion. All that lolly she must be making. Rack my brains figuring how to persuade her to set up a joint bank account. Get call from studio landlords. The studio will definitely be ready for me this Monday. Since I've not managed to make it over all week because of events, the delay's no big deal. But still no ideas on the Commission. Suspect I must deliver sketches soon or I'll be slung off the job.

Saturday December 4

Malik still in hospital. I run Ajax midfield at the Aerodrome where we play the Bolsover Angels. We win 2-0. Persuade entire team to make surprise visit to Debbie's bedside. Malik passes baby round proudly. Debbie hides under blanket. Ira says baby looks like a Wimbledon striker. A square head and long, strong legs. Baby pukes up on Ira. This makes team's day and we all go home happy. Baby will be our mascot.

Sunday December 5

Siobhan rings demanding have I seen Filo? Rings off in a huff when I say no. Wonder what Filo's done to upset her. Nikki decides to visit her mum alone. She says this scrap metal fella her mum's taken in is a gold digger. She's going round there to throw him out. I sneak over to my new studio. It's vast, airy and uncluttered. Can't wait to move in.

6 p.m. Nikki bursts into tears when she gets home. Seems Ruby sent her away with a flea in her ear and she and Randolph are engaged to be married. Nikki says she's going to get a court order to stop the ceremony. Isn't her mum entitled to make mistakes in love like everyone else, I ask Nikki snaps no.

Monday December 6

Fat bill arrives from water utility company. They also include a personalised Christmas card, so that makes it all right then. Debbie rings. She's out of hospital. Explain I can't visit today because I'm going over to my new studio, but will call round tomorrow. Drive over to studio. It's noisy on a weekday, nothing like how it was on Sunday. All around there's the howl of a chain saw, some asthmatic artist coughing and what sounds like someone else sawing a live sheep in half . Guess I'll get used. Lug first load of materials from the Micra boot into studio.

6 p.m. Read in Willesden Courier that MegaWatt is about to initiate further round of downsizing 'though job losses to be kept to minimum'. Meanwhile their profits are up 20%.

9 p.m. Nikki takes me to a casino. InterGlobe Group has appointed a new Chief Executive. He's called Smokin' Joe in the corridors. She met him in the lift and he seemed a nice guy. He wasn't smoking a cigar, though, so why the name? Maybe he's the devil, I suggest. She wins her blackjack hand. I go for drinks. When I get back she's won twice again. She cashes out with five hundred pounds winnings, then we get seriously drunk at the bar. Nikki plays blackjack like a pro. Another of her hidden talents. She tells me she's got plans for making InterGlobe grow.

Tuesday December 7

Do shopping for Debbie and the new baby. The L-Mart Christmas hype is on full. From the PA: (1) "O joy! O joy! Here's something to lift your spirits this Christmas — there's ten percent discount on all spirits above £30. (2) "Yuletide Tuesdays at L-Mart. Love and low prices — the unbeatable combination." Scan babyfoods shelves to find the right kind of powdered milk for little Steve (Gold, newborn) and grab a twenty pack of newborn nappies. Feel sorry for till workers. They have to wear these tinselled hats and say, 'Season's Greetings from L-Mart' to every customer they serve. Admire the one who serves me though, because he manages to make it sound like an insult. Drop Debbie's shopping off (why am I doing it. Where's Malik?) then my own, then stroll down to Bergmann's. It's the only place where tinsel has not spread. Strangely cheered by this.

Nikki comes home and can't get enough of me. I have to satisfy her again and again. Lucky I'm such a stud. I solve algebraic equations in my head as I'm thrusting to stop myself from coming too quick (If $2x + y = 80$ and $3x + y = 116$, what is x? etc). Nikki finally shouts out '36! 36!' and I realise I must have started saying the equations out loud. Later, I give her MegaWatt's annual report which they mailed me for some bizarre reason. She reads it in about three minutes flat, accounts included and calls it beautiful fiction, and she has designs on them. Her mobile rings and she doesn't explain any further.

Wednesday December 8

10 a.m. Go to studio. All my chrome winks away in the light, begging to be picked up caressed. The studio windows are huge, though filthy with sandblasting dust — the building's just been blasted. Decide I need some sounds in here. All this space. Resist the temptation to fire up the welding equipment and start on another chrome construction. Must pour all creative energies into MegaWatt Commission.

Who should be at Willesden baths with Lola and Siobhan but Filo? They were waiting for me. Filo's smuggled his dog in. He doesn't see why a dog can't be allowed to go swimming like any other species. His arsehole's as clean as the next, he says. Filo comes out of cubicle wearing green, yellow piped, mock Y-fronted bathing trunks. Has dog in his arms. Dog, one of those little terriers, yaps frantically, jumps out of Filo's arms, skids through compulsory shower zone and leaps into pool. Pool attendants scoop out dog. Filo and dog are banned from pool. Filo laughs his head off and watches from public gallery. On the drive home, he and Siobhan are all over each other in the back seat of the Micra. Me and Lola feel like gooseberries. We make small talk. I wonder how long she'll stay at the flat now that Filo's moved in.

Thursday December 9

Debbie-Anne's on bedrest. Or supposed to be. Malik sleeps so deeply, Debbie means, he never gets up when baby cries even if she nudges him in the ribs. And he snores like a grossed-out pig. I listen blissfully to her dissing Malik, though I do wonder if she says these things simply because she knows how much they please me. She asks me how my sculpting's going. I confess I'm totally blocked. She puts baby in my arms and lets me feed him. He gurgles away then smiles at me for a long time. Debbie says it's wind. He looks like his dad, I lie. Debbie changes subject a bit too quickly. Did she really get that blood test done?

Nikki phones her mum, to see how she is. Her mum and Randolph have just got back from Hibiscus Court Retirement Home Christmas Party. They sneaked in four bottles of malt whisky to lively up the old fogeys there, Ruby says. Nikki worried. Never known her mum drink before. On other hand, she's glad she's visiting Retirement Homes, in case she eventually has to be put in one.

Friday December 10

10 a.m. MegaWatt people call and install new electricity meter. I protest but they say I'm a bad payer and they have the right. They leave big mess in hallway. Meter spins round faster than a Catherine Wheel.

Malik calls at studio with crate of Polish vodka. Tells me he's heard I've got artistic block and all the artists in Gdansk use this as a cure. He starts pouring. I don't remember anything else about the morning.

4 p.m. Phone ringing. Grope for phone and simultaneously peer out from under sandbagged eyelids. I'm at home. Germanic voice on line. Lola. She's fed up and wants me to take her away from flat and Siobhan and Filo. What am I, a fireman? I think. Lola tires of having to listen to bedsprings boing-ing and pants, gasps and howls and both of them swanning around like they've come top of some Joy Of Sex exam class. How can she finish her PhD on Theoretical Mathematics with all this Practical Shagging going on? And what Siobhan doesn't know is that Filo propositioned her one day when Siobhan was cutting her toenails in the bathroom. He's also got a guitar and practice amp with him. He's not played it yet but can you imagine what hell it will be if he does? The flat's too small for three people. She says I, Harvey, must persuade him to leave, now. Lola only takes about three breaths saying all this. I say I'll try. Why does everyone think I'm Filo's minder?

Dig out Filo from Siobhan and Lola's. He blows Siobhan kisses as he leaves. The plan is (a) to get him drunk; then (b) put Lola's problems to him. Part (a) works. The (b) part gets a bit mangled on account of the vodka. We go to one of the new Vodka bars springing up, Willesdenik, I think it's called, very good vodka, unlike the decanted anti-freeze Malik brought to the studio. Vodka session ends I think with Filo saying yeah, he'll tape him and Siobhan shagging for me, but he personally thinks I'm extremely weird and he will be noting this in his diary. My brain aches. How did it get tangled up like that? Being called weird by Filo is an achievement of sorts, I suppose. Don't try to explain again, probably only make things worse. Brain is in my socks by the time I leave Willesdenik. Get back and Nikki steers me into a cold shower, ostensibly to sober me up, but really because she just enjoys seeing me suffer. Go to bed extremely hung-over, and freezing.

Saturday December 11

Ira substitutes me after only ten minutes saying I have lost all sense of direction and if I was a racing pigeon he'd have wrung my neck by now. Watch from sideline as we win 3-0. Big Bird scores all three and dances with corner flag. Midfield is being run by podgy new kid with freckles who's the apple of Ira's eye. Micra kangaroos home. Realise at gate had it in second gear all way back. Answering machine winks coyly. Retire to bed for rest of day with sheet over my head Try harmonising with throbbing head (Iron John Session Three). Blame Malik and his Polish anti-freeze. Never before had such a pogoing cyclops of a headache.

Sunday December 12

Was groaning all night. Nikki thought I was masturbating. If only. Try hair of the dog cure: tumbler of rum. Feel better immediately. Siobhan rings. Livid that I asked Filo to tape their lovemaking. I am so depraved, she says, she'll never speak to me again. What?!!! Don't know what to say. Try to explain. Explanation doesn't go down too well, probably because speech slightly slurred on account of the rum.

1 p.m. Strike out to Bergmann's. Sappho there. Band rehearsals under way. Forty strong Salsa band. Sonic bedlam. Whistles, drums, brass. Head throbs, but calms after third double vodka. Dance with Sappho. Whole joint jumping by evening. Drag self home at too-far-gone a.m.

Monday December 13

Have my morning tipple of vodka. Can now instantly tell the real (Russian) thing from imitations. Wander around house with duster. Rearrange pile of dirty laundry. Run tap water over dirty plates. Wipe fridge door down. Open can of beans, and eat them cold with thimble of vodka.

7 p.m. Nikki back and complains about smell from pile of dirty laundry and my neglecting housework which she pays me to do. I ask for a rise. She says no, to avoid overheating the Willesden economy. This passes off as humour in her circles no doubt. I ask why she keeps hiding my vodka. She alleges (again) I'm an alcoholic. She won't say where she's hidden the bottles. She expects row but I merely smile and retreat to kitchen where I stir slow-acting garlic into tonight's fish stew. She laps stew up and apologises for her tough-love action but says she's doing it because she loves me. I smile sweetly. Midday tomorrow she will reek of garlic. Later, find carton of duty free cigarettes. Smoke them all to hold off the shakes.

Tuesday December 14

Debbie rings. I am to take Malik shopping and point out the difference between new-born and toddler size nappies. Agree because it'll take my mind off the shakes. Me and Malik trundle down the Baby aisle of Asda. I push trolley, he talks into switched off mobile phone ("in case any of my business contacts see me. I have an image to maintain"). Malik tells me to get going on the MegaWatt Commission. Once I've established a reputation for large scale work, he says, the commissions will flood in. I show him the aisle and the colour code for new-borns. Then demonstrate how a store loyalty card works. Realise Malik's just had me pay for his shopping. No wonder he's a tycoon.

Read in Willesden Courier that MegaWatt are installing

pre-payment meters wherever they can. Nikki comes home and leaps in shower. Emerges asking if I think she has a BO problem I answer honestly no. Feel guilty about garlic, but not guilty enough to confess. Go training. It's so cold my testicles retreat into my stomach. Pitch just right consistency for crocodiles wanting a decent wallow. Think I did enough to impress Ira though. Discover podgy new kid is good at keep-up, but hates the rough stuff. Knock him off ball a couple of times to make the point.

Pillowtalk: confess my garlic sin to Nikki. Nikki whacks me with her pillow. A thousand feathers in air. We have feathered sex on pink bedroom carpet until she suddenly howls with pain. Antony's navel ring has pierced her left buttock. I pluck out navel ring and she dabs her bum with iodine. Bedsheets stink of iodine all night. Can't sleep. Kept awake wondering why I can't come up with an idea for MegaWatt? I've tried meditation, vodka and hash. Nothing works.

Wednesday December 15

Go early to studio. Hang around doors. Meet Genevieve, another sculptor. She's making large-scale moulds. Get glimmer of an idea: I could cast Commission piece, whatever it turns out to be, in aluminium. Genevieve says this would be expensive, but worth it for the finish I'd get. Admire Genevieve. She radiates calm and purpose. Do some preliminary sketches while in her studio. Have something. Genevieve says go with it, see what happens.

12 p.m. Get back. Two messages on answering machine. The first is Siobhan: "You won't see me at pool today. I'm searching for a new flat." She sounds angry with me. Next is Filo: "You won't see me at pool — if my dog's not clean enough for Willesden Baths, then neither am I!" Willesden Baths would probably agree with him on that. Ring the flat. Lola answers.

There's been an argument. Siobhan has just cut up all Filo's underwear, she says. Meanwhile Filo is at a tattooist having 'Filo loves Siobhan' heart tattoo removed. Lola happy telling me this. Says she knew it wouldn't last etc. Lola and me go swimming.

Thursday December 16

Dig out HomeWorld catalogue and teleorder from it more or less randomly — Christmas presents. Cable laying gang arrive outside house and begin pogoing on tarmac with drills, rammers etc. Retreat to studio meaning to get productive but end up watching Genevieve make casts for her Frozen River project. She's stocky, fifty-six, descended on her mother's side from Appalachian Native Americans, and on her father's from English peasants. She went to Slade School of Art for two terms. I tell her about my Commission and how I'm planning to research the invention of electricity on a scientific and mythological level. She says it sounds like I'm farting around and why don't I just sculpt? She has a point.

Friday December 17

Who is my first loyalty to? Filo or Siobhan? How do you choose between friends when you are forced to choose? Dilemmas, dilemmas! Filo and Siobhan are unravelling fast. Siobhan told me to "come round and remove Filo's belongings from the flat, else I'll burn them!" Filo meanwhile left a message on my answering machine saying: "Harvey, you are the stench of rotting rats intestines!" Just that, no explanation. Manage to persuade Siobhan not to chuck Filo's stuff out onto the street. Then find Filo at Bergmann's. He rants "You are the LoveGod of the slug population, you, are the powdered, reconstituted and reshaped contents of a sick bag!" etc. He then goes maudlin on me. He can't face living without Siobhan. Persuade him Siobhan isn't everything. Someone else will come along and he's always got Truffle, his dog. He laps this up. I thank the stars I've watched so many Oprah shows.

10 p.m. Get call from Siobhan. She's impressed with how I made Filo see sense. They're splitting, but it's amicable. They're holding a disengagement party tomorrow and I'm invited. Filo comes on the line to confirm this. When two people part, there's no need for all the grief they usually give each other, he says. Better to part with a party, than a slanging match. Mr Rationality himself. I tell them I'll show. Have vague sense of foreboding.

Saturday December 18

We're playing at the Greyhound Track. Limber up in changing room, stretch, do jumps, deliver pep talk like the natural captain I am. Stunned when Ira says I'm third substitute. Ira takes me to one side and explains he's saving me for the real rough Cup stuff in January when there'll be more at stake. Me, Gonzo and Scooby, the three substitutes, are too valuable to be risked in a mere team match. On the pitch, Ira's teamed Malik up with Kid Wonder in midfield. Our opponents are chefs from Mayfair. Expect without best players, especially me, we'll get rolled out, pastried and stuffed. Even Ira's surprised when we win 7-0. Team carries Kid Wonder on shoulders to dressing room, shouting Zola! Zola! If he's Zola, I'm Maradona. Besides, the cooks could hardly play. If they cook the way they defend they're not fit to peel sprouts.

10 p.m. Filo and Siobhan's disengagement party. Motley crowd of starving students, randy lecturers, blagging liggers and freeloading artists. Don't touch a drop. Mid-party, a chucking-out ceremony is enacted. As crowd watches, Siobhan heaves basket of Filo's clothes out of the door, calls him a total and utter slob who's got a foul mouth, rancid underwear, but very good, slow hands. Filo bows, says she is the second most vile person he has ever known, that she has all the brainpower of a stoned ant and all the sex appeal of cold kebab meat, but that nevertheless she's a great kisser and will always remain in his heart. Siobhan and Filo then take a bow. Filo rejoins the party. Everyone suitably impressed and say will adopt same ceremony when they split up. I prefer the conventional shouting match myself. I mingle, watching Filo. Can tell, deep down, he's hurting, but he manages to keep up appearances for a while. Finally pull him away from party when he's drunk too much neat whisky. Order a taxi. He sobs all the way to the studio where I let him kip for the night.

Sunday December 19

Nikki and I share a bath. Nikki says I wasn't far wrong about Smokin' Joe being the devil. Behind his nice guy exterior he's a corporate barracuda. He's set up automatic recording of all internal calls. The quality and quantity of office chat has sunk to zero as a result. But she's been through it all before and InterGlobe wouldn't be stupid enough to cause another huge wave of disruption after what they've only just ridden out.

She asks about my work, I lie that things are fine. Don't tell her about Filo. She'd tell me to chuck him out. She says there's a big story on MegaWatt in papers, how they've by-passed law against disconnection by installing pre-payment meters, a form of self disconnection so there'll be lots of old people shivering this winter. They have the regulator in their pocket (free plane tickets, free holidays to "conferences"), and the directors are awarding themselves share options willy nilly. Ask Nikki why she doesn't become a director of a company like that and get us rich fast. She smiles that she's working on it. In the evening I cater to Nikki's passion for rhubarb pie and cold custard. Late night thought: MegaWatt are a bunch of shits. What kind of a sculpture do you do for a bunch of shits?

Monday December 20

Visit studio. Stale air and heaving sleeping bag reminds me Filo's here. Ignore him. Have germ of an idea for Commission piece. Sketch it fast. Filo stirs, pops head out of bag, fixes himself breakfast; crisps and Bovril from vending machine. Invite him home so he can take a shower. He accepts humbly. At Cherryville, he strips off, dashes upstairs to shower, and comes down wearing my clothes. Begins grazing my fridge. I throw the rags he was wearing into washing machine for a quick spin . Machine loads with water, door locks, then nothing. Nikki back and asks what Filo is doing in my clothes. Explain Filo's broken heart, his eviction and temporary lodgings, the absence of food at studio, his need for clean clothes, and the non-functioning of our washing machine. Nikki shouts from upstairs that it looks like a typhoon has blown through the bathroom. Moves on to bedroom and makes sarcastic comment that maybe we have poltergeists because there are clothes scattered everywhere. Filo whispers that Nikki's not in happy-clappy mood. I agree. We sneak out to The Last Drop while Nikki in shower. Filo and Tommo click, which scares me. On their own, they're just about bearable. Together they could really blow up the planet. Tommo tells us he knows Honest Al, used to go to school with him and Honest Al used to work a credit card scam, but now he just wrings suckers dry with his washing machine business. Tommo laughs in a funny way telling me this, then promises Filo he'll let Honest Al know we two are friends so he'd better fix the washer, priority, like. I tell him it's very kind of him but not to bother. It's only a washing machine. Filo protests he wants his clothes back.

"It's embarrassing walking around in your threads, they're so . . . square!" I suggest he takes them off then if they're so square. Being Filo he does, and parades out of pub wearing nothing but my L-Mart Big Lover boxers. I chase after him

217

with clothes and beg. He puts clothes back on and I avoid being an accessory to an indecency offence. Back at The Last Drop Tommo slaps me on the back and says I look just the kind of guy who'd wear L-Mart Big Lover boxers. Filo laughs with him. With friends like these . . .

12 a.m. Get home to find Nikki not in. She crawls between the sheets around 2am, smelling of wine and smoke. I can smell Malik's cologne on her neck.

Tuesday December 21

Get to studio to find Filo has installed microwave and Baby Belling cooker. He's a good cook and does a roaring trade in vegetarian samosas and dim sum to all studio lessees. Genevieve feasts off them. Visit Debbie. She's fine, more mobile now.

7 p.m. Go training even though there's no match — this Saturday being Christmas Day. I concede Kid Wonder has brilliant control with both feet. Whole team stands and gawps at his ability. Malik is there and comes over to me all friendly (sign of a guilty conscience over last night?). I ask Malik directly if he's been messing with Nikki. He says no way I've got the wrong guy, he was on the phone to Gdansk all night. I'd believe him but it's definitely his cologne. If he is messing with Nikki he's got amazing sang-froid because next breath he's telling me he's flying to Gdansk tomorrow, more Lada shipment problems, and can I look after Debbie? I agree reluctantly.

Wednesday December 22

Lola rings. Now Filo's gone, everything is 'wunderbar'. Yes for you, I think, but I'm the one who's stuck with him. Go studio. Nightwatchman says he knows Filo is in occupation, but it's comforting to have someone else on site besides robbers, so he's going to let it lie. His only complaint is my friend plays Hendrix riffs in middle of night. He would prefer early Bee Gees. Nightwatchman then does Bee Gees' Jive Talking routine, complete with falsetto pitch and Bee Gees hand jive. Suspect early Bee Gees not in Filo's repertoire. Filo still depressed about Siobhan. Begs me not to go swimming with her and Lola. After the way they treated him I owe it to him as a friend, he says. What can I do? Spend afternoon in studio and finish all the sketches I need for Commission work in a mad scrawl of charcoal.

1 p.m. Filo gets the Baby Belling going, then surprises me by doing a guitar take on Elvis Presley's "It'll Be Lonely This Christmas" while the pot cooks. Maybe he does know some Bee Gees. He gets an ovation from the studio artists who've all gathered to watch. Also gets a dozen Christmas party invites. Filo flogs them cheese fritters at a quid apiece. He makes at least thirty quid. He starts talking to me about my maybe putting up some curtains for him here. Tell him he's got two more days to find a place then I'm chucking him out. He protests where's my Christmas spirit? I repeat, two days.

6 p.m. Go Bergmann's with Filo. Filo bores everyone by moping and sighing about Siobhan. He'll always be here for her, she doesn't know how much she loves him, they had something special etc. etc. until he slumps in a drunken stupor under the table. No one bothers waking him.

11 p.m. Nikki pores over her laptop way into the small hours. Wakes me at 3 a.m. and says Smokin' Joe has acquired a sidekick, Thin Al. Thin Al is actually quite fat, but is so called because he likes his Corporations to have very thin staffing levels. As key personnel, Nikki herself does not personally feel threatened, she tells me at 3.30 a.m. She adds that she wants me to get a Christmas tree tomorrow. It must be a real one, and large.

Thursday December 23

At studio early morning, working on commission sculpture. Sleeping bag heaves more than usual. Filo's head pops up, followed by Genevieve's! Refuse to be surprised. They cook breakfast as I work. Today is Josie's Naked Art day. We all dutifully troop from Bergmann's to park for the event. 'A political act to protest against the waste of environmental resources at Christmas' it says on Josie's manifesto which she hands out to waiting photojournalists. Then she gets her kit off. The cameras flash. Filo says the freezing cold's making Josie's nipples ping out. I check. He's right. Seems Filo's over Siobhan.

1 p.m. No roof rack on Micra, so wedge Christmas tree in back and passenger seat and motor home. Use hacksaw to remove tree from Micra. Erect it. Post hacksaw, it's a very narrow tree. Do shopping for Debbie. She's up and about now. Visit Siobhan and Lola and drop off their Christmas presents. Siobhan gets a HomeWorld Woodland Pot Pourri Dish. Lola gets a HomeWorld Cat Figures Key Rack. They don't know this yet because I've wrapped them.

Nikki gets call from her mum: they can't come on Christmas day. Randolph made a small profit from sale of his scrapyard and they're blowing it on a Christmas cruise to Egypt. Think Nikki is relieved. She didn't want Randolph here. Mention possibility of Filo staying over Christmas. Nikki disapproves, but I hold my ground. Long negotiations produce the following guest list: Malik, Debbie-Anne, Antonia and whoever she brings if she brings anyone (She broke up with Ralph only two weeks ago!) I allow Anthony, the cute young man who lost his belly button ring on our bed, so she accepts Filo 'so long as he's sufficiently clean'; also Joseph, aka Smokin' Joe ('if he wants to come, I haven't actually asked him yet') and whoever he wants to bring. Get Nikki to concede Filo can bring Genevieve if he wants.

Friday December 24

Drive Ruby and Randolph to National Express coach station, first leg of their Egypt cruise. Never heard of a cruise that begins with a National Express coach trip but say nothing and wish them well. Randolph bearhugs me. Don't know why Nikki objects to him. He seems OK. Malik phones for Nikki. Tell him she's at office party.

He's back from Gdansk. Claims he was shot during negotiations with mafia and he's pulling out of Gdansk operation altogether. He made thirty k out of it while it lasted, but he's going to find something safer now like East End pool table management.

Go Christmas Jam at Bergmann's. Rowdy and jumping. Everyone manically happy. Air thick with green leaf ganja. Stand back from it all, sipping orange juice. Tell Filo he can come to our place Christmas day if he wants. Everyone's shimmer-bugging (new, naff dance craze) or snogging or substance abusing. Filo doing all three by the time I leave. Nikki back and sober enough to help with food preparations for tomorrow but flags half way through and attacks the sherry. Who's the alcoholic now? I ask. She gives me a drunken leer and takes another slug.

Saturday December 25

Filo arrives, clean shaven and tuxedoed. No sign of Genevieve. Antonia arrives, again on her own, and is very glam in slinky, silver lamé dress. Smokin' Joe turns up, with Thin Al. The two of them are holding hands. Nikki doesn't bat an eyelid.

Things a bit stiff and formal but liven up during the

Christmas meal after crate of wine knocked back. Malik wants baby Steve circumcised and Debbie doesn't. Everyone takes sides but the drink wins because it all gets muddled and separate arguments break out about whether the stock market for pharmaceuticals has peaked, why privatised trains don't run on time, and chaos theory's challenge to Darwinians. It ends with this subject because no-one actually understands it, except Genevieve who introduced it. There's a pause. Then Malik fills the vacuum by confessing he's had an affair with Nikki recently. Before anyone else can react Debbie confesses she had an affair with me, but it's not my baby — she has the blood test results for both me and Malik and can prove it. All hell breaks loose. I object we did not have an affair, we just had sex. Fierce, six way arguments ensue between me and Nikki, me and Debbie, me and Malik. Plus Debbie and Malik, Malik and Nikki and Nikki and Debbie. Meanwhile, Smokin' Joe and Thin Al cha cha on the patio. I ask if they're fine. They say yes, lovely party. Go back inside and intercept Antony trying to steer a well-drunk Nikki upstairs. Threaten to punch him. He switches his attention to Antonia and has soon got his skilful hands round her lamé waist. I go to rescue her but Antonia brushes me away saying she loves these young bucks, or at least that's what I think she said. Downstairs, Debbie and Malik are arguing on the sofa. Filo's disappeared. Nikki corners me and says we have some serious talking to do. After what seems like hours of soul searching, we agree to forgive give each other one last chance.

Sunday December 26

Malik and Debbie ring. They're tying the knot. Nikki invites them over to celebrate. I groan that we haven't even cleared away yesterday's mess yet. Nikki screams from kitchen. She's found Filo in pile of dirty laundry and thought he was dead. He wakes, nips upstairs, showers, then comes down in fresh set of my clothes. Malik and Debbie arrive. Five hours later I've tried everything and can't get rid of them: Filo, Malik, Debbie and baby all wedged on sofa watching sci-fi movie. Filo says we are all aliens without love. Debbie says that's profound. Me and Nikki say we're going to bed and the last one out should close front door firmly. Pillowtalk: Nikki tells me she heard from Smokin' Joe that InterGlobe will be making hostile takeover bid for MegaWatt in New Year.

Monday December 27

10 a.m. Siobhan rings, distressed. Filo in hospital. He's taken an overdose. He was outside her flat in street late last night. He threatened to kill himself if she didn't let him in but she refused. She didn't think he was serious. She saw him lying on grass outside flat and thought he was fooling. Then she got scared and checked. Found an empty tub of Paracetamol. He'd drunk all this vodka with them. She called an ambulance. They pumped his stomach. She got to him just in time, the doctor said. She doesn't want to go back to the hospital, but thinks somebody should. She didn't think he'd go to such extremes, she repeats. I tell her it's OK, I'll go, and not to blame herself.

12 p.m. Visit Filo in hospital. He says he's been a fool etc. He looks weak. Hospital manager thrusts clipboard at me. I ask if he's been seen by a psychiatrist. The manager laughs and says he's fine, it's him (manager) that needs the psychiatrist. Adds that the hospital needs the bed with it being the season of merriment and suicides, so can I please sign. I sign discharge form reluctantly and take Filo home. I wonder where Truffles, his dog is, but don't ask. Nikki says he can sleep over, but one night only. He is definitely not moving in.

Tuesday December 28

Nikki comes back from work with pyjamas for Filo. She doesn't want him sleeping naked. We agree he can crash out temporarily in the garage. Filo still apologising. Says Christmas always has this effect on him and he'll be right as rain soon. In evening, spend time in garage just talking with Filo, till he drops off to sleep.

Wednesday December 29

Go studio and finish commission sculpture. Modesty aside, it's stunning. Ring round and remind everyone about my MegaWatt Sculpture Unveiling Party at Beehive Studios, New Years Day. Check on Filo. He has installed his Baby Belling and microwave in my garage. Wants to know if he can have some more powerpoints fitted around.

7 p.m. Nikki back from work. Smokin' Joe has spared her Department. She comes in for particular praise in Smokin' Joe's report. Privately I think it's my Christmas Day cooking that did it. Few can resist the charms of my Roast Muscovy Duck Breast With Pineapple. Smokin' Joe told her they're going ahead with the MegaWatt Takeover plan. InterGlobe and MegaWatt. Far as I can see, they deserve each other. Nikki and me agree we need to spend more time together to make this relationship work. Cable gang set up with mini JCB, rammers, floodlights, diesel pumps and all. Must get paid double for nights.

Thursday December 30

Siobhan rings about the party — will Filo be there? If he will, she won't be coming. Persuade her to come, for Filo's sake if not for her own. They should be able to be friends. She agrees only after I promise to control Filo firmly throughout the evening.

8 p.m. Look over the House-husband Contract nostalgically with Nikki. It's up for renewal, she says. The cooking has become microwave meals, the shopping should have a variety clause added to it; I get a big fail on laundry duties As for the sex, she says that I'm good on the plentiful bit, but like my shopping, it lacks variety. I promise to read up on the Kama Sutra but she says no need, she'll take me through it herself. We make our way upstairs. Just as we get twisted into an interesting position, the cable gang strike up. We try to bonk to the rhythm of cable gang's rammer.

Friday December 31

We spend New Year's Eve at Antonia's. Antonia asks how we've coped with the role switch, my doing housework and Nikki bringing home the bacon. Nikki says yeah, we cope fine. I say since I do the shopping, strictly speaking it is I who brings home the bacon — from L-Mart. They both smile patronisingly at me.

Saturday January 1

10 p.m. My unveiling party. A packed crowd surges into the studio. Among them are Siobhan and Lola. Filo is by the sound system, Genevieve in dungarees and paper hat, Big Bird, half the rat pack, Ira in golf casuals, and the Kid Wonder whose name I forget in Karl Kani gear; Tommo saunters in wearing a black polo neck and with his hair slicked back; Honest Al is on tow two steps behind Tommo, shirt tucked in, knuckles scrubbed, teeth flossed I'll bet. A Brooks-shirted, MegaWatt Exec swaps civilities with Sappho, who's wearing a Nigerian headwrap and has the frowning, Yoruba art expert, Ade, by her side. There are at least twenty others. The air is sodden with footballers' strength aftershave and exotic perfume, making the studio a souk of smells. Nikki, radiant and sober, is by my side. The MegaWatt Exec has a speech on index cards he's due to read out. He asks me to do the unveiling sooner rather than later as he's not feeling well.

10.30 p.m. On cue, Filo plays the taped fanfare and I yank the wrap off my sculpture. It's a huge vulture, grasping a rod of lightning. All in weathered aluminium. Sappho shouts out "Woah ! Woah! Yes! Yes!" The footballers cheer, the artists nod, everyone applauds. Everyone except the MegaWatt Exec. He clutches his Brooks shirt top button, goes red, then purple, then falls. Everyone stares at him. Nikki goes to revive him. Malik rants at me. I'm an idiot. I won't get commissioned to design a paper clip after this. I should prostrate myself, grovel on all fours to that man when he's revived, promise to melt the thing down and start again, say I copied the wrong bird from the library book and I meant an eagle. I decline Malik's advice. Malik calls me dumb. I don't like being called dumb. Especially by a man who's been having sex with my woman. I knee him in the groin. He flails wildly, catches me with a lucky punch and we sprawl to the floor. I'm getting the upper hand when suddenly there's water everywhere. It's Filo with a fire hose. Removal of hose from wall sets off building alarm. Caretaker arrives and announces building has to be evacuated. Notice Filo and Siobhan leaving together, Filo holding Siobhan by the waist, Siobhan looking dreamily into his eyes. Lola says they're both drunk, that's the only explanation.

Get home. Cable guys wave to me as I park. Phone rings. It's Malik and Nikki. They've talked the MegaWatt Exec round. He will give me another chance if I apologise. Apologise natch, I tell them. Harvey Robinson's principles are not for sale.

Harvey's Robinson's Survival Guide To Relationships.
aka The Truth On A T-Shirt

Never believe in the possibility of a long term relationship with someone who likes to sleep on the same side of the bed as yourself.

A man with a dishcloth over his shoulder is never accused of being idle.

If your lightbulbs blow all the time, it is not an international conspiracy of lightbulb manufacturers that's causing it. It is the faulty wiring in your house.

Your guests will be able to tell the difference between roast chicken and blowtorched chicken.

If the drill goes in very easily, the shelf will fall down very easily.

More salt does not always improve the taste of things. Some things are meant to taste bland.

If all else fails, the woman next door might just know how to switch on the hammer action of your new drill.

You cannot cook food in engine oil, so don't even think about it.

You cannot take apart something you've cooked and put it together again. You have to get it right first time. This involves not only reading the instructions, but actually following them.

A watched kettle must be plugged in if you want it to boil.

If you do not want someone to open the oven door, do not tell them not to open the oven door (Think about this one).

A stitch in time will keep your pants from splitting later.

Apart from round the edges of barbecued ribs, if food is black it usually means you have overcooked it.

BABY FATHER BY PATRICK AUGUSTUS

"Baby Father…an entertaining look at four black guys on the town who
enjoy womanising but suddenly discover the joys of parenthood."
Daily Mirror

BERES and Sonia are the model upwardly mobile professional couple, until
the day she walks out of and leaves their seven-year-old daughter behind.
Successful fashion photographer LINVALL'S one night of passion has come
back to haunt him just as he enters a new relationship.
Thirtysomething GUSSIE is worried that he'll miss the boat if he doesn't
find a woman to have children with soon.
JOHNNY is wondering just how he'll explain to his mother that she's got
two grandchildren and two new 'daughters-in-law'…AND TO CAP IT
ALL, THE MEN ARE DEMANDING THE SAME RIGHTS OVER
THEIR CHILDREN AS THE MOTHERS!

ISBN 1-874509-05-0

BABY FATHER 2 BY PATRICK AUGUSTUS

"Baby Father…an entertaining look at four black guys on the town who
enjoy womanising but suddenly discover the joys of parenthood."
Daily Mirror

When JOHNNY finally decides to spend some quality time with his baby
son, he is vexed to find that his parental duties have been taken over by his
baby mother's new lover.
Thirtysomething BERES discovers that his new wife's baby father isn't too
happy about the recent developments in their domestic arrangements either.
LINVALL'S neglected his role as a father for so long that now, when he's
called to play dad, he's long forgotten how to do it!
Eligible bachelor GUSSIE yearns to have kids but he still can't find a
woman whose 'rateable market value' is as high as his…AND TO CAP IT
ALL, THE WOMEN HAVE GOT THEM UNDER MANNERS!

"A superb follow up to the massive hit novel Baby Father."
Paperbacks Reviewed

"Patrick Augustus writes with a voice that is totally unique. He deserves all
the success he's had."
The Voice
ISBN 1-874509-15-8

X Press Black Classics

The masterpieces of black fiction writing await your discovery

❏ The Blacker the Berry   Wallace Thurman   £6.99
*'Born **too** black, Emma Lou suffers her own community's intra-racial venom.'*

❏ The Autobiography of an Ex-Colored Man   James Weldon Johnson   £5.99
'One of the most thought-provoking novels ever published.'

❏ The Conjure Man Dies   Rudolph Fisher   £5.99
'The world's FIRST black detective thriller!'

❏ The Walls of Jericho   Rudolph Fisher   £5.99
*'When a buppie moves into a white neighbourhood, all hell breaks loose. **Hilarious!**'*

❏ Joy and Pain   Rudolph Fisher   £6.99
'Jazz age Harlem stories by a master of black humour writing.'

❏ Iola   Frances E.W. Harper   £6.99
'A woman's long search for her mother from whom she was separated on the slave block.'

❏ The House Behind the Cedars   Charles W. Chesnutt   £5.99
'Can true love transcend racial barriers?'

❏ A Love Supreme   Pauline E. Hopkins   £5.99
'One of the greatest love stories ever told.'

❏ One Blood   Pauline E. Hopkins   £6.99
'Raiders of lost African treasures discover their roots and culture.'

❏ The President's Daughter   William Wells Brown   £5.99
'The true story of the daughter of the United States president, sold into slavery.'

❏ The Soul of a Woman   Zora Neale Hurston, etc   £6.99
'Stories by the great black women writers'

I enclose a cheque/postal order (Made payable to 'The X Press') for

£ _____
(add 50p P&P per book for orders under £10. All other orders P&P free.)

NAME _____

ADDRESS _____

Cut out or photocopy and send to: X PRESS, 6 Hoxton Square, London N1 6NU
Alternatively, call the X PRESS hotline: 0171 729 1199 and place your order.

WHEN A MAN LOVES A WOMAN BY PATRICK AUGUSTUS

"One thing's for certain...no man is ever gonna love you the way I do..."

Campbell Clarke grew up poor, whereas Dionne Owen came from a wealthy and respected buppie family. When they met a week before her marriage to City broker Mike Phillips, Campbell knew instantly that Dionne was the woman he wished HE was marrying.
The following years took their lives down very separate roads, but Campbell is prepared to wait as long as it takes to win Dionne's love.

"Excellent...a modern romance that every man and woman can relate to."
The Voice

"A compulsive read...written with humour and a real understanding of the soul of a black man."
Yvette Richards

ISBN 1-874509-24-7

X Press Children's Collection

THE DRUMMOND HILL CREW

The No. 1 Bestselling Range Of Children's Books

Set in Drummond Hill comprehensive, this series of books for 9-12 year olds, show a group of school friends in a variety of exciting adventures.

AGE AIN'T NOTHING BUT A NUMBER
by Yinka Adebayo £3.99
Remi, Tenisha, Darren, Tyrone and the other Drummond Hill pupils go on a summer holiday to the mysterious Headstone Manor and find themselves bang in the middle of an adventure full of GOOSEBUMPS!

BOYZ TO MEN
by Yinka Adebayo
£3.99
Best friends Darren and Tyrone used to be the naughtiest children in the school. Now twelve years old, Tyrone is the model pupil but Darren hasn't changed. He's even started hanging out with the notorious Smoker's Corner Crew. This puts their friendship to the test. THE MORAL: GROWING UP CAN BE PAINFUL.

LIVIN' LARGE
by Yinka Adebayo £3.99
When a show-off arrives at school, Tenisha, Remi, Darren, Tyrone and the rest of the Drummond Hill Crew all decide that he's acting too big for his boots. It can only be a matter of time before there's TROUBLE!

These books are already HOT property. Order your kid's copies today!

Please rush me the following Drummond Hill Crew title(s) at £3.99 each

Title	Quantity	£
❏ Age Ain't Nothing But A Number		
❏ Boyz To Men		
❏ Livin' Large		

(add 50p P&P per book for orders under £10. All other orders P&P free.)
I enclose a cheque/postal order (Made payable to 'The X Press') for

£ _____

NAME _____

ADDRESS _____

_____

Cut out or photocopy and send to: X PRESS, 6 Hoxton Square, London N1 6NU

Alternatively, call the X PRESS hotline: 0171 729 1199 and place your order.

Keep updated with the
HOT
new novels from
The X Press.
Join our mailing list.
Simply send your name
and address to:

Mailing List
The X Press
6 Hoxton Square
London N1 6NU